"Hop on."

"Matt!" Helen said, shocked. "You aren't going to steal this!"

He met her gaze, deadpan. "No, Helen, I'm going to find the owner and tell him I'm taking it, so he can call the police."

She looked around furtively. "What if the owner comes back?" she said.

"Well, maybe if we stand here debating about it long enough, he will," Matteo said impatiently, pointing to the space behind him. "Get on. The idiot left the keys in the ignition. He deserves to walk."

Helen hesitated, looking unhappy.

"Look, Miss Abe Lincoln, you just defrauded the Puerta Lindan government by entering the country under false pretenses and you're on the lam with a wanted man. If I were you, I wouldn't let a little thing like a stolen motorbike stand in my way."

Dear Reader,

When two people fall in love, the world is suddenly new and exciting, and it's that same excitement we bring to you in Silhouette Intimate Moments. These are stories with scope, with grandeur. These characters lead the lives we all dream of, and everything they do reflects the wonder of being in love.

Longer and more sensuous than most romances, Silhouette Intimate Moments novels take you away from everyday life and let you share the magic of love. Adventure, glamour, drama, even suspense— these are the passwords that let you into a world where love has a power beyond the ordinary, where the best authors in the field today create stories of love and commitment that will stay with you always.

In coming months look for novels by your favorite authors: Maura Seger, Parris Afton Bonds, Elizabeth Lowell and Erin St. Claire, to name just a few. And whenever you buy books, look for all the Silhouette Intimate Moments, love stories *for* today's women *by* today's women.

Leslie J. Wainger
Senior Editor
Silhouette Books

IMRL-7/85

Doreen Owens Malek

Montega's Mistress

Silhouette Intimate Moments
Published by Silhouette Books New York
America's Publisher of Contemporary Romance

SILHOUETTE BOOKS
300 East 42nd St., New York, N.Y. 10017

ISBN: 0-373-07169-8

First Silhouette Books printing December 1986

All the characters in this book are fictitious. Any
resemblance to actual persons, living or dead, is
purely coincidental.

America's Publisher of Contemporary Romance

Printed in the U.S.A.

Books by Doreen Owens Malek

Silhouette Romance

The Crystal Unicorn #363

Silhouette Special Edition

A Ruling Passion #154

Silhouette Desire

Native Season #86
Reckless Moon #222
Winter Meeting #240
Desperado #260
Firestorm #290

Silhouette Intimate Moments

The Eden Tree #88
Devil's Deception #105
Montega's Mistress #169

DOREEN OWENS MALEK

is an attorney and former teacher who decided on her current career when she sold her fledgling novel to the first editor who read it. She has been writing ever since. Born and raised in New Jersey, she has lived throughout the Northeast and now makes her home in Pennsylvania.

Chapter 1

An opalescent moon hung over the Atlantic, dappling the shoreline and streaking the frothing waves with a silver path, as a wounded man stumbled up from the beach. Half crawling, trying to run, he was gasping for breath and glancing nervously over his shoulder at the flashing blue lights of the police cars gathering on the sand. Scrub grass and sea oats littered the slope, impeding his progress, and he staggered, almost falling several times. He clutched his injured arm with his other hand, the fingers slippery with his own blood. A small revolver dangled loosely from his forefinger and thumb, and he stuck it in the waistband of his pants so that he could wipe the sweat and seawater from his eyes. His vision thus cleared, he saw a light at the top of the embankment, and he headed for it, feeling a surge of hope. According to his information, this area of the beach was supposed to be deserted during the off-season, the vacation homes empty, and he hoped to find refuge in one of them. He dropped to the ground suddenly as the beam of a

searchlight passed over him and then stood unsteadily,
reaching for his gun again and scrambling for the ridge. He
had to make it before he passed out; he had been shot before and could feel the remembered weakness flooding his
limbs.

The light blurred and danced in the distance, coming
closer by inches as he dragged himself toward it. When he
drew near he saw that it was an arc lamp above a patio,
probably left on for security reasons when the owners departed. He paused for a moment, surveying the landscape.
The house stood alone, surrounded by artfully placed trees
and bushes that provided privacy, as well as a beautiful setting. Satisfied, he lurched onto the cement deck, supporting himself with one hand flat against the redwood siding of
the house as he peered through sliding glass doors. They
were covered by heavy woven drapes that effectively concealed the interior from view. He looked back at the beach,
at the distant figures of uniformed men swimming dizzily
before his eyes and then down at his arm. In the dim light his
sleeve seemed covered with a substance the color and con-
sistency of spring mud. Making his decision, he lifted a
folded tarpaulin from the railing behind him and wrapped
it around a small deck chair. Gathering the last vestiges of
his vanishing strength, he raised the chair above his head
and crashed it into the right-hand panel of the doors.

The glass cracked and he kicked it loose from its frame,
taking care to do so quietly. When he had created an opening large enough to admit his body, he slipped through it.
He slumped against the inner wall with relief, then shot bolt
upright as a switch was thrown and the room filled with
light.

A woman faced him—young, pretty, terrified. She was
dressed in a floor-length flowered nightgown, pale hair cas-
cading over her shoulders, and it was obvious that she'd
been reading at the dining table with a small study lamp

whose glow was not visible outside. Her hand went to her throat as her blue eyes widened in alarm, and his heart sank. Oh, no. Not a woman. A man he could have knocked out, or tied up, but this was impossible. . . .

Her eyes moved toward the telephone, and he stepped forward before she could act on her thought. She went white, staring at the gun in his hand. Her fright was palpable, flowing in waves across the distance separating them. He had to reassure her, fast, or panic might cause her to do something reckless.

"I'm not going to hurt you," he said hoarsely, weaving on his feet as he spoke. "I'm not a criminal. Just do what I say, and everything will be all right."

Helen Demarest looked back at him, trying to accept the reality of his alien presence in her father's house. Her trancelike gaze moved over his form, registering that he was tall and slim, wet and very disheveled, with longish dark hair and tattered, filthy clothes. His features were handsome, or would have been under normal circumstances, without the sickly pallor that underlay his olive skin and made his brown eyes too large for his face. As she hesitated, unsure whether she should listen to him or run for the door, he shivered violently and several drops of blood sprayed from his fingertips, spattering the beige carpeting with carmine stains. Helen lifted her hand, as if to aid him, and he acted reflexively, raising his gun.

She flinched visibly, and he knew he had made a mistake. He had to convince her that she was safe, not act like the thug she thought he was.

"Sit down," he rasped, gesturing with the barrel of the gun toward one of the Breuer chairs surrounding the table. She sat stiffly, her body rigid with apprehension, and he sank gratefully into a deep leather lounge chair. His dizziness subsided, and he studied her more closely. Barefoot, her face washed clean of makeup for the night, she was a slight, porcelain blonde who looked back at him without expression, her hands clasped tensely in her lap.

"I'm not going to hurt you," he said again, meaning it, aware how empty it sounded after his intimidating entrance, but trying anyway. In his debilitated condition he might not be able to control her without harming her if she decided to make a break for it.

He couldn't tell if she believed him. She kept looking at his arm, and finally he did, also, realizing what a gory mess it must seem to her. She didn't look the type to be familiar with gunshot wounds.

"Can you get me a rag?" he asked. She rose slowly, went to the space-age kitchenette on the other side of the oak bar and returned with a dish towel. She handed it to him, and he bound it clumsily around the wound, watching her all the while. She stood, unmoving, in front of him, obviously afraid to take a step except on his command.

"And a glass of water," he added. She got it for him, and he drank eagerly, feeling a delicious slaking of his fierce thirst.

"Juice would be better," she said in a light, steady voice, and it was a moment before he realized she had spoken. He blinked, startled.

"You've lost a lot of blood; you should have some orange juice. Would you like me to get it?"

He nodded, amazed, hoping that this was not some kind of trick that would force him to take action against her. But she appeared to be in earnest, going to the shiny, stainless-steel refrigerator and removing a quart carton of juice. He noticed that the whole place was done up like a designer's dream: coordinated neutrals, recessed lighting, rich fabrics and heavy, polished woods. Whoever this girl was, she was not poor.

When she gave him the carton he refused the glass and drank straight from the container, wiping his mouth with the back of his good arm. Their eyes met over his sodden sleeve and he said, "What's your name?"

"Helen. Helen Demarest. What's yours?"

It almost struck him as funny, the way she sounded so American, like one of the coeds he had gone to school with, making chitchat at a frat party. "Matteo," he answered truthfully, playing along, buying time.

"Did the police shoot you, Matteo?" she inquired evenly.

She was nothing if not direct. He decided to answer her in kind.

"Yes."

"What you were doing is illegal," she said. It was not a question.

"It is illegal, but it is not wrong."

Their attention was distracted by the wail of a siren in the distance, moving closer. Helen's head turned toward it automatically, and he stood abruptly, the room spinning around him. He rocked back on his heels, and his eyes closed as he fought for equilibrium. The threat implicit in the sound seemed to defeat him, and when he opened his eyes again he extended the gun to Helen, butt first.

"No police," he said huskily, falling heavily against the wall, sliding along it, his lashes fluttering. He was losing consciousness, the gun slipping from his fingers. As he passed out Helen ran to his side, grabbing the gun and easing his descent to the floor. He rolled bonelessly onto his back as she stood up uncertainly, the gun like a live thing in her hand.

Her first impulse was to throw it out the window, but she feared it might be needed later. She tried to think of an unlikely place to hide it, and she saw the door of the refrigerator standing slightly ajar. She ran to the kitchen and tossed the gun into the crisper drawer, glad to be rid of it. Then she hurried back to the man sprawled on the rug, knelt next to him and lifted his wrist. His pulse was rapid and thready, his

heart working overtime to make up for decreased blood
volume. Helen wondered how badly he was hurt; the wound
looked awful, but she was no judge of such things. Perhaps
he was going into shock. She tried to remember long ago
first aid classes and could only recall something about
keeping victims warm. She was going for a blanket when she
was halted by the echo of screeching tires at the end of the
lane. This was followed by the sound of doors slamming. It
had to be a squad car; nothing else would be abroad at this
time of the night. The people in it were searching for the
fugitive at her feet. She glanced at the door; help was just
beyond it, a hundred yards away. She looked back at Matteo and, as if in response to her examination, his eyes
opened. The lashes stirred, then lifted to reveal onyx eyes
that locked with hers.

"No police," he whispered, then faded out again.

Helen swallowed. There was something pathetic, even
touching, about his insistence in the face of his failing
strength, and she found she couldn't deny his request.
Making an impulsive and possibly foolish decision, she ran
to the wall and snapped off the overhead light. With her
heart pounding she listened to the activity outside, waiting
until the sounds indicated that the search was over and the
police had left. Then, after making sure all the drapes were
closed, she picked up the study lamp, extended the cord to
its full length and examined her nocturnal intruder more
closely.

He was still unconscious, but breathing regularly. His face
was beaded with sweat, his clothes already drying in the air-
conditioned room. The bleeding from his wound seemed to
be slowing, but his color was alarming, making his tan seem
like a coat of greasepaint. Helen got up to fill a basin with
water and then bathed his face, stroking his brow and tem-
ples until he revived. When he saw her, he tried to sit up, but
collapsed.

"It's all right," Helen soothed him. "The police have gone, and I've put your gun away. You can't stay here on the floor; you need some proper rest. You'll have to get up now. I'm going to take you to my bed."

It was clear that despite his dazed state he understood she was going to help him. He looked stunned for a second, then rapidly decided to accept without question the boon that fate had sent him. He draped his good arm over Helen's shoulders and hoisted himself first to a sitting position, then to his knees. He didn't wince or cry out, but perspiration broke out afresh on his forehead, and his mouth became a grim line.

"It's just down the hall," Helen said gently.

He nodded stoically, determined to make it. She put her arms around his waist and hauled him upward, swaying with his weight. His scent overwhelmed her, a combination of musky masculinity and the coppery, heated smell of blood. He was muscular, heavier than he looked, and she had to pause to catch her breath when he was finally on his feet.

"*Cálmate,*" he murmured, looking into her eyes, lapsing into his native language in his attempt to encourage her. "We can do it together."

Cálmate. That was Spanish. Helen recognized it from her childhood, when her mother had had a Costa Rican maid. It was the Latin equivalent of "take it easy," an expression used between friends. She had earlier noticed his slight accent, discernible only with certain words, and this, along with his name, confirmed her initial suspicion that he was not American.

It was a short distance to the bedroom, but the walk seemed to go on forever. It had taken everything he had left to get to the house, and Helen almost had to carry him to the bed. She could tell that he was humiliated, frustrated by the frailty of his body, whose instant obedience he had evidently come to expect. By the time they reached their goal

one side of Helen's nightdress was drenched with his blood.
When she released him he sank heavily onto the edge of the
bed, then fell back on it, passing out almost immediately.
Helen did what she could to arrange his limbs comfortably,
hoping that she would be able to move him to change the
linen. The bed already looked like a murder had taken place
on it. She covered him with a light blanket from the closet
and then sat on the satin-draped chaise next to the bed,
trying to collect herself.

She almost couldn't grasp what had happened. An hour
before she had been studying the details of Christopher
Marlowe's death in an Elizabethan barroom brawl, and now
she had a wounded outlaw ensconced on her stepmother's
Oscar de la Renta bedspread, as if the one event had influ-
enced the other. She had to do something to care for his
wound; it could become infected if not dressed, and she
didn't even know if the bullet was still in it. Helen bit her lip
thoughtfully, instructing herself not to panic. She was a
graduate student in sixteenth-century literature, not a nurse,
but surely common sense had to play some role in an event
like this. Soap and disinfectant, that's what she needed. She
picked up a notepad from the end table next to the bed and
began to make a list.

Her life had not prepared her to deal with such a crisis.
She was the daughter of a millionaire, but far from being the
pampered princess some supposed, she was a postscript to
the youth of both her parents, who had gone on to succes-
sive remarriages, behaving dutifully but not lovingly toward her. Raised by a socialite mother who had little time
for her only child, Helen had been shuttled from boarding
schools to expensive European summer camps, always an
afterthought, always alone. She grew up seeking solace in
the intellectual pursuits that became the butt of jokes and
misunderstandings among her family and friends. Occupied with fashion shows, shopping expeditions, tennis and

skiing, they could not fathom her interest in books and knowledge. Considered an oddity, almost an outcast, Helen was driven further into her studies, trying to find a meaning in them that seemed absent from the aimless, hedonistic lives of her relatives. She was now pretty much on her own, living on a trust fund, maintaining minimal contact with her imperious, dictatorial mother and a father far more interested in his stockbrokers than he was in her. For the child of generations of money, Helen was singularly idealistic, almost naive, having been raised apart from the financial pursuits of her family in the rarefied atmosphere of strictly run private schools. With money to support her and little interference from the father who supplied it, Helen went on with her studies, absorbed by a rich and timeless past she found much more rewarding than sterile reality. She had been immersed in her work for three weeks, isolated in her father's vacation house, when the man on the bed had disturbed the quiet, satisfying pattern of her days with his unexpected intrusion.

Helen suddenly threw her pencil on the floor and pressed her palms to the sides of her head. A man could be dying not five feet away from her, and she was making a *list*, for heaven's sake. She got up hurriedly, realized she was still wearing the stained nightgown, stripped it off impatiently and slipped into a terry robe. She checked on Matteo, who was sweating profusely, muttering to himself. It was clear that his temperature was rising, and Helen wondered if there was alcohol in Adrienne's medicine cabinet. She left her patient to rummage in her stepmother's bathroom, looking for supplies. Adrienne was more into fifty dollar an ounce wrinkle cream than gauze bandages, but Helen did manage to find some peroxide and large sterile pads that would have to do until she was able to get out to a pharmacy. What she really needed was an antibiotic, and since Adrienne was something of a hypochondriac, with a coterie of doctors and no shortage of cash to command their attention, she had a separate glass cabinet stocked with little plastic vials of prescription medicines. Helen had never looked in it, but she did so now, passing over the many bottles she was unable to identify until she came to one labeled "erythrocin stearate." She had taken that once herself for a strep throat, so she set it aside, hoping that its time of potency had not expired and that Matteo was not allergic to it. The date on the label was obscured, but there were ten tablets left, enough to help if he responded to it. Helen also found a half-empty container of Percocet, with directions indicating that Adrienne had taken it for an abscessed tooth. It had to be a pretty powerful painkiller, then, because her stepmother raised the roof if she got a hangnail. Helen put the two bottles in the pockets of her robe and rapidly replaced everything else, then went back to the vanity and assembled what she thought she would need to dress the wound.

When she returned to Matteo's bedside, she tried to slip the sleeve off his injured arm, but he fought her hands, twisting away, seemingly slipping further into delirium. Taking an alternative tack, Helen picked up a pair of shears and began to cut away the sodden material around the wound. But once she uncovered it she wished she hadn't.

It was a jagged mass of torn flesh, carbon stained and flayed raw, with the reddish streaks that indicated infection already radiating out from the bloody center. Helen stuck her tongue in the corner of her mouth, fingers busy, muttering a prayer under her breath. When she realized she was reciting the Girl Scout oath, she stopped short and began again, encouraged by the familiar words as she washed away the coagulated blood, splashed the gaping wounds with antiseptic and covered them with sterile pads. She hadn't been able to feel anything under the skin, and she could see the bullet had passed clean through the meat of his upper arm, exiting out the back. She finished by tearing an old pillowcase into strips and tying them around the dressing to hold it into place, securing them just above Matteo's biceps. Her handiwork, when complete, looked like a neat little package, but the patient did not seem improved. He was still mumbling incoherently, his skin fiery, and she didn't know how she was going to get him to take the pills in her pocket. Finally she crushed them up in a glass of water and forced the liquid down his throat a little at a time, tilting his head back and dribbling it between his lips. It was a tedious and exhausting process for both of them, and when the glass was empty she didn't feel like struggling with him any further, but she knew that the rest of his damp shirt had to come off. She peeled it from his body by inches, noticing the foreign label inside the collar. She also noticed that his torso was beautiful, the dusky skin flowing silkily over his well-developed arms and chest. A spray of dark hair spread over his breast and formed a line down his abdomen to his belt. She paused to wipe his face, heavily beaded with perspiration, studying his long, spiky lashes, the heavy shadow of beard on his upper lip and chin. His thick, wavy hair was damp and matted, and she brushed it back from his forehead, wondering whether it was black or dark brown; in its current state it was impossible to tell. When she was finished she tidied the bed and got up to wash the instruments she had used. On her way out the bedroom door the telephone rang, and Helen glanced at the clock on the dresser as she went to answer it. The night had passed, and it was morning. As she picked up the receiver Helen thought that it had to be one of her parents, since they alone knew she was at the beach house.

It was the long arm of Switzerland, otherwise known as Helen's mother, Sophia Chamberlain Demarest Collier Nyquist. Sophia lived in Gstaad with her third husband, the chocolate baron, who commissioned his secretary to send Helen a ten-pound box of bonbons every Christmas. Helen had long ago stopped reminding her stepfather that she was allergic to chocolate and routinely dropped the gift off at an orphanage near her apartment in Cambridge. And now Sophia, with her exquisite timing, was calling up for her semi-annual clothes lecture while her daughter was harboring a gunshot victim.

"Darling, just ringing up to remind you that the collections are coming out next week, and I'm expecting you to go with me to pick out a few things," Sophia began in her breathless, confidence-sharing voice, broaching the expected topic.

Sophia had been born in Darien, Connecticut, but ever since she had lived in England with her second husband, she was fond of dropping Britishisms like "ringing up" into her conversation. Helen looked at the ceiling. She had never accompanied her mother to this ritual orgy of spending, but that did not deter Sophia from behaving as if it was an obligation which Helen would be rude and insensitive to ignore. Helen sighed as her mother rattled on about the trip, wondering how much her stepfather would be expected to pay for this latest indulgence. "Pick up a few things," to her mother, meant packing off her entire current wardrobe to a secondhand house for a tax deduction and starting over from scratch, ordering up originals from a range of designers.

"Sophia, I have enough clothes, and I really have to go," Helen interrupted when her mother paused for air. "I have to get to the library."

"Don't be ridiculous, sweeting, one never has enough clothes," Sophia replied, laughing lightly and ignoring the rest of her daughter's statement. "I've already bought your ticket; you can meet me in Rome at Claudia's villa."

Claudia Fierremonte, a friend of Helen's mother's who had inherited a sports car fortune, shared Sophia's attitude toward life and the continual pursuit of the perfect wardrobe. Helen would rather do battle with Medusa than be trapped in the Eternal City with the two of them.

"I can't make it, Sophia, I have too much work to do." Helen glanced at Matteo as he kicked off his cover, wishing that she was churlish enough to hang up in Sophia's ear. She wanted to get back to her patient, who was now cold again and shivering. She put down the phone while her mother was still talking and unfolded the quilt from the foot of the bed, drawing it up to his chin. He settled down, and Helen picked up the receiver again to hear her mother say, "And Roberto will be there."

As if that were an enticement. Roberto Fierremonte was Claudia's brother, a handsome, charming playboy who, like Claudia, had never done a day's work in his life. Sophia thought that he was love's young dream and considered Helen's low opinion of him to be just another of her daughter's many aberrations.

"I thought we had closed the subject of Roberto," Helen said wearily, mentally tapping her foot. She had to hand it to her mother; Sophia was relentless as a tidal wave. She never surrendered, never seemed to consider doing so. "And my research can't wait. I'm sorry."

"Helen, really, your obsession with that...project... simply defies comprehension," Sophia observed, the first note of irritation creeping into her tone. "You absolutely must do something about the way you look. When you arrived for Bobbie's shower in that...jacket, I almost died. I mean, died, right there in the Sherry Netherland. Darling, I hate to say this, but you are embarrassing me."

Helen had thought her mother's cousin Bobbie should be embarrassed, throwing herself a shower for her fourth wedding. "That jacket was a pea coat, Sophia. Millions of people wear them."

"That's just my point, dear, you're not millions of people. You have an image to project; you can't go around in

rags you've picked up in the basement of an army-navy
store. I'll bet that thing isn't even wool.''

"I don't know; I didn't interview the sheep," Helen replied sarcastically, but the gibe was lost on her mother, who
switched to her other favorite subject, Helen's stepmother.

"I hope you're comfortable there in your father's place,
Helen," Sophia said unctuously. "It was so chic and stylish when I decorated it; I can only imagine what it looks like
now. That woman your father married has the Manhattan
town house done in Reign of Terror, I think; I can't understand why everything is red."

Matteo stirred, and Helen waited until he relaxed again
before answering. "It's Mediterranean, Sophia, and you
know her name is Adrienne. Dad's been married to her for
five years." Helen glanced around the room, desperate to
get off the phone quickly without provoking a follow-up call
by Sophia. Suddenly inspiration struck, and she added,
"Actually, maybe you're right. I really should get out of
here soon because Adrienne needs the place for a house
party Debra wants to have. She told me so a few days ago."

Sophia's most cherished guiding principle was to thwart
her successor's plans whenever possible. "Well, I certainly
wouldn't let Adrienne drive you out so she can throw a
shindig for that fat little adolescent of hers. Take as long as
you like, dear. Forget about the collections. I know you have
things to do. Shall I call your father and tell him you need
to stay a little longer?"

"That's okay," Helen answered, grinning, "I'm sure
Adrienne and I can work it out. Have a good time, Sophia.
Goodbye."

"*Ciao*, darling."

Helen hung up gratefully, going immediately to check on
Matteo. Fresh blood was already staining the gauze above
the wound, but it wasn't running in rivulets anymore. She
hoped he didn't need a transfusion, because he wasn't going

to get one lying in Adrienne's bedroom. She realized that there was nothing more she could do for him and that she should just let him rest, so she completed the task Sophia's call had interrupted: cleaning up and putting everything back where it belonged. Then she stretched out on the chaise next to Matteo, propping a pillow behind her head and closing her eyes. She was exhausted, and it wasn't long before she slept.

Helen awoke in late afternoon, to find that she had slept through the time to give Matteo his pills. She found him bathed in perspiration, still feverish, and drifting in and out of consciousness with a rapidity that scared her. During one of his lucid moments she told him that she was calling a doctor, but he reacted so violently that she retracted the statement in order to calm him. She changed the dressing on his wound and then gave him a dose and a half of the medicine, praying that it wasn't too much. After drinking the liquid, Matteo fell back on the bed, his eyes closed, and Helen thought he was unconscious again. But as she moved away the fingers of his good hand encircled her wrist, squeezing it. Too weak to talk, he nevertheless communicated his gratitude, and Helen felt the sudden sting of tears behind her eyes. She was glad that she had sheltered him, sure now that she had not been wrong to do so.

After she had taken a quick shower and dressed, she made coffee and toast and took them back to the bedroom. She felt the disorientation that doing morning things in the evening brought, but forgot it when she saw that Matteo was shaking so badly that the bed rattled. He was wracked with chills. She grabbed extra blankets and piled them on top of him, crawling up on the bed to hold him when his trembling didn't cease. She held him tightly, cradling his head against her shoulder, and after several minutes his shivering lessened. He relaxed into her arms, and Helen remained in her awkward position, loath to disturb him. When he seemed to be sleeping peacefully she let him slip back to the bed, turning his pillow so that the cool side touched his cheek. He sighed deeply, and she was happy that she was able to make him more comfortable.

Helen went back to her tepid coffee and cold toast, wondering how old he was. It was difficult to tell from his appearance, because he had probably never looked worse in his life than he did right now. That he was young and, under normal circumstances, quite attractive in a dark, Latin way was obvious. The rest was a mystery. He had no identification on him, which was undoubtedly not an accident, and his knowledge of English could have been gained anywhere. Resignedly she finished her toast and brought the dishes back to the kitchen.

For two more days Helen cared for Matteo, while he plunged in and out of fevers, sometimes seeming to improve, then losing ground when his diminished strength was not equal to the struggle. At times it was clear he knew she was there, but at others all his concentration appeared to be focused on fighting off the infection that sought to conquer him. And he was a fighter. He wrestled with his illness the way Jacob wrestled with the angel, a mere mortal against a powerful force, but a fierce, stubborn mortal who would not acknowledge an enemy greater than himself. Helen, silent witness to the battle, fed him juice and medicine and stormed heaven with pleas for his recovery. Her papers gathered dust on the dining room table, and her books went unread as day merged into night while she kept her vigil by his bedside. She changed his linen and his dressings, forced soup on him when he seemed capable of drinking it and left him alone only once, to slip out to the local drugstore for supplies. Convinced that he would be dead when she got back, she ran headlong into the bedroom, relaxing only when she saw the rise and fall of his chest as he breathed.

By the afternoon of the third day she thought he looked better. His color had improved and the skin around his wound felt cooler. At suppertime she ate a container of yogurt and made a cup of tea, sitting on the edge of Matteo's bed to drink it. She couldn't remember ever being so tired; she ached with it, and for the first time in her life understood what it meant to be "bone weary." Letting the empty cup fall to the rug, she lay down on the other side of the bed, where she would be able to hear Matteo if he made the slightest sound. She thought she should set the alarm to give him his medicine, and that was the last thing she remembered before she awoke because someone was touching her hair.

She sat up, startled to find him looking at her with eyes that were clear and steady.

"You're better," she whispered.

He didn't answer, merely continued to gaze at her as if trying to put the pieces of a puzzle together.

"Do you remember me?" she asked.

"Helen," he replied, in a disused, rusty voice.

"That's right. Do you remember how you got here, what happened?"

He nodded.

"You've been very sick. You wouldn't let me call a doctor, so..."

"How long?" he interrupted hoarsely.

"How long have you been here?"

He nodded again.

"Three days."

"Three days?" He seemed unable to believe it.

"Yes. You...arrived late Friday night, and it's now Monday evening."

He attempted to clear his throat, wincing slightly. "And you've been taking care of me all this time?"

"Yes. I'm so glad you're feeling better."

He glanced around the room, then looked back at Helen. "Where is my gun?"

"I put it away."

"Where?"

"In the refrigerator," Helen mumbled, dropping her eyes.

He looked blank. "What?"

"In the crisper drawer of the refrigerator. I didn't know what to do with it, and I figured it was the last place anyone would look."

For the first time he smiled. It wasn't much of a smile, just a slight upward turning at the corners of his mouth, but it changed his face. "Good girl," he said, and suddenly her action didn't seem ridiculous anymore, and she smiled back at him, proud of herself.

"Has anyone been here?" he asked, closing his eyes, visibly running down, the strain of even this short conversation tiring him.

"No one at all. We've been quite alone." Helen moved to check his bandage, and his eyes opened as she bent over him. The gauze bore a dried brown stain, small and unintimidating.

"Why did you help me?" he inquired huskily, holding her gaze with his.

Helen had been asking herself the same question ever since the first night, and she hadn't been able to come up with an answer more complicated than the one she now gave him.

"I guess because you needed help," she replied. She stepped back and eyed him levelly. "Matteo—is that your real name?"

He indicated assent.

"Matteo, what are you mixed up in?"

He turned his head. "I can't tell you. For your own protection, it's better if you don't know. I'll leave as soon as I'm able; if anyone traces me back here you can say I forced you to hide me at gunpoint, took you for a hostage.''

''Why? Would someone come looking for me?''

''For me,'' he murmured. Helen's brow furrowed, but as she opened her mouth again to press him for more information, she realized that he had fallen asleep and she felt ashamed. Now was not the time to grill the man; he was two steps away from an intensive-care ward. She tucked his blanket around him and resolved to let the questions wait until he felt up to answering them.

She didn't know then that as far he was concerned they would not be answered.

When Matteo awoke again, it was to the smell of food.

Helen was sitting next to the bed with a plate of scrambled eggs. She extended a forkful to him, raising her eyebrows.

He glanced at the offering without enthusiasm, then turned his head away.

''I know your appetite is gone, but it'll come back once you taste something good,'' she encouraged him.

He brightened. ''Got any Angel Bites?''

Helen stared back at him in amazement. ''Angel Bites? You mean those chocolate covered marshmallow snacks the kids like?''

He looked offended. ''I never heard they were just for kids.''

''That sound like an advertising campaign,'' Helen said dryly. ''Sorry buddy, no Angel Bites. I'll pick some up when I go to the store. In the meantime you'll have to make do with this.'' She handed him the fork.

He eyed her warily.

''Eat, or I'll feed you,'' she threatened.

He picked up the plate and obediently swallowed several mouthfuls, then pushed the dish back into her hand. Helen allowed him the round and presented him with a cloudy glass of dissolved pills.

"What's this?" he asked suspiciously.

"An antibiotic and a painkiller crushed up in water," she answered.

When he still hesitated she added, "You've been belting it down since Friday night, so I wouldn't worry. I do believe it's the reason you're not dead, so drink up."

He drained the glass and said, "You're the reason I'm not dead, Helen."

She didn't answer, unable to think of a suitable reply to such a tribute.

"Where did you get the medicine?" he asked, handing the empty tumbler back to her.

"My stepmother keeps an entire pharmacy in the bathroom. I just went through the bottles and picked out something from the assortment."

"The right stuff, apparently. That was clever."

"Not really. Adrienne has enough drugs in there to outfit the peace corps. It was only a matter of looking. She's probably got the cure for the common cold buried in that closet."

"Well, you don't mind if I think you're clever, do you?" he asked, teasing her.

Helen permitted herself a small smile. He talked just like an American, yet she had seen the foreign labels in his clothes, and sometimes she could hear a faint accent. And he had consumed enough Angel Bites to develop a fondness for them. What was going on here? Why was he in Florida, and why had he been shot? The pieces of the puzzle didn't fit together, and it was driving her crazy, but she stuck to her resolution not to interrogate him. She wanted to keep the conversation light until he was feeling stronger.

"This house belongs to your stepmother?" he asked abruptly.

"My father, but he never comes here anymore. Adrienne and her children use it mostly; I came during the off-season because I wanted privacy and quiet."

"Which lasted until I arrived," he concluded.

"It's still quiet," Helen said, and he grinned. The effect on Helen was considerable; she looked away so he wouldn't see the response in her eyes.

"You're much more alert," she observed neutrally, fussing with his pillows. "You fell asleep in the middle of our last conversation."

He sobered instantly. "No more painkillers. They're knocking me out, and I have to get moving." He tried to sit up, but fell back, his face pale. A fresh stain began to seep onto the gauze covering his wound.

"What are you doing?" Helen cried, grabbing his hands to hold him down. "You're in no condition to get out of bed, do you want to open up that arm again?"

He subsided reluctantly. "I've been here too long already; there are people who need me, people waiting for me."

"Well, they'll just have to wait. If you go anywhere now, you'll be scraped off the sidewalk in ten minutes and wind up in a hospital, a hospital full of doctors. And do you know what doctors have to do when they treat a gunshot wound? Call the police. How would you like that?"

The question was rhetorical. His eyes slid away from hers, and she picked up his dishes and took them to the kitchen. She made a production out of rinsing them off to give herself time to consider what he had said. Of course he would want to leave. Whatever had brought him to her door was still waiting to be accomplished. If he had succeeded in doing it, he would not have been shot. But the thought of his departure was painful in a fundamental way she didn't wish to examine too closely. During the past few days Matteo had become the central feature of her existence; his total dependence on her had forged a bond between them that she wished, she now realized, could continue. But he intended to return to his original objective without a thought for her except the gratitude he had already expressed.

Helen dried a dish thoughtfully and replaced it in the cabinet above the sink. Had she expected something more?

When she returned to Matteo's room he was staring out the window at the ocean. "This is a beautiful spot," he said to her as she entered.

"Yes, my father had this house built for my mother as a wedding present because she loved this part of St. Augustine so much. It was originally sort of a log cabin, very rustic, but it's been redone a couple of times since then."

"Your parents are divorced now?"

Helen noticed that he wanted to know all about her, while offering no information about himself. But then again, she had nothing to hide.

"Yes, and both have remarried twice. I've had assorted stepmothers and stepfathers, as well as, let's see, nine stepsiblings at various times. We're a very modern family." She tried to make a joke of it, but he didn't miss the forlorn expression she banished as soon as it appeared.

"Something tells me you won't follow that pattern," he said quietly. "You seem like a one-man woman to me."

"I hope so," she said lightly, turning her back on him deliberately. "Things are confusing enough right now."

He sensed that the issue was a sensitive one and sidestepped it. "You must have an interesting time at family reunions," he said lightly.

She faced him with a grateful smile. "Oh, we'd never get together all at once," she said. "Too much potential for open warfare. My mother would probably knife Adrienne."

"Is she jealous?" he asked.

"You bet."

"Why?"

"Adrienne currently holds the position my mother used to have."

"And that's enough?"

"For my mother it is. She regards men as property, once acquired, always owned." She didn't have to add that she disagreed with this philosophy; her tone as she said the words spoke volumes.

"Is she still in love with your father?" he asked, not caring about the answer, but about the insight he was getting into Helen's character.

"I think she is, in a way, although she would never admit it. He was her first real love, and you never forget the first one, no matter who comes after him."

"You sound like an expert."

Helen hesitated. "No as a matter of fact, I'm not. But I know *I'd* never forget."

He noticed the way she phrased it. The event was still in the future for her, and somehow he wasn't surprised.

"I don't think Sophia has felt the same way about another man since my father," Helen went on. "Or maybe I just like to think that he was special to her. I don't know."

"Sophia? You call your mother by her first name?"

"I'd better. She'd have a stroke if I ran around calling her Mom. She likes to tell people that we're sisters and see if they believe it."

"Do they?"

"Sometimes. More often than you'd think." Sophia's lifetime preoccupation with her physical appearance had paid off handsomely. At forty-seven she was remarkably well preserved.

"You look alike, then?"

Helen smiled wryly. "I don't know if you'd say that. We have the same coloring, similar features, but my mother is far more flamboyant, stylish. We're sort of like the original and the photographic negative.''

Matteo was watching her face, noting its changing expression as she spoke about her mother. "I can't imagine your being a shadowy imitation of anyone," he said softly, and she looked up to meet his eyes. They were closing, but he smiled at her before he fell asleep.

Helen got up in the middle of the night to check Matteo's dressing, and as she touched his shoulder his good hand flashed from beneath the covers and caught hers in a viselike grip. Helen recoiled from the pain; for someone recovering from such a severe illness, he was remarkably strong.

"Matteo, it's me," she said quietly. "Helen. I just want to change the gauze pad on your arm."

He studied her in the half light admitted by the open door to the hall and then released her, moving his fingers up to lay them against her cheek.

"I'm sorry," he whispered. "You took me by surprise."

Not a good idea, Helen thought to herself as she discarded the stained dressing and replaced it with a fresh one. He must have had some rude awakenings in the past.

When she stepped back he grasped her hand and pulled her toward him. She couldn't read his face, but his intent was clear as he drew her onto the bed and into his arms.

"Stay with me," he murmured. "You're too far away."

Helen lay next to him, snuggling up to his uninjured shoulder and putting her head on his chest. He encircled her with his arm, moving his leg so that she could fit comfortably against his side. He felt warm and solid, and she could hear his voice rumbling in his chest as he said, "While I was sick I dreamed that we were together like this."

"That wasn't a dream," Helen replied, feeling her face flame in the darkness. "You had the chills and couldn't seem to stop shaking. I got on the bed with you and held you until you quieted down.''

He didn't answer for a moment, but she felt his lips moving in her hair. When his voice came it was low and husky.

"I don't know how to thank you for what you have done," he said quietly. "You probably saved my life. And I've got to live long enough to do what must be done."

There it was again, the hint that his business encompassed more than he could say. Since he had brought it up, she pressed her advantage, asking, "Can't you tell me what you were doing when you were hurt?"

"No."

"Why?" She cast about for an idea. "Did you steal something?"

His whole body stiffened, and she was immediately sorry she had said it.

"Do I seem like a thief to you?" he responded softly, and his grip on her shoulders relaxed, as if he didn't want to touch the person who could ask him such a question. "I told you once I was not a criminal, and I wasn't lying."

Helen half sat, looking down into his face. "You admitted that what you were doing is illegal. Most people would say that makes you a criminal."

"Is that how you see the world," he replied coldly, "all clear choices, everything black and white?"

"I see," Helen answered, frustrated by his obstinacy, his distant tone, "that you are treating me like a child."

"You act like one," he stated flatly. " 'Tell me, tell me,' as if this were a game we are playing, keeping secrets. It is not a game. When I say that I do not want you to know in order to keep you safe, you refuse to believe me. You kept me alive when I might have died without you. Should I pay you back by putting you in danger? What kind of friend would I be if I did that, Helen?"

She didn't answer, unable to argue with him. She noticed that his English became less colloquial when he was upset. He dropped the familiar conjunctions and adopted a more formal style, speaking the way he must have when he first learned the language.

He sighed heavily and reached for her again. "Come here. I don't want to fight with you."

Helen curled up with him again, unwilling to pursue the discussion, but still troubled.

"Can you trust me, Helen?" he asked, twining his fingers with hers and inching her closer. "Can you accept that I am making the right decision?"

"I guess I'll have to," she replied grudgingly, settling against him.

There was a smile in his voice when he directed, "Go to sleep, my stubborn little American."

Helen was tired and, despite her misgivings, found it surprisingly easy to obey him. She was almost out when she murmured, "The Chinese believe that you are always responsible for someone whose life you have saved. Do you think that's true?"

He waited a beat before he answered soberly, "I wonder."

But Helen didn't hear him.

She was asleep.

Chapter 2

Helen was reading in the chair next to the bed when Matteo opened his eyes the next morning. He didn't speak, but studied her covertly, taking in every detail.

She was wearing a blue robe with white lace ruching at the neckline, her blond hair flowing over her shoulders loosely. Her pose and her clothing reminded him of a painting he had once seen; it had depicted a golden girl in a blue dress sitting in a shaft of sunlight, bending her head over a book in her lap. Helen was absorbed, turning the pages without looking up, her expression rapt.

What an unexpected delight she was, Matteo thought. By all indicators, she should have grown up to be a vain, self-indulgent woman like her mother. Instead she was a dreamer, a loner who had come to this out-of-the-way place to escape the heedless life her family led. And when he had burst into her self-imposed isolation and ruined it, she had saved him with a spontaneous act of kindness.

"What are you reading?" he finally said, and she started, glancing toward him.

"You're awake," she said. "Are you hungry?"

"What is that book?" he persisted, and she held it up for his inspection.

"*Faust in Hell*," he read aloud, "*The Tragedy of Christopher Marlowe*. Why tragedy?"

"Oh, because he died so young, in such a senseless way. He might have been greater than Shakespeare, if he had lived."

"'Sweet Helen, make me immortal with a kiss,'" Matteo recited. "Is your name a coincidence?"

Helen shook her head, putting the book aside. "No, my father is a Marlowe buff; he named me. Dad also introduced me to his work when I was young." She smiled ruefully. "I think it's the only interest we have in common."

"Something, anyway," Matteo said gently, and she nodded.

"I have to get through this during the next week or so to remain on schedule," she said, standing up.

"What schedule?"

"My own. I'm working on my thesis and I have it all mapped out, what areas to cover and how long each should take." She folded her arms and examined the patient. "You're looking remarkably chipper today. I have to go to the store; we're out of food. It won't take me long. I'll be back before you know it, okay?"

He forced her to meet his eyes. She seemed to know what was coming, but he said it anyway. "Helen, I'd like you to get me some clothes. I have to take a shower and get dressed."

"You're going to leave soon," she responded.

"Yes."

"Today?" she asked dismally.

"We'll see," he said quietly, relenting. He studied her clouded face and added, "I have no money."

"I do," she replied simply. "What should I get?"

He looked thoughtful, trying to remember his American sizes. "Shirt: fifteen and a half, thirty-four. Pants: waist, thirty-four; inseam, uh, thirty-two, I guess. And shoes, see if you can get that tennis kind, what do you call them . . ."

"Sneakers?" Helen supplied.

"That's right, sneakers. Size ten. Is that all right?"

"Fine," she replied briskly, turning for the door.

"Helen," he said.

She paused.

"I have to go. I don't want to, but I must."

She didn't answer, merely left the room and went across the hall to change. He heard her leave a few minutes later.

As soon as she was gone he swung his legs over the edge of the bed and tried to stand. His knees gave way and he had to grab for the back of Helen's chair to steady himself, but he was on his feet for the first time in days. He maneuvered into position and sat down slowly, stretching his long legs in front of him. It felt good to be out of the bed, but even he had to question whether he was going to be doing any traveling right away. He felt punchy and light-headed, which he ascribed partly to the lingering effects of Helen's miracle pills. As they wore off the wound in his arm began to feel like it was being gouged by a hot poker, but he wanted to be clearheaded when he left.

He had to get back to his men. But just as important, he had to protect this girl who had taken such a risk for him. In his diverse life he had seen other acts of selfless behavior, but nothing quite the equal of this. That a rich, beautiful American woman would shelter a wounded stranger from the police and drop everything to nurse him back to health seemed unbelievable, but it had happened. To him.

And now he had to make sure that he got away clean, so that she wouldn't suffer any repercussions.

Unlike most of his compatriots, Matteo liked Americans, having gone to school in the United States for years. He had developed a solid affection for their open, easy manner, fierce independence and amazing resourcefulness. What he liked best was their romantic unpredictability; this young woman would have had every reason to throw him to the wolves and go back to studying literature and cashing her trust fund checks, but she had done exactly the opposite. And now he had to get out of her life without satisfying her legitimate curiosity or getting her into trouble with the authorities, who were surely still looking for him.

It was not going to be easy.

When Helen returned she came into the bedroom carrying several wrapped packages and a brown paper grocery bag.

"Angel Bites, as requested," she announced, tossing a cellophane packet into his lap. "And what are you doing out of bed, may I ask?"

"It's time," he answered flatly.

"Clothes," she said, dumping the parcels on the bed. "In the stated sizes. I don't think you'll make the cover of *Gentlemen's Quarterly*, but they should do the trick as long as you don't take off the shirt and display that shoulder to anybody."

"Thank you. Will you help me to the bathroom? I want to get cleaned up."

"Are you sure you're strong enough for that?" she asked, challenging him.

For an answer, he stood and took a step toward her. She moved to aid him, slipping her arm around his waist and walking at his side. She could feel the resurgence of his natural strength; it wouldn't be long before he would depart her life as suddenly as he had entered it. She led him to the bathroom and took him past the whirlpool and the sauna closet to the sunken bathtub, made to order for Adrienne and inlaid with imported Italian tiles. The gold-plated faucet had more gadgets and dials then a ship's boiler, and Helen showed him how to regulate the temperature and flow. She left him leaning against the wall and went to the closet for the things he would need. She returned to find him unbuckling his belt, favoring his injured arm but otherwise holding up very well. Too well.

He paused as she handed him a stack of Lord and Taylor towels, a bar of Adrienne's gardenia-scented soap and a bottle of her henna-herbal "specially formulated for the client" shampoo. Adrienne kept the place stocked like a Paris salon, and so Helen had seized the opportunity to travel light and leave her own toiletries at home. She wasn't sure Matteo would appreciate the amenities; he would probably emerge smelling like a high-priced bordello. But he would undoubtedly be clean.

"I'll be right outside the door if you need me," she said, watching as he set the towels on top of the rack and turned to face the tub. He was moving slowly, but gaining assurance with each passing second. He glanced at her and nodded.

"Go ahead. I'll be fine."

Helen left and closed the door behind her, listening as the rush of water began shortly afterward. It continued for a long time, sounding like Victoria Falls in the narrow hallway. When the shower stopped she waited anxiously, hoping that his impaired balance wouldn't cause him to fall on the slippery tile floor. Seconds later the door opened, and a cloud of steam emerged. When it cleared she saw Matteo standing in front of the mirror over the sink, wearing a towel knotted around his waist. Barefoot, dripping, his soaking hair pushed back from his forehead, he was frowning down at Adrienne's Lilliputian sterling silver razor. It was totally inadequate to handle his five-day growth of coarse black beard.

"Is this all you have?" he asked. "Your father didn't leave a razor here?"

"No, but I have a disposable one in my luggage. I'll get it."

She went for the razor, and when she came back he was lathering his face, grimacing at his own image.

"I look like a bus station degenerate," he said grimly, and she had to laugh.

"What bus station have you been hanging out in?" she asked playfully.

"Port Authority," he answered, before he thought. "At least I used to pass through there, years ago. I don't imagine it's changed much."

"How long since you've seen it?" Helen asked innocently, and his eyes met hers in the mirror.

"All right," she conceded grumpily. "I'm probing, I admit it, but I can't understand why..."

The razor fell from his fingers as he gripped the edge of the sink with both hands, his knuckles white.

"What is it?" Helen asked, moving in to steady him.

"Nothing, just felt a little dizzy." He went to pick up the razor again, and Helen grabbed it out of his hand.

"That's it," she said firmly. "You sit down and I'll shave you."

"You're not shaving me," he protested as she tried to push him into the vanity chair, objecting to the servile nature of the task.

"Yes, I am, or you keep the beard. And unless you want little children to run screaming out of your path, I suggest you get rid of it."

"That bad, huh?" he replied glumly.

"You said so yourself."

He sat down, subsiding with surprising meekness. Helen had a strong feeling that it was a rare thing for him to succumb to another's will. She relathered his face, noticing that his drying hair was the color of bittersweet chocolate, a shade lighter than his brows and lashes, which were jet black. Shining now with cleanliness, it fell in loose waves onto his forehead and around his ears. And as she drew the razor over his skin, his features emerged, more clearly than she had ever seen them; even on the first night they were already shrouded with stubble. The face that evolved was that of a young grandee in a Goya court portrait: fierce, proud, beautiful. Careful to avoid glancing down at his near nude body, Helen finished shaving him, wiping his cheeks with a towel and removing daubs of cream from his ears. He watched all the while with his alert, cola-brown eyes; they moved with her, following her to the medicine chest as she removed a fresh gauze pad from a shelf and stripped off the paper wrapper.

"Just hold still for a minute," she instructed him. "I want to cover your arm with this."

The wound was scabbing over and healing nicely, draining just a little clear fluid. Helen swabbed it with alcohol and fastened the new bandage in place, smoothing the surgical tape with a meticulous fingertip.

"You take such good care of me," he said, looking up at her from his sitting position.

"All part of the friendly service," Helen answered lightly, putting away the shaving gel. "Now on your feet, buddy. You should be back in bed."

She took both his hands and hauled him upward, while at the same time he rose on his own. The result was that he stumbled forward and lost his balance for a second, falling against her. Helen caught him, supporting his weight. As he straightened, the towel around his waist came loose, falling to the floor, and Helen suddenly found herself in the arms of a naked man.

He smelled wonderful, not feminine at all; Adrienne's goodies took on a distinctly rugged flavor in combination with his masculine flesh. His skin was smooth and fresh, like satin, with the hard base of muscle underneath it. She wanted to cling but drew back, flustered, until he reached out with his good arm and pulled her tight against him.

Matteo's hands slipped to her hips, and he molded her to him, shifting his position to straddle her. Helen gasped as she felt his arousal, and he groaned in response, his head dropping to her shoulder. He nudged her neck, moving his mouth inside her collar, and Helen closed her eyes as the delicious friction of his lips on her throat made her weak with longing.

"Helen," he muttered, caressing her through her clothes, moving his mouth to the swell of her breasts above her bra. She sighed luxuriously, running her fingers through his damp hair, trailing them to the firm column of his bare neck. He reacted swiftly, stepping back from her slightly to reach for the top button of her blouse.

She tilted her head back to look into his face, and her movement seemed to snap him out of the drugged haze of sensuality that had enfolded both of them. He released her so suddenly that she almost fell.

"What am I doing?" he rasped, slumping against the wall behind him and closing his eyes. "Helen, get out of here. Shut the door and leave me alone."

Helen obeyed because she didn't know what else to do. She went into the living room and sat down woodenly, wondering what would happen next. In the space of a minute everything had changed between them.

Still in the bathroom, Matteo rubbed his mouth with the back of a trembling hand, then reached for the new shirt that Helen had bought for him. He started to remove the pins from its folds, then threw it on the floor in frustration.

So much for his lauded self-control. He had been deluding himself that if he could just get away without touching her, everything would be all right. But of course that had focused all of his concentration on avoiding physical contact, which was the same thing as pining for it every moment. Restricting himself to affectionate embraces and kisses on the cheek had only inflamed him more. He had been injured, but he was far from dead. Every day of his recovery had brought him closer to acting on his feelings, and finally he had.

It didn't help to know that he would still have to leave her, and thanks to this incident, more bereft and alone than ever. He could tell that she wasn't used to letting people get close to her. From what she had told him of her life, she obviously preferred her own company. He couldn't blame her. Her background was hardly conducive to instilling faith in enduring relationships. She wasn't cynical or jaded, just understandably wary. But circumstances had changed her perspective in his case, before she even realized it, and now it was too late. The tie was there between them, indestructible, permanent. She had saved his life. There was no more to be said.

Matteo scratched around the edges of his bandage, his expression bleak. The healing skin was itchy, but he barely noticed what he was doing, his mind racing. His whole adult life had been dedicated to one goal. It had never occurred to him that anyone or anything could interfere with his desire to reach it. Until now.

He understood with a deep sense of alarm that he didn't want to leave Helen. The realization was revolutionary, disturbing. No single person had ever meant enough to him to threaten his purpose. He was used to thinking in terms of hundreds, thousands; individuals got lost in a scheme like that, even when the individual was himself. But Helen, with her gentle persuasion, had reminded him that he was a man, who needed not just commitment to noble ideals, but love, too.

He picked up the shirt, wincing as a knife blade of pain shot through his injured arm, and slipped it on, careful to slide it slowly over his wound. The thing was a constant annoyance.

Matteo had no patience with physical infirmity, and consequently he frequently compounded any illness he had by getting up too soon—or never lying down in the first place. This instance was certain to be no exception. He was planning on leaving the next night, well before any doctor in his or her right mind would have let him out of bed. But in a real sense his imminent departure was flight; flight from the one woman who could become more important to him than his cause.

He finished dressing, taking about five times longer than usual because his arm, and his general weakness, fought him all the way. He emerged from the bathroom to find that Helen had changed to an oversized T-shirt that left her slim, tanned legs bare and was sitting at the dining table, making notes on a yellow legal pad. She didn't look up as he came into the room, but said, "Would you like some lunch? I bought sandwich rolls and cold cuts at the store."

He realized she was going to pretend that nothing had happened. Well, that was probably for the best, and he decided to go along with it.

"That sounds good," he answered, his resolution lasting until she got up to walk past him and he saw that her brief outfit barely grazed her hips, immediately conjuring up all sorts of images in his overstimulated imagination.

"Do you think you could put something else on?" he snapped irritably, turning away.

Helen glanced down at herself, momentarily puzzled. "What's wrong with this? I always wear it to work in; it's comfortable and . . ."

"What's wrong is there isn't enough of it," he interrupted stiffly.

"Oh," she said, reddening. "I didn't think; I was just used to wearing anything while you were sick."

"Helen, I'm not sick anymore," he informed her, feeling idiotic and wishing he hadn't brought the subject up at all.

"Go into the bedroom and take a rest," she said, dismissing the topic. "I'll bring the food when it's ready."

He followed her instructions, wondering, as he sat on the edge of the bed, how he was going to keep his hands off her until it was safe for him to leave.

The next day was going to be his last, and they both knew it. Silence reigned for most of the morning as Matteo studied the local maps Helen had gotten for him. Helen remained in the dining room, pursuing her work, trying to forget what he was doing. Even the briefest conversation was painful, reminding them that soon there would be none at all.

Around noon Matteo emerged from the back hall, rubbing his arm and tucking in the shirt that was his usual size, but too big for him now with the weight he had lost during his illness.

"Do you know the Camache Island boat basin?" he asked Helen.

She looked up from her papers. "Yes, it's just a couple of miles away, down Route A1A. Why?"

"I'd like you to take me there, in your car. After it gets dark, so there's less chance of us being seen. All right?"

"All right," she agreed, determined to be as stoic as he was.

He looked out the glass doors at the sun-swept panorama of sandy beach and aquamarine ocean.

"Georgeous day," he said.

"Why don't you go out on the patio? You've been cooped up in here for almost a week; the fresh air would do you good."

He hesitated. "I might be seen."

She looked incredulous. "Here? Matteo, there isn't another house for half a mile down the beach either way."

"I meant from a boat. With binoculars."

She was speechless for a moment and then said quietly, "Your enemies would go to such lengths?"

He shrugged slightly. "They have before."

Helen was staring at him in consternation when they both heard a noise on the front walk. Moving with lightning speed, Matteo grabbed Helen and clamped one hand over her mouth, stopping any sound she might have made. He drew his gun, which he had earlier retrieved from its hiding place, and pointed it at the door, continuing to hold Helen in a throttling grip that immobilized her completely. After a couple of seconds several letters fell through the slot in the door and slid onto the floor. It was only the mailman. Matteo released Helen slowly, and she stumbled away from him, fingering her bruised lips and fighting tears.

"Why did you do that to me?" she gasped. "Do you think I took care of you all this time in order to betray you now?"

He had the good grace to look ashamed and was unable to meet her eyes. "I'm sorry. It was an instinctive reaction."

Helen stared back at him, outraged. What kind of life did he lead, that his "instinctive reaction" was not to trust anyone, including herself?

He continued to look away from her, and she tried to brush past him, tired of waiting for him to acknowledge her. His hand came out to stop her, and she shook him off.

"Helen..." he began.

"I don't want to hear it. There is no excuse for treating me that way. If I had wanted to I could have called in a legion of police while you were flat on your back and out of your head."

"I know that. I was startled, Helen, that's all. I didn't expect to hear anyone come to the door."

"He comes to the door every weekday, Matteo. We have mail service here just like everyplace else. You haven't heard him because before today you were spending all of your time in the bedroom. Now will you let me get by? I have work to do."

He grabbed her shoulders and spun her around to face him. "Helen, don't do this. I don't want to go with things all wrong between us."

"Why not?" she answered cruelly. "You'll be gone, what difference will it make?"

"Helen, I have no choice!"

"Oh, yes, yes. I know," she replied sarcastically. "How could I possibly forget? You have your all-important mission, whatever on God's green earth that is. And everyone is after you, and it's bigger than both of us, but you can't tell me about it. Did I miss anything, any of the bad movie clichés you've been feeding me since you came here? To tell you the truth, I'm sick of listening to them, and I am heartily sick of you, so why don't you just..."

She didn't complete the sentence because he pulled her into his arms and covered her mouth with his. She resisted futilely for a few seconds, but they both understood that she didn't really want to get away from him.

For a first kiss it was remarkably free of tentative exploration. Matteo knew what he was doing, and Helen's response was elemental, total. This was Matteo, whom she had saved, and who might yet save her.

Matteo was as lost as she was, moving his lips to her cheek, her ear, lifting her against him to merge her body with his, then opening her mouth with his tongue. Helen responded eagerly, her desire to please making up for her lack of experience, and he ran his hand down her back, forcing her closer. He was still holding the gun, and it slipped from his grasp as he embraced her, clattering to the hardwood floor exposed at the edge of the rug. They broke apart, looking down at it, then at each other. The weapon was a brutal reminder of their true situation, and Helen stepped back, out of the circle of Matteo's arms. She didn't say a word, but went straight to the bedroom and shut the door. Matteo did not follow.

Miserable and exhausted from her long vigil at Matteo's side, she fell asleep and woke in late afternoon, sticky and uncomfortable. She listened, but couldn't hear anything from the rest of the house. For a brief moment she thought that he had already left, but then realized he would have no way of getting to the marina other than hitchhiking, and he would never risk the exposure. She emerged to find him reading one of her books, a treatise on Elizabethan poets. The contrast struck her immediately: earlier in the day he had been ready to shoot the mailman, and now he was calmly reading a textbook, looking for all the world like a graduate student in the stacks of a library. Even the clothes she had brought enhanced the illusion; the jeans and ox- ford shirt would not have been out of place on any campus in the country.

"I'm going to take a shower," she announced. "I as- sume we'll be leaving later."

He looked up, putting the book aside. "Feeling better?" he asked.

"Not really," she answered, unwilling to comfort him. "You should eat something before we go. You don't know how long it will be before your next meal."

He didn't dispute her assumption that his upcoming schedule would not exactly be routine. He nodded, and she left him to prepare for the coming night.

When she returned, dressed, like him, in jeans and a shirt, he was setting out food on the bar, a conglomeration of the leftovers from her last shopping trip. Helen sat next to him on an adjoining stool, noticing that he ate methodically but without enthusiasm, as if he were forcing himself to consume fuel, knowing he would need energy later.

The atmosphere was thick with undercurrents, very tense. Helen could manage only a few bites and then he cleared everything away, walking a wide circle around her as if she might explode at any moment. Helen felt that his caution was justified; she didn't know whether to scream at him or burst into tears. He was actually going to leave, without apology and without explanation. It seemed incredible, but there was no mistaking his attitude of quiet determination. He was looking to the future, in his mind already on his way.

"Let me check your dressing one last time," Helen finally said, breaking the silence that had lasted for almost an hour.

He sat in the chair he had occupied the night he arrived, and she knelt before him, unbuttoning his shirt and pulling off his sleeve, exposing the wound to view. She peeled away the bandage and saw that there was nothing to be done; it was clean and dry. She retaped the gauze in place, and then, unable to help herself, she leaned forward and pressed her mouth to his naked shoulder, hiding her face.

His arm came up convulsively, his fingers tangling in the fine mass of her hair.

"Oh, Helen," he said brokenly, and in that one moment she almost believed he would stay.

But then she moved back to look into his face, and what she saw there seemed too much like pity for her to allow it. She straightened at once, rose to her feet and turned away. He was not going to feel sorry for her. She had tried, and she had failed. Whatever called him was more important to him than she was, and that was that.

He rose, also, buttoning his shirt. "Can you go to the store once more for me?" he asked quietly. "There are a couple of things I need."

"Have I ever refused you anything?" she said bitterly, and he rounded on her, his dark eyes blazing.

"Helen, do you think I wanted it to work out this way?"

"I don't know what you want, other than to get back to whatever it was you were doing last Friday night. And judging from appearances, that wasn't good."

He looked away, his face closing. "You'd better get going to the store. It's getting late."

Helen sighed resignedly. "What do you want?"

"Dark glasses..."

"Sunglasses?"

"Yes, and a knit hat to cover my hair. And a penknife."

"That's all?"

"That's it."

"I'll go right now."

She picked up her purse and was on her way as he called after her, "Thank you."

She ignored him, pulling the door closed behind her.

By the time Helen got back it was full dark, and Matteo was waiting for her anxiously, pacing the living room floor. When she handed him her purchases he donned the glasses and the hat and put the knife in his pocket.

"Won't people think it's odd that you're wearing dark glasses at night?" Helen asked. "If they see you, that is."

"They'll probably just think I'm a drug addict," he answered, and she couldn't help smiling.

He saw her expression and shrugged. "It's better than being spotted," he added, smiling a little himself.

As she watched he pulled the .38 from his belt and depressed the hammer, sliding the cartridge out to check it.

"Do you have to do that in front of me?" she inquired tightly, and he glanced at her quickly.

"I'll be ready in a minute," he replied quietly, going into the bedroom and shutting the door.

Helen waited, trying not to think how empty the beach house would seem without him.

He returned shortly, the gun concealed beneath a pullover sweater Adrienne's son Andy had left behind. She had to admit that he looked like a local. His dress was appropriate for early spring weather in north coastal Florida; the days were warm, but the nights were usually cool and breezy.

"Let's go," he said, and Helen turned on her heel for the door.

Matteo followed her to the Mercedes 300D her father kept in the attached garage and got into the back, lying down on the seat. Helen opened the windows and drove out the palm-lined lane to the road, turning left for A1A.

The salt wind blew through the car, stirring her hair, as she glanced in the rearview mirror. Matteo could not be seen. Although his precautions seemed almost paranoid, Helen didn't comment on them. After all, someone *had* shot him.

It was a short distance to the boat basin, and when they arrived Helen drove past a restaurant and a string of shops to the dock. It was almost deserted at that hour. Boats bobbed at anchor in their slips, the water was calm, the sky spangled with stars. She slowed to a stop and announced, "We're here."

"Do you see a boat called *Estrellita*?" he asked, his voice sounding spectral and disembodied floating toward her from the back seat.

"I can't read the names from here; it's too dark," she responded, turning her head toward him. "I'll have to get out and look."

He hesitated, then said, "Be careful. If anyone sees you just turn around, get back in the car and drive away."

"All right."

Helen got out and strolled along the wooden dock, reading a succession of names emblazoned on a long row of power boats. She passed *Sunshine Superman*, *Blue Lagoon*, and a number of others, but could fine no *Estrellita*. She turned around and came back, looking again, but it was not among them.

She returned to the car and said, "It's not there."

"Are there any other boats docked here?" he asked.

"Just the commercial craft on the other side of the lagoon."

"Take me there."

Helen started the car again, noticing that his tone was changing as he assumed command of the venture. It was obvious that he was used to issuing orders, and he was back to his old form.

She circled the marina, pulling up at the commercial dock and getting out to look. It didn't take her long to find the boat, a medium-size cruiser with a large, powerful engine. She glanced around her. No one was near. She could see a young couple walking hand in hand in the distance, but they were going the other way.

Helen returned to the car and opened the door. "I found it," she told him. "It's right nearby. You can get out now; the dock is deserted."

He emerged feet first, straightening and looking around him. When he satisfied himself that she was right, he followed her to the boat and jumped down into it, reaching up with one hand to pull her after him.

"How did you know this would be here?" she asked, thinking that the question was probably an exercise in futility, but trying anyway.

To her surprise, he answered. "This is the boat I came in on," he said shortly. "My men were told that if anything happened to me they were to leave it here."

"Sort of like an alternate escape route, huh?" Helen said.

He examined her in the feeble light, trying to read her expression.

"Sort of," he finally replied, and she let it go at that.

He went to the control panel at the front of the boat and looked over the instruments, seeming to find that everything was in order.

"How will you get it started?" she asked. "You don't have a key."

"It's hidden on board."

"But the customs check, the harbor police, Matteo."

"I'll be all right, don't worry." He turned to face her, and she knew that this was the farewell she'd been dreading.

"When you get off the boat," he instructed her, "don't wait for me to leave. Just take your car and drive directly back to your house."

"And forget you?" she concluded for him, hating the betraying tremble that invaded her voice.

He put his arm around her and pulled her tight against his shoulder, rocking her gently. "No, *mi corazón*. Remember me, as I will always remember you."

He let her go, taking her face between his hands and kissing her lips lightly.

"Mi corazón," he whispered again, still brushing her mouth with his.

"What does that mean?" she asked, fighting the growing tightness in her throat.

"My heart. And you are my heart, even if I never see you again."

Helen closed her eyes, unable to bear the thought of it.

"Mi princesa americana, mi señorita dolorosa blanca," he murmured, stroking her hair.

She understood only that he was saying goodbye.

He embraced her once more, quickly, fiercely, and then pressed something into her palm.

She glanced down at it, glinting gold in the harbor lights, and realized that it was the small ring he wore on the little finger of his left hand. It had a signet ring's flat surface and bore on its face, not initials, but the symbol of a tropical bird inscribed in a circle.

"It's the only thing I have of value," he said, "and even that is more sentimental than monetary. Please keep it, so that you'll think of me when you see it."

Helen slipped it onto her ring finger, closing the hand that wore it into a fist.

"Now go," he said huskily, pushing her toward the dock. "I can't delay any longer."

Helen accepted his assistance in climbing up to the wooden walkway, turning to look down at him once she was out of the boat.

"Go," he urged her. "Walk to your car and don't look back."

She hesitated.

"My safety is in your hands," he warned her. "Farewell, *majita.*"

That convinced her, as he had known it would. She hurried back to the car, not risking a glance at the basin until she was behind the wheel.

The *Estrellita* was still there, but its deck was empty. He had gone below.

Helen started the car and drove out of the marina, seeing the road before her through a blur of tears.

Chapter 3

The night Matteo left was the longest night of Helen's life. It was ridiculous, but she couldn't sleep without him. She, who had prized solitude since childhood and had lived alone since she graduated from high school, was surrounded by the emptiness of the beach house as if lost in the Siberian wasteland. The compact, functional rooms seemed cavernous, and the bedroom where he had slept was a desert. She wound up dragging her pillow and blanket out to the living room couch and sleeping there, where the memories weren't quite so painful.

In the days that followed she tried to go back to her old routine, but the 1500s no longer held the charm for her that they once had. She found she didn't much care any more what had inspired Christopher Marlowe to write *Tamburlaine*; she had met her own twentieth-century adventurer, and he was the one on her mind.

Helen spent a lot of time sitting on the beach, staring out to sea, thinking about the changes Matteo had brought to

her life. She finally decided that she wasn't going to get any
work done as long as she remained in St. Augustine, so she
made arrangements to go back to her apartment in Massachusetts. On the day before she was to fly north she went to
the supermarket for cleaning supplies, intending to leave the
house the way she had found it. Her father employed a
housekeeping service, but Helen always felt an obligation to
tidy up before she left. When she was younger her mother
used to tell people laughingly that Helen cleaned her room
before the maid could get to it; she didn't want the poor
woman to face a mess.

After she parked her car in the lot, Helen entered the air-
cooled supermarket, picked out a cart and wandered the
aisles aimlessly. She stared at the array of sprays and
cleansers, soaps and scouring pads, seeing instead the empty
deck of the *Estrellita*.

She missed him terribly. She felt half alive without him,
purposeless, incomplete. She didn't realize until he was gone
that she had admired his dedication, the single-mindedness
that took him away, because while he was with her she had
also resented it. She felt, no, she knew, that he had wanted
to stay with her, but he put his ultimate goal before his personal desires. And after twenty-five years of her mother,
Helen found his attitude a refreshing, even enlightening,
change.

She picked up a box of steel-wool pads, looked at the
price stamped on it and put it back. She couldn't organize
her thoughts enough to make a decision and finally started
tossing items into her basket in rapid succession, eager to
finish. She was at loose ends. Taking care of Matteo had
made her feel needed for the first time in her life. She had
never before experienced the fulfillment associated with
helping someone she had grown to care for, and she felt its
loss deeply.

She got in line at the checkout counter and picked up a newspaper on a nearby stand, scanning the stories for word of Matteo, as she did every day. She had seen nothing and, as desperate as she was for answers, she kept silent and made no inquiries, determined to keep his presence in her life a secret, as he wished.

As Helen paid her bill, she wondered idly how long it had been since her mother had shopped in a supermarket. Queen Sophia, as Helen's father still called her, never bought her own groceries. Clothes and jewelry, however, being far more important, commanded her personal attention. One of Helen's earliest memories was of being dragged around to various salons while her mother tried on samples, took fittings for alterations and ordered up originals from designer sketches. Helen could also recall very clearly sitting in the reception rooms of Tiffany's or Van Cleef and Arpels, fidgeting with a crystal paperweight on the salesman's desk while her mother shopped. Sophia sipped tea with lemon from a Limoges cup and shook her head repeatedly, waving away the trays of rings, bracelets and necklaces presented for her inspection. The patient clerks, hoping for a big sale, tried to amuse the fractious child, but Helen was finally sent away with her nanny so Sophia could get on with the important business of selecting a new bauble to add to her collection. What a disappointment I must have been to her, Helen thought suddenly. She really wanted a friend to share her interests, and since Helen's lay elsewhere, Sophia was forced to resort to the likes of Claudia Fierremonte. Claudia, who lived in Rome but didn't know who the president of Italy was, could pick out any dress at a charity ball and tell you which designer's house had made it.

Helen realized that she was standing in the store's foyer, carrying her bag and looking through the plate glass window at nothing. She shook herself and walked out to the parking lot, blinking in the blazing sunshine and pausing to extricate her keys from her purse. When she reached the car, she inserted her key into the door lock. As she did so, a black sedan came roaring to a stop next to her, and two figures bolted from the rear doors on either side. Before she could react one man snatched the bag from her hands and the other one took her arm in an iron grip and hustled her into the back seat. In the space of several seconds she found herself sitting with a captor on either side of her as the driver took off again, tires squealing, the car bulleting into the street and rounding a corner almost instantly.

"What's going on?" Helen sputtered, looking from one man to the other. "Who are you?"

Neither answered, gazing directly ahead.

Helen's first thought was that she had been kidnapped for her father's money. Once, when she was about ten, he had been having trouble with the union at one of his plants, and the fighting had been bitter, finally resulting in threats against Helen's life by anonymous members of the local. The dispute had been resolved eventually, but she always remembered the incident, which served as a warning that wealth carried its penalties as well as its privileges.

"Where are you taking me?" Helen demanded, trying to sound braver than she felt.

The man on her right turned to look at her. "Do not be afraid," he said, in thickly accented English. "We mean you no harm."

"What is this about?" she said slowly, beginning to change her mind about the purpose of her abduction. His accent, though cruder and far more pronounced than Matteo's, sounded hauntingly familiar. Could it be...? Her heart leaped into her throat as he reached inside the collar of his shirt and withdrew a silver chain. A medallion hung from it, and he held it out, displaying it for her. A tropical bird inscribed in a circle glowed in the filtered light from the tinted windows. Helen looked down at her ring; the symbols were the same.

"Matteo," she whispered. "Does Matteo want to see me?"

Her companion nodded. "*Sí*, Matteo. We take you to him; you come with us. Yes?"

Helen didn't ask why Matteo hadn't come himself or why he had chosen such a dramatic method of providing her with an escort. She knew from experience that he had his own reasons for doing everything, and she was so happy at the prospect of seeing him again that she didn't question them.

She sat back in her seat and watched the passing scenery as the driver, who was clearly familiar with the area, skirted St. Augustine and Crescent Beach and headed for the highway, turning toward Jacksonville. They drove for almost an hour in silence, while her guards stared out the windows and the efficient driver piloted them through downtown Jacksonville and into a seedy, rundown area near the docks. It was the sort of neighborhood Helen would not have ventured into alone, but she was sure that her two companions, both the size of pro linebackers, were under orders from Matteo to protect her with their lives. When the car pulled to a stop and they got out, the men materialized on either side of her like secret-service men flanking the president.

Helen looked over the facade of what appeared to be an abandoned warehouse as her companions led her to a rear entrance. It was approached by walking through an alley littered with refuse remaining from a time when business was conducted inside. Sheets from newspapers, handbills and pamphlets crunched underfoot as one of the men opened a door set into the barnsided wall and they stepped through it.

The interior was vast and empty. The man who had spoken to her in the car gestured for her to follow him, and he

took her to a small inner office, which must have served as
the center of commerce in its day. The second man fell in
behind her as Helen entered the glass-walled room and was
asked to take the only available seat. She did so, wondering
uncomfortably where Matteo was. The guards remained
with her, obviously waiting for him, also.

Helen sighed and tried to get comfortable on the folding
chair, ready to remain until he arrived.

As Helen was settling in to wait, Matteo was on his way
to the warehouse by another route, lest anyone should be
following his car. He was driving; two of his lieutenants sat
in the back seat. As he looked into the mirror he saw the two
men exchanging glances. He knew exactly what they were
thinking, though they would never be bold enough to say it.

Before leaving for this meeting he had explained his plan
to the two of them, and it had met with a less than enthu-
siastic reception. Disputing their leader's judgment was out
of the question, but their covert looks, their unspoken in-
credulity, had said it all. They thought Matteo had finally
lost his mind.

Relying on the help of an effete American heiress was
preposterous. If Helen Demarest did what Matteo pro-
posed, she would be required to fly off to the jungle of a
country she'd barely heard of to aid people she didn't know.
To even suppose that she might do so was absurd.

Matteo disagreed. His men were sincere, but their
knowledge of Americans was limited to what they heard in
political diatribes and read in slanted newspapers. Matteo
had lived in the United States for thirteen years while attending school. He knew that Americans loved underdogs
and causes, but most of all they loved their freedom, and
they admired others who wanted the same thing for them-
selves. Helen might help him, not in spite of her nationality
but because of it.

Matteo turned into the alley leading to the warehouse, schooling himself to keep his inner conflict from showing in his expression. His main reason for leaving Helen in Florida, without the promise of future contact, was to keep her out of danger. Now he was about to ask her to immerse herself in it. He had to dismiss the contradiction, because he was desperate. He knew that her feelings for him would convince her to go along with his scheme when other arguments might not, and he was out of options, forced to use it. He saw no alternative.

He stopped the car and got out, followed by his men, who trailed him closely, their hands at their belts. The local police were still on the alert for him, and extra patrols had been assigned to the waterfront area. Matteo strode purposefully into the warehouse, heading for the room where Helen had been sequestered.

He had wanted to be there when she arrived, to minimize her anxiety, but his men had pursuaded him that it would be better to arrive later and be certain that she was not tailed. He could see the back of her head through the glass as he approached, and his steps quickened.

Helen got up the minute she saw him, momentarily taken aback by the change in his appearance, and then flinched when the men with her took a step toward her as she rose.

Matteo lifted his hand as he came through the door, and they fell back. Helen looked at him, and he returned her stare. Neither said a word.

He had undergone a remarkable transformation. His hair, which she remembered as longish and wavy, was cut short in a contemporary style, and tinted to give it an auburn cast. He had a short beard, but unlike the one she had shaved off, this was clipped and neat, like the three day growth worn by models in sportswear advertisements. While it gave him a stylish and slightly rakish air, it also had the desired effect of making his features less sharp and identifiable. He wore aviator glasses with grayed lenses for the purpose of concealing his eyes; Helen knew that his vision was perfect.

His clothes completed the picture. Helen had spent enough time in expensive stores to recognize top quality merchandise: pleated linen pants with a cowhide belt, cotton lisle shirt, soft lamb's-wool sweater. The total image was chic, upscale, preppie. For reasons she didn't understand he wanted to look that way.

Helen glanced nervously at the guard nearest her, and Matteo nodded toward the door, dismissing the men. All four departed immediately without a questioning glance, but she noticed that one remained just outside the door, within calling distance, his back to the room.

Once they were alone, Matteo opened his arms, and Helen ran into them. He held her for a long moment before she said, "Matteo, you're all right. I was so worried."

He stepped back to look at her, brushing a strand of hair from her brow. "I'm fine. I hope my men didn't frighten you. There was no safe way to get in touch."

"I was scared at first, but then the bigger one showed me his medallion, the one with the same figure that's on the ring you gave me. After that I knew they were from you and I would be okay." She touched his cheek, roughened now as it had been when he was sick. "How is your arm?"

"Good as new. You're an excellent nurse."

Helen's hand fell away and she said guardedly, "Matt, why did you bring me here? The way you left, I never expected to see you again a week later."

"I didn't expect it, either," he replied simply.

"What happened?"

He turned away. "I can't get out of the country. My plan when I left you was to go south to the keys and use a connection I have there, but apparently I'm too hot to handle." He smiled resignedly. "The local police are one thing, but your FBI is also looking for me, and my friend didn't like the idea of federal charges and a federal court. So here I am."

Helen sighed and folded her hands, as she had when she was little and confronted with a problem. The cloak-and-dagger tactics and unsavory surroundings might be necessary, but they still made her uneasy.

"All right, Matt," she said in a controlled voice, "what is going on? You wouldn't tell me before, but you must have changed your mind, or I would not be standing here, correct?"

"Yes."

"So. What's with your clothes—your hair, for starters. You look like a Wall Street stockbroker out for Saturday lunch at the country club."

"Good," he said with satisfaction. "That's my disguise."

Disguise? she was about to reply when she had to jump out of the way as a mouse scurried by, followed by another in hot pursuit.

"You'd better get a cat in here," she advised him. "You've got mice roller-skating all over the place."

"I don't plan to stay," he answered dryly.

"No? Where are you going?"

"Back home, I hope. That depends on what you do." He held her light gaze with his darker one. "You helped me once, Helen, will you do so again?"

"Tell me about it," she said warily, "and I'll let you know."

Matteo gestured for her to resume her seat, overturning an orange crate next to it. He arranged the box so that he would face her and sat down. "Ask, and I'll answer," he said.

"Who are you?"

"I am Matteo Salazar de Montega," he replied solemnly, humoring her, like a child reciting his lunchtime menu for his mother.

"And where is your home?"

"My country is Puerta Linda," he replied, producing a map from his pocket and opening it for her. He had come prepared.

"Here," he added, pointing to the coastline of Central America. Helen followed his forefinger to a tiny state divided from its neighbors by a river on one side and a mountain range on another. She continued to look down at the map as he took off his tinted glasses in order to see better.

Puerta Linda. The name struck a chord in Helen's mind, and she remembered news reports of the turmoil in that country, the clips filled with shots of men in fatigues toting rifles and aerial views of verdant jungles.

"The night we met I was buying guns for the revolution there, and your Coast Guard interrupted the sale," Matteo went on evenly. "That's why the federal government is in on it, too; they're looking for me on illegal purchase of weapons charges."

Helen listened, absorbing each piece of information as it came. Puerta Linda was a world away, the current government a corrupt dictatorship threatened by bands of rebels who sought to overthrow it. Rebels like the man before her, who watched her calmly with obsidian eyes, waiting for her reaction.

And now his name began to assume its full significance, and her mouth went dry. Montega. He was the leader of the revolution, a young turk who was trying to organize the various factions to make a disciplined assault on the sham democracy in power. He had been described as well spoken and American educated, a brilliant organizer with a keen mind and limitless personal courage. Matteo Montega was the most prominent figure in his country's evolving history, and Helen had been hiding him in her father's house for a week, feeding him erythrocin and Angel Bites. It was incredible.

"What do you want me to do?" Helen asked quietly, subdued by the enormity of it.

"Your government knows that I will try to get back to my country," he answered. "Agents are watching the airports, monitoring all flights to Puerta Linda. There aren't many, so it isn't difficult to screen the passengers. I want to leave the country as part of a couple because they will expect me to be traveling alone. But I need someone, a real American who would not arouse suspicion, to pose as my wife."

"And that's where I come in," Helen whispered.

"Yes. There is more involved here than just my breaking American law, although that is what they would use to imprison me. The current government in my country is allied with the United States, and the Puerta Lindan officials would like nothing better than for the American authorities to throw me in jail and let me rot there. I'd be out of the country and out of their hair, permanently."

Helen swallowed, realizing that he was right.

"You must understand," he said, leaning forward earnestly. "My country would be ripe for a Communist takeover if the current government fell and the rebels were not organized and ready. I must be there, Helen, or Puerta Linda will go from a lesser evil to a greater one."

"I'm not a very good actress," she said feebly. "I don't know how convincing I would be."

"You would just have to be yourself," Matteo replied. "You are an American, you have the right accent, the right attitude; you could answer questions correctly if you were challenged. We've got all the paperwork; you wouldn't have to do anything except get on the plane with me and sit there until we arrived."

Helen stared back at him, her eyes wide.

Matteo took her hand. "Helen, I speak English very well, but I have never been able to lose my accent completely. And it gets more pronounced under stress; it would give me away in a minute. At the very least it would make the authorities suspicious, and closer investigation would prove disastrous. But if you were with me you could do most of the talking, provide me with cover, don't you see?"

"I see," she murmured, not looking at him.

He thought she was about to turn him down and said, "Before you say no, let me tell you more about me and my country, and why it is so important for me to get back there."

Helen's gaze returned to his face as he said, "The bird on the ring I gave you is the aquatar. It is native to my country and a freak of evolution, able to survive under conditions that would kill other wildlife, able to eat almost nothing for long periods and store its own water. It is a survivor, tough and smart and as tenacious as the spirit of freedom in my people. That's why we took it for our symbol."

Helen listened, intrigued.

"My country has not been in the hands of the people for a long time. The 'elections' the government holds are a farce; the officials talk about registering and voting, and then perpetuate a dictatorship that has kept the same faction in power for twenty years."

"Puerta Linda always calls itself a democracy," Helen said. "But most people know better."

He snorted. "Do you think so? Americans don't seem to care."

"They just don't understand, Matteo. It's all so confusing, so many different groups and it's happening so far away."

"But you should try to understand!" he said passionately. "You Americans take too much for granted; when I was in school here and would hear on the news about the lack of 'voter turnout' during an election, I would be enraged. Do you know what the opportunity to vote in a free election would mean to any Puerta Lindan? And so many of you throw it away; softball games and appointments for a haircut are more important.''

Helen dropped her eyes, remembering an election day when she had been immersed in her research and had forgotten to vote.

"I want to bring to Puerta Linda the same kind of government you have here. My father made a mistake in sending me to America to school. I learned what it's like to live in a free society, and once you've done that, you can't go back to a lifetime of indentured servitude.''

"Your father?" Helen said.

"Yes. He was a minister of the current regime who served it until he died three years ago. He had all the wealth and privileges its favorites enjoy: a seaside villa, a staff of servants to wait on him and his family, the best of everything. Nothing was too good for a man so high in the government, a trusted cog in the most corrupt machine in Central America.''

"It must have been hard for you growing up in his house," Helen offered softly.

"I didn't," Matteo responded, meeting her gaze directly. "I am illegitimate. My mother was my father's maid.''

"Oh," she said in a small voice.

Matteo stood and began to walk around, gesturing to make his points. "I was raised with my mother's people and saw things from their point of view. She was poor and I was poor, dirt poor, while my father and his legal wife, and their legal children, lived in a big house, and were driven around in a fancy car, and ate off china plates.''

Helen didn't say a word, fearful he would remember that she was a lot closer in origin to the father he described so bitterly than to Matteo himself.

"We ate off the clay dishes my mother made by hand, when we had anything to eat at all," he continued, lost in the past. "And she was ignored once she got older and lost the beauty that had attracted my father's attention. But he did do one thing for her, something that changed the course of my life and made me glad, for once, that he had sired me."

"What was that?"

"He listened to my mother when she asked for me to receive an education. She knew it was the one route I could take to escape the cycle of poverty that had trapped her and everyone like her. She begged and pleaded and I guess she finally wore him down, or maybe I was getting old enough to become an embarrassment and he wanted me out of the way. I don't know. But when I was ten he arranged for me to go to boarding school in Connecticut. He had a lot of diplomatic ties here because the ambassador to the U.S. at that time was a close friend of his."

Helen sensed that he had almost forgotten she was there, his memories were so vivid. He smiled slightly.

"So I found myself living and studying with a bunch of rich Americans, the sons of doctors and lawyers and big businessmen. And there I was, the Puerta Lindan bastard without a word of English transplanted to the wilds of New England. The first winter I almost froze. I had never seen snow, and we had two blizzards, drifts up to the windowsills. I thought I was at the North Pole. And I couldn't even say Connecticut." He grinned suddenly. "When I get nervous I still can't."

Helen smiled back at him, glad that his reminiscence had taken a humorous turn. "I can't imagine your ever being nervous," she said.

"It happens," he replied lightly.

"What school was it?" Helen asked.

"Longfield Academy, in Westport."

"I know it." She didn't add that she had a cousin there.

"And so," he went on, "I began my American education. The people in charge at the school knew who my father was, and they were very anxious that he should think everything possible was being done for his son. In enrolling me, he neglected to mention that he had never married my mother, so they treated me like the scion I never was in Puerta Linda—private tutors to help me with my English, the best accommodations, the roommate of my choice, and so on. It was a very schizophrenic existence; in America I was the Puerta Lindan prince, and at home I was the Montega bastard."

Helen could feel the pain in his voice as he spread his hands and said, "It shouldn't come as a surprise that I began to spend more and more time in America. On school vacations I would go to the home of a friend and have my bed changed by a maid who might have come from my village in Puerta Linda. I saw less and less of my mother, finding ways to remain on campus over the summer: sports camp, an extra course, a school job. She finally died the fall I started college at Columbia."

"Matteo, you were young," Helen said gently. "No one would choose to be treated the way you were at home when there was an alternative available."

"She had no alternative," he said flatly. "And I almost forgot she existed while I was so busy grabbing at the good life."

"You're remembering now," Helen stated quietly.

He looked at her, really seeing her for the first time in several minutes. "That's right. What I want to do is for her and everyone like her. If I can change their lives maybe hers won't have been in vain."

"Did you go back to Puerta Linda after college?" Helen asked.

"Not right away. I had majored in engineering, and I took a job at a firm in New York. I had a big salary, a flashy apartment and a fast sports car. I dated blondes and red-heads with names like Sharon and Tracy and Beth."

"And Helen?" she supplied softly.

He nodded. "They thought I was exotic, primitive, dangerous. What a laugh. The most dangerous thing I did in those days was forget my slide rule."

"As opposed to now, when your life is a powder keg," Helen said unhappily.

He ignored that. "And then one day I was assigned to go to Puerta Linda on a job, to scout out a location for a new bridge near San Jacinta, the capital. I hadn't been back in so long—not since my mother's funeral, and then only for a couple of days—that I almost felt like a foreigner myself. But the management thought I would be able to deal with the natives better since I had lived there, so I was on my way."

He paused, staring into the distance. "And something happened when I got there. I went to visit my mother's sister and saw again the way she lived, saw what I had been actively trying to forget since I was ten. And I knew why I had never become an American citizen, why the engineering degree and the G. Fox clothes had polished me but never really changed what was inside of me." He shrugged. "I resigned my job and stayed."

"And you started to work to change the government," Helen said.

He folded his arms. "At first I was naive. I actually thought I could organize the vote, the way I had seen my friends do for a campus election. Then it gradually became clear that there *was* no vote, that it was all fixed and controlled from the top and that the only chance for change was revolution. So I went underground and got together with others who felt the same way I did." He lifted one shoulder eloquently. "That was eight years ago."

"And now you are the leader."

He made a deprecating gesture. "So they tell me on American television. You know the media, they like to hang tag lines on people."

"And with all the Sharons and Tracys you knew, there's no one you could ask to go to Puerta Linda with you?"

Matteo knelt on the floor before her and took both her hands. "Not one of them could do what you did for me when I broke into your house. You're the one I want."

"Oh, Matt." The directness of his plea was disarming.

"I wouldn't ask this of you if there were any other way, Helen. I have to get home."

"I know you do," she responded softly.

"The terms would be the same as when I stayed at your house," he added. "If you're caught, I'll say you were my hostage and that I forced you to go along in fear for your life."

Helen didn't answer, wondering if it was possible that he was proposing this scheme, and even more unbelievable, that she was actually considering it.

"I would offer to pay you," Matteo said finally, a note of despair creeping into his voice, "but my men have investigated your background. I know that your family is wealthy and that money would not persuade you. I hope the cause of freedom will."

"You investigated me?" Helen asked incredulously.

"It was necessary. I had to know more about you before I asked you to help. I could see that the house where you were staying was expensive, and I knew that your family must be well off, but there's rich and there's *rich*." He smiled thinly. "I used to see the name Demarest on the trucks delivering fuel to my dormitory at school in New

York. I didn't realize you were *that* Demarest until I got the report."

"And you still trust me?" Helen asked. "I would think that would be difficult for you now."

"Why?" he asked, his brows knitting. "I know you; I know what you did for me. Information about what your father has in the bank or in stocks doesn't change that. I just wanted to make sure that you didn't have any... encumbrances."

"Like what?"

"Like somebody who would come after you if you left the country."

"Oh, I see. And you discovered that nobody really cares much what I do, right? I should think that would make me ideal for your purposes. Is that why I was chosen for this dubious honor?" she said flatly.

"You were chosen for my faith in you," he answered huskily, and she closed her eyes, not wanting him to see the emotion there.

Matteo held both her hands to his mouth, kissing them. "As soon as we reach Puerta Linda, you can turn around and go back home. I just need you to get me there."

Helen gazed into his lean, handsome face, unsure of what to do. He was asking her to take a terrible chance, and she didn't delude herself about one thing: if he had made it back to his country on his first try, he would never have contacted her again.

But, on the other hand, this man had a purpose and a direction her whole family had always lacked. Everyone she knew was like the parasitic aristocracy he described in Puerta Linda. His dedication appealed to her strongly; she found it almost irresistible. He had given up the very things that her relatives thought spelled success and happiness for something that meant more to him, and she wanted to help him.

"The risk isn't all on your side, Helen," Matteo concluded. "I'm taking a chance in telling you this, because if you say no, as soon as you leave here you could turn me in. But you didn't let me down before, and I don't think you will now."

Helen smiled. Part patriot, part con artist, he was all persuasiveness and all charm. He used his natural gifts to get what he wanted, and she guessed she wouldn't be the first person who found it impossible to turn him down.

"All right," she said.

He bowed his head, too moved to speak.

"I'll leave a message with my mother's secretary that I'm taking a vacation."

"Anything you need to arrange is fine," he said quickly, finding his voice.

"If your men could take me back to my car, I'll go home and pack," she said.

Matteo knocked on the glass window, summoning the guard who still stood outside. The man entered, and Matteo issued a rapid command in Spanish.

"He'll take you back," Matteo said to Helen. "He is my best man; you'll be safe with him."

"He looks like a skyscraper, Matteo; I'm not worried."

Matteo chuckled, then kissed her quickly on the forehead.

"Go. Bring light clothes, summer things. It's very hot in Puerta Linda. I'll take care of everything else."

"Okay."

He put his hand on her arm as she turned to go.

"Helen, I haven't the words to thank you."

"You've thanked me enough for a lifetime, Matteo."

"You've done me a lifetime of good, *mi corazón*."

"Tell me that when you're safely back in Puerta Linda," Helen said.

"I will be soon. I know it."

He raised his hand in farewell as she walked out with the guard, and Helen squared her shoulders, telling herself that she had made her decision and was not going to lose her nerve now.

And she didn't.

When she got back to the beach house she left the guard, who seemed to understand a lot more English than he was able to speak, in the car and went inside to get her things together.

She telephoned her mother's personal assistant and left her message, then packed up the piles of books and papers on the dining table and stowed them in a closet. The thesis would have to wait, and she didn't want Adrienne's kids making paper airplanes out of her notes while she was away.

Then Helen riffled the drawers for suitable clothing. The weather in Florida was never really cold, and over the years she had accumulated a wardrobe of sorts which she left at the house for her occasional use. As she folded blouses and pairs of cotton slacks she tried not to think about what she was preparing to do, because if she considered it rationally she knew she would chicken out. In her whole life she had done few unconsidered, spontaneous things, and now she was about to make a quantum leap into the realm of rash, impulsive behavior, leaving good sense far behind.

For once she had an opportunity to follow her heart, and she was going to take it. She believed that it was not the mistakes that haunted people in later life, but the chances missed, the roads not taken, and this was one road she was going to follow as far as she could.

Helen snapped the tabs on her suitcase and picked it up, along with her purse.

She was ready. She glanced around the beach house for a last look and then marched out the door to share Matteo's fate.

Chapter 4

When Helen returned to the warehouse, Matteo was waiting for her. He took the suitcase from her hand and said, "It's a rare woman who can pack for a trip with one bag."

He was trying to lighten her mood, and she smiled briefly. Now that she saw the car standing ready for them and realized that she was actually going, the butterflies in her stomach were turning into hummingbirds.

"We're leaving from the Jacksonville airport," Matteo said as they walked out to the black sedan in the alley. "We'll be taking a commercial flight; the private planes are being watched too closely." He handed Helen's bag to one of the guards and said something in Spanish. The man stowed it in the trunk.

"They don't think I can be trusted, do they?" she asked Matteo suddenly, and he shot her a quick, intent glance.

"Why do you say that?" he asked.

"It's just the way they look at me. Like they'll go along with anything you want to do, but they have their doubts."

"You're very perceptive," he replied quietly.

"That's not exactly encouraging."

He smiled reassuringly, touching her hair briefly. "You let me worry about them. They can't help their prejudices. The only thing they understand is that the United States is an ally of the government we're trying to overthrow. But they don't know you."

"Why do you do business here, if they distrust Americans?"

Matteo shrugged. "Best prices on black market guns, the best supply. You have to go where the trade is, and you have to deal with whoever is running it."

He handed Helen into the back seat of the car and slid in beside her. "The flight leaves in an hour. We have to go straight to the airport."

"Is there a price on your head back in Puerta Linda?" Helen asked as the driver started the car and pulled out of the alley and onto the road.

Matteo turned to look at her and then faced straight ahead.

"Don't think about that," he answered.

"Is there?"

"Of course, Helen. You know the answer to that. I'm an enemy of the government. My picture is in every post office."

He picked up a briefcase from the floor and snapped it open. He handed her a sheaf of documents, some in Spanish, some in English.

"These are your passport, identity papers, everything you'll need to get into Puerta Linda. Look them over. I doubt very much that you'll be asked any questions, but just in case you are, try to get familiar with the information."

The papers said that she was a textile importer out of Dallas, Texas, going to Puerta Linda to buy raw silk, which was apparently one of its biggest exports. Matteo was her husband, and they were planning to stay for five days.

"Do you think these things will hold up?" Helen asked doubtfully. "This picture that's supposed to be me is so grainy it could be anybody."

"The usual method of entry into Puerta Linda these days is by bribe," Matteo answered dryly. "The papers are just a formality; few people actually look at them. All the airport officials are on the take. Getting a job there is considered a great coup."

Helen thought that over; no wonder he wanted to reform things back home. "What about on this end?" she asked.

"Don't you know how it works in America?" he said, turning to smile at her. "They'll always let you leave; it's getting back in that's hard. And for that you have your real passport, right?"

"Right," she said. He seemed to have all the answers.

He reached over and sqeezed her hand. "Relax. I'm going to take care of you."

Since she really didn't have a choice, Helen decided to follow his advice.

When they reached the airport the driver took off and left them in the company of the other front-seat passenger, the man who had shown Helen his medallion. As they walked along the concourse and headed for the ticket counter, Helen was sure each person who saw them could tell that he was a bodyguard. He walked two paces behind Matteo and watched everyone who passed as if they were about to pull a gun.

At the counter Matteo produced two tickets and handed over Helen's bag.

"You were pretty confident that I'd go along with this, weren't you?" she said to Matteo as they walked to the passenger gate. "My ticket was in your pocket when you asked me."

"I was hopeful," he responded. "But there was every chance it would go unused."

They left Matteo's comrade at the luggage check. Matteo embraced him and said something softly to him in Spanish, and the man nodded. He remained watching them as Helen put her purse on the conveyor belt to be screened.

As she and Matteo passed through the line Helen glanced nervously at the security guards, waiting for Matteo to be recognized. He actually bore little resemblance now to the man who had burst into the beach house, but she was sure one of them would see through the beard and the Fifth Avenue haircut to the revolutionary hiding underneath. She walked through the arch of the metal detector, and then froze as it went off when Matteo followed her.

"Just a minute, sir," the guard said, coming to stand by his side. "Please empty your pockets."

"Sure thang, officer," Matteo responded in a deep Texas drawl.

Helen almost fainted. He sounded like a B-movie cowboy.

Matteo displayed the contents of his pockets, and the guard held up a metal keyring.

"This must have done it," he said. "Go on through now."

Matteo complied, and the buzzer was silent. The guard handed him the offending object, saying, "Thanks for your cooperation."

"You bet," Matteo yodeled, and Helen grabbed his arm, pulling him after her toward the passenger lounge.

"What is the matter with you?" she hissed at him as soon as they were out of earshot. "Did you think you were in a Marlboro commercial? I've heard more authentic accents in fourth-grade Christmas pageants."

"The papers say I'm from Texas, and I had to talk that way because they might have checked them. I had a roommate in college from Abilene; I thought I sounded just like him."

"Do me a favor, will you? Next time you order up a set of dummy papers, get them to say you're from Jersey City."

"We have to take what's available," he replied, grinning at her.

Helen stared back at him, beginning to realize one thing that she should have understood from the start. He actually enjoyed this. He enjoyed the close calls, the aspect of living on the edge, which was so much a part of his work. She sank gratefully into a lounge chair, hoping that her heart would hold out for the duration of the journey.

When their flight was called, Matteo put his arm around her shoulder and walked next to her as they lined up for the plane, like any husband. He squeezed her gently as he handed their boarding passes to the bored stewardess, who glanced at them routinely and gave them their stubs.

"See how easy?" he whispered to Helen as they took their seats.

"Don't give me that," she muttered in response. "We're much more likely to encounter trouble on the other end, and you know it."

"Still mad about my Texas accent?" he said to her, smiling slyly.

She turned her head to stare out at the landing strip, and he laughed.

"The flight is four hours," he added. "You'd better get some rest."

Helen thought she would be far too nervous to sleep, but it wasn't long before the drone of the motor and the comforting presence of Matteo beside her had lulled her into slumber. She woke to find herself curled up in his arms, her head on his shoulder and one hand draped loosely over his muscular thigh. He was calling her name.

"What is it?" she said, sitting up and stretching.

"You have to fill out your landing card. The stewardess just distributed them."

She searched his eyes, concerned.

"It's all right. Just use the information on the papers I gave you, and everything will be fine."

Helen did as he directed, listing her name, address, age, and the purpose of her visit to comply with the documents in her purse. She handed hers in when the stewardess collected them and then glanced at Matteo when the pilot announced that they had begun their descent to San Jacinta.

"You're doing fine," Matteo said.

Helen didn't answer, wondering what conditions were like in Puerta Lindan jails. Every scene in *Midnight Express* flashed across her mind. That was Turkey, she reminded herself. Puerta Linda had to be a little more advanced, a little more civilized.

She changed her opinion as soon as they stepped off the plane and onto the tarmac. She looked around apprehensively, instantly wishing that she were back in the land of the free and the home of the brave.

Soldiers in green fatigues were everywhere, all carrying machine guns, riding three and four in a jeep or walking in incessant parade to and from the reception terminal. Barbwire fences surrounded the open area leading to the debarkation building, and marksmen were perched in gun turrets at strategic places all along the route.

"Welcome to Puerta Lindan democracy," Matteo said sarcastically into her ear.

"Oh, my God, Matteo," she responded, clutching his arm. "This is awful."

"This is what I want to change," he answered simply.

Helen tried not to gawk as they walked with measured pace to the long white building at the end of the paved lane. The humidity was crushing, stealing the breath from her lungs and causing her clothes to cling damply to her skin. The sky was overcast, threatening rain as they entered the reception area and got in line.

"Here we go," Matteo whispered. "Courage."

"Matteo, I'm frightened," she answered. There was no doubt in her mind that those military men in mirrored sunglasses, carrying Israeli Uzis and American M-16s, meant business.

He embraced her and held her close for a couple of seconds, kissing her hair.

"So am I," he answered. "I always am, and I've never been caught yet. Take a deep breath, Helen, and try to calm down. I didn't bring you this far to let anything happen to you. You believe me, don't you?"

Helen nodded, looking up at him. Strangely enough, she did.

"I just keep thinking that all of these people must have seen your picture," she said, putting her lips directly to his ear.

She thought of the price on Matteo's head, and her heart sank. In a poverty-stricken country like Puerta Linda, a reward could be a pretty powerful motive.

They were moving closer to the desk, and just as Helen was telling herself not to panic and to leave everything to Matteo, a dispute arose in front of them. A woman who had traveled on the plane with them was led away, screaming and crying, between two soldiers.

Helen stared out the terminal window at the palm trees swaying in the breeze. She couldn't look at Matteo because she didn't want him to see the terror in her eyes.

They were next. After she placed her papers on the table before the official examining them, Helen shoved her hands in her pockets to conceal their trembling.

"Mr. and Mrs. Caldwell, from Dallas, Texas," the man said in a heavy accent. "You will be staying here for five days?"

"That's right," Helen replied, staring straight ahead. Why was he asking her that? It was written on her card.

The man looked up at Matteo. "Mr. Caldwell?"

Here it comes, Helen thought.

"Yes?" Matteo said, drawing out the word, making it two syllables, as an American would.

Good boy, Helen told him silently.

"The stamp on your passport expires in two weeks," the official said. "Make sure you have it renewed."

"Thanks, I'll just do that," Matteo replied, and Helen saw him shove a wad of folded bills across the counter when he took back his passport.

"Bienvenida a Puerta Linda," the man said. "Welcome to Puerta Linda."

Matteo nodded and took Helen's arm, steering her toward the door. They had almost made it when another voice interrupted their progress, calling, "Mr. Caldwell."

Matteo stopped in his tracks, and Helen went rigid. A uniformed official appeared at Matteo's side and said in stilted English, "Come with me, please."

Matteo looked at Helen, telling her without words that they should comply. The official led them to a small side office while Helen mentally recited the first line of every prayer she knew. Once inside the room the man shut the door, breathed a sigh of relief and started to babble in rapid, excited Spanish.

Helen looked from one to the other. If she and Matteo were about to get arrested, every film she had ever seen had been wrong.

Matteo saw her confused glance and held up his hand for the other man to stop talking.

"He's a friend," Matteo said to Helen, "sympathetic to our cause. He works at the airport and saw me arrive. He says that one of the top government officials, who might recognize me because he used to work with my father, is here on an inspection tour. We have to get out another way so we don't pass him."

Helen sagged against Matteo, who hugged her for a brief, encouraging moment. She smiled at their companion.

"Gracias," she said. It was almost the only Spanish word she knew.

"De nada, señorita valiente, amiga linda del jefe," he responded, bowing graciously.

"What did he say?" Helen asked.

"He said, 'You're welcome, brave lady, beautiful friend of my leader.'"

"How lovely," Helen murmured, inexplicably near tears. The strain was proving to be almost too much; she felt close to collapse.

Perhaps reading her expression, Matteo said something to their rescuer, and he gestured for them to follow him.

"He has a car out back," Matteo explained as they hurried in his wake.

"Matteo, I don't like this. He recognized you; someone else might."

Matteo shook his head. "No, he knew I was coming, and he was watching for me. My men told him what I would look like, what I would be wearing. *Cálmate, niña,* it's almost over."

Their ally led them to an old Fiat parked by the service door they used to exit the building and handed Matteo the keys. Matteo thanked him and the man hurried back inside as Matteo opened the passenger door and hustled Helen into

the car. He ran around to the other side and jumped in,
starting the motor as he pulled his door closed.

"Now we just have to get through the check at the exit
gate," Matteo said grimly, glancing in the rearview mirror
as he pulled into one of the moving lanes of traffic. "There's
a pistol in the glove compartment. Get it out and give it to
me."

Helen complied, handing over the weapon and staring
ahead at the wooden booth as a light rain began to fall.
Matteo slowed the car, pulling into line and rolling down his
window. A uniformed soldier accepted their papers without comment and, after examining them for several seconds, peered into the car at its occupants.

Helen hoped that the sound of her teeth chattering was
not audible. The gun was concealed under Matteo's seat; if
he decided to search the car it was all over.

The guard asked Matteo a couple of questions, but his
tone sounded routine, and Matteo answered briefly. The
man handed their papers back through the window, eyeing
Matteo closely as he did so. Then he seemed to come to a
decision and waved the car on.

Matteo lost no time, gunning the motor as the guard lifted
the crossbar to let them through. Then, as they passed the
booth, Helen saw one of the other soldiers speak urgently
to the man who had stopped them. He whirled and shouted
something after the car, and Matteo cursed violently under
his breath. He floored the gas pedal, and the Fiat lurched
forward as the guard dashed through the door of the booth
and leveled his rifle at the fleeing car.

"Get down!" Matteo shouted, grabbing her shoulder and
shoving her onto the seat. She soon heard the whine of near
misses, and then the explosion of a hit as a bullet cracked the
rear glass and sailed over her prone body to exit through the
front window.

"Don't move," Matteo yelled as she cowered on the floor, her hands over her head, and he yanked down his window to fire back at his antagonist. Helen could hear the sound of other gunfire and knew that some of the soldier's comrades were joining the attack. Bullets whizzed around the little car, and ricocheted from its metalwork, as Matteo pushed it at merciless speed through the exit lane of the airport and toward downtown San Jacinta.

Helen was flung from side to side on the floor as he made turn after turn, evidently trying to lose the pursuers he had picked up at the exit turnstile. There was unrelieved tension for several minutes as he raced pell-mell through the old city, and the Fiat's well-used transmission was strained to the limit from the frequent downshifting. The smell of burning rubber and leaking transmission fluid soon filled the air, but Matteo drove on, manuevering the car with fierce concentration until he finally said, glancing in both mirrors and then looking at Helen, "I think we lost them."

Helen unfolded herself from the floor of the car and fell back in her seat. "What happened?" she asked shakily, in a voice that sounded several octaves higher than normal.

"The guard's buddy recognized me," he answered. "The first guy was a little suspicious, but when the second came in he nailed me." He shot Helen an intent glance and added, "You look a little pale."

"Is that all you can say?" she replied, staring at him. "Does this sort of thing happen to you all the time?"

"Not all the time," he answered mildly. "Now and then." He pulled a handkerchief out of his pocket and handed it to her, saying, "Wet this from the canteen and wipe your face."

Helen took the handkerchief, marveling that he seemed more concerned about her faintness than their recent narrow escape. Not to mention that they were fleeing from the airport police in a rapidly expiring car and would soon have no other means of transportation.

"We've got to ditch this car," he said as if reading her mind. "It's on its way out, and besides, the police will have a description by now." He slowed down to drive through the busy, crowded downtown streets, turning into a narrow lane flanked by rows of stores. He guided the little car into a parking space and left it there, signaling for Helen to get out on her side and follow him. When she reached him he took her hand and they strolled along the street, blending in with the other window-shopping young couples.

"They'll be able to trace us here when they find the car," Helen said, looking around for policemen, unused to the role of fugitive. "One of the passing citizens is sure to notice the bullet holes in the glass."

"We'll be long gone by then, Dick Tracy," Matteo replied, grinning at her.

"Oh, really?" Helen replied, amazed at his nonchalance. "How are we getting out of here?"

"You'll see."

They continued to walk, and Helen realized that he was scrutinizing the racks of motorbikes parked along the street. Suddenly he halted and said, "Wait for me at the corner."

Helen went ahead, turning when she reached her destination. She watched as he walked one of the bikes out to the road and jumped on, kicking the motor into life. He idled for a moment and then glided up to her, saying, "Hop on."

"Matt!" Helen said, shocked. "You aren't going to steal this!"

He met her gaze, deadpan. "No, Helen, I'm going to find the owner and tell him I'm taking it, so he can call the police."

She looked around furtively. "What if the owner comes back?" she said.

"Well, maybe if we stand here debating about it long enough, he will," Matteo said impatiently, pointing to the space behind him. "Get on. The idiot left the keys in the ignition—he deserves to walk."

Helen hesitated, looking unhappy.

"Look, Miss Abe Lincoln, you just defrauded the Puerta Lindan government by entering the country under false pretenses and you're aiding and abetting a wanted man. I wouldn't let a little thing like a stolen motorbike stand in my way."

Helen climbed on behind him, winding her arms around his lean waist. A cool breeze lifted her hair from her neck, relieving the wet heat for a moment, and she wished that she were doing this with Matteo under other circumstances, when she might have been able to enjoy the ride.

"Okay?" he said, turning his head.

"Okay," she confirmed, and he took off with a surge of power, negotiating the streets with controlled efficiency, making his way out of town. When they stopped at a light Helen said into his ear, "Where are we going?"

"A friend of mine has a *taberna* in the hills. We can rest there and try to think what to do."

"About what?" Helen said.

"About you," he answered, and then roared off as the light changed.

Helen hung on as he rode steadily toward the outskirts of San Jacinta, climbing all the way. Spanish street signs and shops with names like *Bodega Escorial* and *Mendeja—Zapatos Para Toda La Familia* passed in a blur as the rain, which had stopped, began to fall again. It was a soaking mist that penetrated Helen's thin clothing and returned Matteo's hair to the ringlets that the stylist who had cut it had managed to eliminate. They were driving into the setting sun, and darkness was falling with the swiftness of equatorial night.

Helen pressed her cheek to the curve of Matteo's damp
spine and imagined that they were traveling together through
the tropical paradise Puerta Linda might have been, without the ominous presence of the soldiers and the constant
threat of civil strife. The palms and jacaranda trees lining
the streets of the capital bent slightly under the weight of the
prevailing wind as they skirted the thinning traffic and left
the city, following a winding trail that moved upward
through overhanging cliffs. After a while Helen could see
the gleam of the ocean below, and Matteo turned on the
bike's single headlight. The air grew cooler with the height,
and the road they were traveling was no longer paved. The
bike kicked up a spray of loose dust, which covered them
both and adhered to their wet skin and clothing. Helen knew
she had never been filthier in her life, or in greater danger,
but she couldn't seem to muster much concern about either
condition. She was exhausted, and the hibiscus and olean-
der growing in profusion along the high stone walls they
passed intoxicated her with their heavy perfume. She lin-
gered in a dream state in which the feel of Matteo's strong
body under her hand, the heady fragrance of the wild
blooms and the enclosing darkness merged to convince her
that everything would be all right. Matteo could perform
miracles; hadn't she seen him do it? He would get both of
them out of this, and she was not going to be afraid.

Helen's eyes were closed, her head slumped against Matteo's back, when the bike ground to a halt and he dropped
the kickstand. She sat up groggily, and he took one look at
her and lifted her bodily off the motorcycle. He shushed her
feeble protest that she could walk, and she caught only the
barest glimpse of whitewashed walls and a handmade
wooden sign over the door that Matteo carried her through
before she put her head against his shoulder and shut her
eyes again. It was so much easier just to let him handle

everything, and after all, this was his country and he was used to such adventures.

She was aware of the low murmur of Spanish, and then felt the sweet comfort of a soft bed receive her weight. She meant to protest the loss of Matteo's arms, but found she was too tired. When he let her go she fell fully asleep immediately, and she didn't feel him cover her with a light blanket or hear him leave the room.

When Helen awoke she didn't know where she was. It took her a moment to remember the trip into the hills from San Jacinta and her arrival at their destination. She sat up and looked around her, taking in the rustic room with oak beams overhead and the darkness outside the single window. It must have been the middle of the night. The furniture was spare and mismatched: the bed on which she lay, covered with a faded patchwork quilt; a washstand with a pitcher and bowl, both cracked; and a cane chair by the window, some of the latticework missing from its seat. The window itself was bare, and the only covering on the floor was a rag rug made from bits of yarn, a washed-out riot of dulled colors like the quilt.

Helen listened carefully and could hear the faint thrum of music from the floor below. She remembered Matteo saying something about a *taberna*. Was that a restaurant or hotel? It seemed as though it was both. If so, some of the patrons downstairs must be keeping late hours. And she was in one of the rooms to let on the second floor.

The first order of business was to find Matteo. She got up, putting aside the sheet draping her legs, and went to the door, opening it a crack. The music got louder, but the hallway was almost dark, illuminated by a single electric bulb. Helen felt her way along it to the stairwell and was about to descend when a door on her left opened abruptly. A large woman in a sunny yellow peasant blouse and a lip-stick-red skirt confronted her, clapping her hands together with obvious delight.

"¡Ah, la señorita de Matteo!" she exclaimed, beaming at Helen. Her shining black hair was scraped back into a severe bun, which did nothing to detract from the bright good humor of her expression. Gleaming gold hoops dangled from her ears, and a hand-embroidered apron was tied about her ample waist.

"¿Tiene usted hambre?" she asked Helen, and when Helen indicated that she didn't understand, the woman mimed the use of a knife and fork.

Helen nodded. She was, in fact, famished, but locating Matteo was of even greater interest than food at the moment. She tried desperately to remember the phrase for "where is" that the Costa Rican maid had taught her and finally came up with it.

"¿Dónde está Matteo?" she said triumphantly, and was gratified when the woman's smile became even wider. She answered with an incomprehensible flood of Spanish, however, and Helen wished she hadn't tried to get cute.

"Matteo," she said again, desperately, hoping that the woman would take the hint. *"¿Dónde está Matteo, por favor?"*

The woman responded by taking her hand and leading her back to the room she had just left.

"Siéntese," she said to Helen, pointing to the cane chair.

Helen understood that she was to sit and did so.

Satisfied, her companion nodded vigorously and then launched into a short speech in which Matteo's name figured prominently. She was either going to get him or telling Helen that he had left for parts unknown, never to return. Helen decided that it had to be the former and settled in to wait.

The woman departed, closing the door behind her. Downstairs, someone started to sing, accompanied by a number of guitars. Helen was listening to the music, feeling like a third grader waiting for the principal to arrive, when the door opened and Matteo walked through it.

Helen jumped up and flung herself into his arms.

"Hey," he said, laughing and nuzzling her, "I'm going to leave you alone more often if this is the kind of greeting I get."

Helen's erstwhile companion followed him in, carrying a tray. When she saw the two of them embracing, she made a remark to Matteo and cackled loudly, winking at Helen.

"What did she say?" Helen asked, her face beginning to flame.

"I think I'll leave that one untranslated," Matteo said dryly, shooting the woman an exasperated look. "Elena brought you something to eat; she said you told her you were hungry."

The woman put the tray on the bed and stood grinning at Helen, obviously waiting for an introduction.

Matteo sighed, shaking his head.

"Helen, this is Elena, the innkeeper's wife. The man who owns this place is an old friend of my mother's family." He turned to Elena and said something in Spanish.

Elena curtsied with remarkable grace and said prettily, *"Con mucho gusto, la señorita bonita de Matteo. Mi casa es a su servicio."*

"I'm very pleased to meet you too, Elena," Helen answered.

The ritual observed, they all looked at one another.

Matteo then stared at Elena and nodded toward the door.

Elena made another crack, and he took her arm and escorted her into the hall, slamming the door with a resounding thud.

"Matteo, what was she saying about me?" Helen demanded when he returned.

"Never mind her, she has an overactive libido. Did you sleep well? You'd better eat something; we have to get an early start in the morning."

"Where are we going?" Helen asked, sitting on the bed and picking up the piece of buttered bread Elena had left.

Matteo sat next to her and looked into her eyes. His own were direct, sober, and very dark.

"To my camp," he answered her. "You can't get out of the country now, Helen. You were seen with me at the airport. They'll have your description posted everywhere by now, and they'll know the name you were using, as well."

Helen dropped the bread back onto the plate and swallowed hard, her throat suddenly closing.

Matteo tipped her chin up with his forefinger and said huskily, "You have to stay with me."

Chapter 5

Stay," Helen repeated, unsure whether she should burst into tears of joy or have hysterics. She wanted nothing more than to be with Matteo, but here, where they were both still fugitives...

"For a while," he added. "Until I can find a way to get you back home safely."

Helen didn't know what else to say. Matteo picked up the bread she had dropped, added a slab of cheese and put it in Helen's hand again. She took a bite and chewed obligingly, washing the sandwich down with a healthy drink of the dark brew Elena had provided. She swallowed it, then coughed and began to blink rapidly, inhaling deeply.

"What is that stuff?" she asked Matteo, when she could talk.

"Agua de fuego," he answered. "Firewater."

"I'll say. You could have warned me."

"I thought you might like to go native," he teased her, enjoying her discomfiture.

"Haven't they heard of iced tea around here?" she said, and he laughed.

"I'll see what I can do," he offered, standing up. "Is there anything else I can get you?"

"How about a bathtub?" she asked.

"I think you'll have to make do with that basin in the corner," he said, "but I'm sure Elena can heat the water for you."

"And a change of clothes?" she went on, raising her eyebrows questioningly. "I'm wearing half the road we traveled to get here."

"I don't think you and Elena are the same size, but she has a daughter who might fit the bill. Finish that food and I'll be right back."

Helen polished off the meal while she was waiting, and was inspecting the sorry state of her shoes when he returned.

"Tea," he said, handing her a glass. "Sorry, no ice."

Helen drank it anyway; it was wet, and at least tasted familiar.

"And," Matteo said, holding out his other arm, "for my lady's toilette."

Helen took the bar of crude yellow soap, the pair of rough, ribbed gray towels and the square of fleecy material to be used for a washcloth.

"I seem to remember getting these things for you," she said to him, piling the items on the bed.

"The supplies you provided were a little more refined," he replied ruefully.

Helen lifted one shoulder negligently. "Soap is soap."

She was pinning up her hair with barettes from her purse when he stilled her hands with his and said gently, "You're something else, lady. This must have been the worst day of your life, and I haven't heard one word of complaint."

Her hair fell over his fingers as she replied softly, "It wasn't the worst day of my life, Matt. I spent it with you."

Matteo twisted a bunch of the silken strands around his fist and said quietly, "I'm sorry I got you into such a mess, *majita*."

"What does that word mean?"

"Little maja, little lady."

"Is that what I seem to you?"

"Yes. A perfect lady: warm, generous, loyal. Look what you've done for me. I don't understand how anyone can give so much and take so little."

Helen was too moved to speak. She had never been paid such an extravagant compliment.

Matteo dropped his hands to her shoulders and said, "What's wrong with that family of yours? How can they ignore you? Don't they see what a treasure you are?"

There was a knock at the door and Matteo went to answer it. He returned carrying a steaming kettle by its wooden handle.

"Here's your hot water," he said to Helen. "Let me pour it into the basin for you, and then I'll see if Elena found those clothes."

He left Helen preparing for her bath and went below to collect fresh clothing from his friend's wife. When he returned, the door to Helen's room was ajar, and as he was about to leave the things in the hall he was stopped by a sight that took his breath away.

Helen was standing in a pool of light from the table lamp, washing. Her skirt and blouse were off, dark shadows on the bed, and her one-piece teddy was folded down to the waist, leaving her torso bare. Her back was to him, but she was turned slightly sideways, so he could see her three-quarter profile. His lips parted as she lathered her upper arms, rubbing the creamy soap over her ivory skin. The fine muscles of her slender back tensed and relaxed as she moved, tilting her head back and stroking the snowy column of her throat.

Matteo's gaze traveled lower, taking in the long, slender legs and narrow hips exposed by the high cut of the teddy. He looked up again to find her hands traveling to her breasts, and he almost groaned aloud. He watched as the dusky nipples rose to her touch, as they would surely rise to his. She picked up the washcloth and glided it over her abdomen, then moved it upward to stroke the valley between her breasts before she lifted her hair with one hand and washed the nape of her neck. Her breasts, free of the confinement of clothing, were more ample than he would have suspected, full and high.

Matteo could not seem to get enough air into his lungs. Perspiration broke out on his forehead. Look away, he told himself. Turn around and go downstairs; wait until she's finished. Voyeurism is pathetic, an invasion of her privacy.

But he discovered that he couldn't move. He had imagined her naked so many times, wondered how she would look, and the reality did not disappoint him. Just a few more seconds, he thought, and then I'll go quietly and she'll never know I was here.

Helen bent and splashed clear water over her skin, and Matteo watched as the sparkling rivulets caressed her like crystalline fingers. She raised each of her arms in turn, rinsing, and her breasts rose, taut and firm, the nipples stiffening even more in reaction to the cooling water. He leaned against the wall, his stomach knotting with desire. This was too much, more than any mortal man could bear. Sweat was trickling down his sides under his shirt as he stared helplessly, spellbound, caught in the same net that had once held David as he coveted Bathsheba.

Helen dipped her cloth in the basin and rinsed her back. Matteo's eye traveled her spine, taking in the beautiful arch from straight shoulders to slim waist, and he longed to trace with his hands the path the water took. When she began to dry herself, he saw a rosy hue invade her skin, saw the imprint of her fingers on her flesh as she cupped each breast and then released it.

Matteo's hand went to his hardening sex and he shifted his weight, easing the stricture of his jeans. He tried once more to leave, but instead found himself pushing open the door and walking toward her. He dropped the clothes Elena had given him on the chair and said, "Helen."

He didn't recognize his own voice. It was low and hoarse, filled with longing.

She half turned before he touched her, sliding his hands under her arms and enclosing her breasts from behind. She gasped at the intimate contact, but then relaxed as he pressed his lips to the base of her neck.

"Oh, Helen, what a picture you make," he moaned, as she lay back in his embrace, closing her eyes as his fingers stroked her nipples, teasing them to new sensitivity. He drew his mouth along the satiny line of her shoulder, and Helen whimpered when he lowered his hands to her hips and forced her back against him.

"Feel what you do to me," he said into her ear. He grasped her waist and turned her to face him, kissing her wildly, the pretense of control he had maintained so carefully for so long gone in an instant.

Helen's mouth opened under his, welcoming the invasion of his tongue. She had never been kissed like this, with such primitive urgency, and she responded in kind, running her palms over the hard surface of his back, reveling in the coiled power she felt there, tension she had created and which sought her for its release. She had touched him often while he was sick, seen to his every need, but this was different; it was almost like discovering him anew. The first time he had held her the day he got out of bed he'd changed their relationship forever, and now she associated this hunger with him, the only man who had ever made her feel it.

Matteo picked her up and set her on the bed, falling with her into a prone position and nuzzling her neck. His lips moved lower, tasting the soft skin, redolent of soap and her own unique scent. They settled on the pink bud of her nipple, and Helen arched her back, sinking her fingers into his hair and holding his head steady as he laved her, then sucked gently. She made a small sound, not of protest, but of pleasure, and he increased the pressure until she was stimulated to a point just below pain. When he moved back to sit up, she tried to hold him, but he slipped out of her grasp and unbuttoned his shirt, stripping it off quickly and dropping it to the floor. Then he lowered himself to her again and she wound her arms around his neck, sighing with the satisfaction of feeling his naked skin against her own.

Matteo twined his limbs with hers on the bed, and Helen's thighs loosened to allow him closer. She felt him, ready, and he grunted when she unconsciously lifted her hips to meet him. She was acting on blind instinct, but her eager innocence inflamed him, urging him onward. He rolled her on her back and laid his flushed cheek against the smooth flesh of her belly, placing a kiss there before peeling back the rest of her chemise and pulling it off her legs.

Helen stiffened, but did not resist; she had already made the commitment to him in her mind. There was only one small concern, and she voiced it as he stood to remove his pants.

"Will it hurt?" she asked, her quiet voice coming at him out of the semidarkness.

Matteo's hand froze on his belt buckle, and he didn't reply for several long seconds. Then he thrust trembling fingers through his tousled hair and sat down slowly on the edge of the bed, moving like a man recently awakened from a dream.

"No, Helen, it won't hurt, because nothing is going to happen," he answered evenly. He retrieved the folded sheet from the foot of the bed and flung it open, drawing it over her from feet to neck.

"What is it?" Helen said, sitting up and clutching the sheet to her breasts. "Did I do something wrong?"

He shook his head. His hands were braced on his knees, and she could see the decreasing motion of his chest as his breathing returned to normal.

Helen reached for him with her free hand, touching his smooth shoulder, slick now with perspiration.

"It's all right, Matteo."

"No it's not," he replied huskily.

"I'm ready," she insisted. "I love..."

He whirled suddenly and clamped his hand over her mouth. "Don't Helen. Don't say it."

"Why not? I feel it," she answered, when he relaxed his grip.

"You don't know what you feel!" he said fiercely, standing and shrugging back into his shirt. "It's just the circumstances, and everything's new, and we've been thrown together so much. You've been waiting all your life to attach your pent-up feelings to somebody, and I'm here, that's all."

"I'm not twelve, Matteo. I know what I want."

"I have nothing to offer you, Helen."

"I'm not asking for anything," she replied heatedly, trying to read his expression in the gloom.

"That's the whole problem," he countered, throwing up his hands. "You should. You deserve better than this tacky room and a one-night stand with a guy who might be dead next week."

"Oh, don't say that," she said, closing her eyes.

He sat down again and took her hand, holding on when she tried to draw it back. Finally she stopped resisting him, and he held it to his lips.

"Helen, your crazy family has been abusing you for twenty-five years. I'm not going to get in line."

"You're not abusing me," she said confusedly. "What are you talking about?"

His shoulders slumped with resignation and he said, "Listen to me. I know I've been a louse, dragging you into all of this, but I'm not that big a louse. There are some things even I won't do, and this—" he pointed at the bed "—is one of them."

Helen withdrew her fingers from his grasp and curled them on the sheet. "I see," she said dully.

"When you get back home," he said firmly, "you'll have a different perspective on everything, and you'll be glad I prevented you from making a mistake."

"Stop lecturing me," she said, turning her head away. "You sound like my father."

His mouth curved in a smile. "I don't feel like your father." He touched her cheek gently. "Save yourself for one of those nice boys back in America, Helen."

"I don't know any nice boys," she replied despondently. "I don't want any nice boys." She rose up quickly and flung herself on his chest, the sheet falling to the bed. "I want you."

He embraced her reflexively, and the instant he felt her, nude and supple in his arms, his resolution began to fade. He stiffened and said, "Don't make this any harder than it already is, Helen."

"I want to make it hard," she whispered, kissing his shoulder, trailing her lips inside the collar of his open shirt until she found the newly healed scar of the wound she had tended. "This is my mark on you," she added, tracing it with her tongue. "Every time you see it you'll think of me."

Matteo sucked in his breath and pulled her back by the hair, looking into her eyes. She was learning very fast.

"No, Helen," he said flatly. "I'm going to take care of you while you have to stay in Puerta Linda, and then I'm going to make sure you get back to the States safely. And that's it." He released her and stood up. "I'm going back downstairs for a while. I suggest you get to sleep. If you need me later, I'll be in the room across the hall."

She watched him button his shirt and head for the door, then slumped down on the bed when he went through it.

He wants me, she thought. Maybe he doesn't love me yet, the way I love him, but he wants me, and that's a step in the right direction.

Helen turned on her side and snapped off the small lamp, which hadn't given much illumination in the first place, and now she was in total darkness.

There was hope yet. She would work on it tomorrow.

Matteo ran down the rickety wooden steps and stopped at the bottom, wiping his face with the tail of shirt. It was cooler now, at night, but the humidity was high, and Puerta Linda's trademark rains still threatened, lending a further touch of heaviness to the air.

He walked through the reception area and out the back to the kitchen, where he opened the rear door, lifting his face to the breeze. That had been a close one. If she hadn't made that remark, it would all be over by now, plunging him deeper into the abyss of guilt he already inhabited.

He left the door open and went back inside, looking in the ancient refrigerator for a can of the brew Helen had earlier refused. He found one and popped the top, swigging it down in huge, grateful gulps.

She was a kid, he had to remind himself, in more ways than one. The years separating them were not so many, but the gulf of experience between them was a chasm. He felt

uncomfortably close to using her, and he was not going to
compound that by robbing her of her innocence.

But God, she was sweet. It had taken every ounce of
willpower he possessed to walk away from her. He didn't
consider himself particularly noble, and the effort of deny-
ing himself what he desperately wanted had left him parched
and drained.

He shook his head, taking another drink. He had really
done it this time. All right, maybe she had agreed to come
with him of her own free will, but he didn't take much
comfort from that. He had done his best to talk her into it,
after all. And maybe his plans had gone awry. If things had
worked out the way they were supposed to she'd be on her
way home right now. But the fact remained that she was
stuck in Puerta Linda because of him, in danger because of
him, and he was not going to leave her seduced and discarded because of him, too.

He looked up as Esteban, Elena's husband, entered the
kitchen and greeted him. The two men sat at the table and
began to plan Matteo's route for the next day. He had to
avoid the roads and travel through the bush to dodge the
police, who, according to Esteban's latest information, were
beefing up their efforts to find him.

Matteo gave brief consideration to leaving Helen with
Elena and Esteban, then realized she would never stay. She
would probably just come after him on her own, which
would be far more dangerous for her than if he took her
with him.

He put down his drink and leaned over the table to listen
to Esteban, concentrating on the older man's directions.

One thing at a time.

He would deal with Helen in the morning.

* * *

When Helen awoke she was naked, and she was startled until she remembered the events of the previous evening with a clarity that made her blush.

She got up and washed quickly with the tepid water left over from the bath Matteo had interrupted. She recalled the feel of his mouth and his hands on her body, and when she noticed a small pink mark on the inside of one breast she felt a thrill, as if it was confirmation that she had not imagined the passionate interlude in his arms.

She dressed in the clothes Matteo had procured for her, a loose cotton blouse and capri pants of the type teenagers in the States were currently wearing. The garments were a little big, but a definite improvement over the bedraggled items she had worn in the rain. She bundled those up and resolved to wash them when she got the chance, which might not be soon.

She was brushing out her hair when Elena knocked at her door.

"Comida, señorita de Matteo," she called.

Helen assumed that was breakfast and opened the door. Elena bustled in with a tray, grinning when she saw Helen dressed in her daughter's clothes.

"I'm glad you find me amusing," Helen said, glancing at the tray. It held a cup of something dark, which Helen fervently hoped was coffee, a flat corn cake and a piece of coral melon.

"¿Café?" Helen said, pointing to the cup, using up another item in her less than immense vocabulary.

"Sí, sí, café con chicore," Elena replied, nodding vigorously.

Helen picked it up and took a sip, wondering, with ominous foreboding, what *chicore* was. But it tasted all right, a little bitter, but recognizable as coffee.

"¿Leche?" she asked, encouraged.

Elena pointed to the little pitcher on the tray, which indeed turned out to contain milk. Helen added it to the coffee as Elena, evidently convinced by this conversational success that they were now going to get along famously, set the tray on the bed and sat next to it, folding her arms.

Helen understood that they were about to have a talk. That should prove to be interesting, since she knew about ten words of Spanish and Elena knew no English at all.

Helen bit into the piece of melon, waiting. She refused to launch into another "*dónde está Matteo*" routine, although she was beginning to wonder where he'd gone.

"*Matteo es muy hermoso,*" Elena offered, smiling knowingly.

All Helen understood of that was "Matteo is." She put on a blank expression and turned her hands palm upward to indicate ignorance.

"*Hermoso,*" Elena repeated, stroking her face with both hands lovingly.

Matteo needs a shave? Helen wondered. No, that couldn't be it. Matteo is...something. He is shaving? She mimed the activity to Elena, who shook her head disgustedly, standing and posing, turning from side to side as if admired by a crowd.

I don't believe this, Helen thought. I've come fifteen hundred miles and been shot at by the Puerta Lindan police so I can play charades.

She shrugged to indicate bafflement.

"*Hermoso,*" Elena said again, louder, frustrated by Helen's stupidity. "*¿Lindo, sí?*"

At this point Matteo strode into the room, since Elena had left the door open and he could see the two women inside. Helen was glad of Elena's presence; she felt awkward seeing him in the light of day after their last encounter and jumped in to ask, "Matteo, can you tell me what Elena is trying to say? She keeps repeating that you're *hermoso*, or something like that, and she obviously expects me to react to it."

Matteo fixed Elena with a baleful stare, and the older woman burst out laughing. Helen knew immediately that she had made a mistake.

"What does it mean?" she asked in a small voice, her curiosity outweighing her judgment.

"Good-looking," Matteo said, sighing. "Handsome. I think our landlady was preparing to enumerate my virtues for you, lining you up for the hard sell. She thinks if I got married and started producing babies my life would be complete."

"Maybe she has a point," Helen said softly. "And you are *hermoso*. Very *hermoso*."

Elena had been following the conversation from the tone of their voices, and she slapped Helen on the back approvingly, which almost sent her flying across the room.

Matteo decided it was time to intervene. He cleaned off the tray Elena had brought and handed her the empty, saying, "Thank you, Elena, it's been real. Goodbye, good luck and God bless."

Helen was laughing when the older woman left, and she said to Matteo, "I can't believe the way you talk. If I didn't know better and I didn't hear that little accent every now and then, I'd swear you were an American."

His reaction was not what she expected. He studied her soberly for a few seconds and then answered, "There are others who would agree with you. And it hasn't made me very popular in some quarters."

She could tell that she had touched on a sore subject and asked quietly, "How do you mean?"

Matteo sat on the cane chair and took a sip of Helen's coffee, grimacing at its bitterness. "Elena's been cutting this with too much chicory," he commented, before answering Helen's question. He drew his finger around the rim of the cup and said thoughtfully, "There's a faction among the rebels that would like to see me replaced."

"Replaced?"

He nodded. "They know that I was educated in the U.S. and had spent more time there than in Puerta Linda by the time I reached adulthood. They want someone who never 'deserted' his country to be their leader."

"Who is *they*?"

Matteo bent his head, staring into the cup. The bright morning sunlight filtering through the window turned his hair into a burnished ebony helmet, dark and gleaming.

"Well, actually, it's only one man, but he has others who would follow him if it came to that. He's one of my best, too, Vicente Olmos. I can tell that he's biding his time, waiting for the right moment to turn on me and seize command for himself."

"But if he wants what you want, a new government for Puerta Linda, why does he waste his energy on divisive action that will only weaken your group internally?"

Matteo rose, putting the cup down and jamming his hands into the pocket of his jeans. "You don't understand about the egos involved here, Helen. Olmos has lost sight of the larger issue; he sees only that he's more suitable for my position than I am. Or so he thinks. He's strong too, a tireless fighter, and he's lived in Puerta Linda all his life. He knows there's anti-American feeling in the camp, and he plays on it, calling me '*nuestro jefe americano*'—'our American leader.' He says I talk like an American, act like an American and think like an American."

"Lucky for him that you do," Helen responded fiercely. "Lucky for all of them. They'll be free one day because you think like an American."

He stared at her, smiling gradually, and then put his hands on her shoulders, putting his cheek against her hair. "You're good for me; do you know that?"

"Am I?" she whispered.

"Yes, you are. Anyway, don't worry about Olmos. He's too afraid of me to do anything, and unless his greed for power outweighs his fear he won't be a threat."

Helen could well understand that the other man might fear Matteo. As gentle as he was with her, she remembered his reaction when the mailman had arrived, and at the airport, and knew that he could be deadly. She shivered slightly and he stepped back, looking down at her.

"What is it?" he asked.

"Nothing. Just thinking about the trip ahead. How far is it to your camp?"

"I got the directions last night from Esteban. If we leave now, we should make it by nightfall, but some of the way will be on foot."

"You need directions to get to your own camp?"

"It's moved every few days in order to hide it from government troops."

"But they find you anyway, don't they?"

"Sometimes. They're always looking." He glanced around the room. "Are you ready?"

"Yes."

"Good. Elena packed us some food, and Esteban fueled up the bike this morning. Let's go."

As they walked down the stairs Helen said, "I still feel bad about stealing that bike."

Matteo halted. "If it will make you feel better, after this is over I'll try to track down the owner and send him the money for it, okay?"

"Will you really?"

"I said I'll try."

"I guess you think I'm silly. I mean, I realize that you probably steal cars and boats and things all the time, but I don't, and well..."

"I don't think you're silly. And as I told you once before, I'm not a thief. But I do what's... necessary."

Yes, he did, Helen thought, as he called Elena and Esteban to say goodbye. He always did what was *necessary*, and that knowledge caused a chill to set in around her heart, belying the stifling heat of the Puerta Lindan day.

Elena hugged Helen goodbye, and Esteban shook hands with her solemnly, like an ambassador bidding farewell to a foreign dignitary. The sun was already scorching as they climbed onto the bike, and Helen began to wish for a return of the rain. At least it provided a temporary cooling effect, and she had a feeling that before long she would think that any relief was welcome.

She was right. Matteo drove steadily for hours, always climbing, and the sun beat down on her back like the hammers of hell. It was rough going, too, as he kept off the main roads and often took tracks that were little more than well-used footpaths. By the time he stopped for lunch she was sunburned and thirsty, and her insides felt like jelly. He pulled the bike into a shaded area and helped her off it. Helen sat immediately, folding her legs under her and closing her eyes.

"You don't look so hot," he said, bending down to peer into her face.

"I am very hot, thank you very much," she replied, not opening her eyes.

"I mean it," he insisted, squatting next to her and handing her a thermos. "Take a drink. Why didn't you tell me to stop?"

"I know how important it is for you to get back to your men," she answered, swallowing the water he gave her.

"Hey. Listen. Nothing is more important to me than you. Got that?"

"I got it," she answered, as he reached into his pocket and withdrew a white paper packet.

"Salt pills," he said, offering her two of them. "They'll help prevent dehydration. You're just not used to this climate, and it can be a killer."

Helen swallowed the pills dutifully, wondering how he could look so fit and hale after the ride they'd just had. And he was the one who had taken a bullet a short time ago, not her.

Matteo got up and unstrapped the pack he had carried on the back of the bike, taking out a bottle of lotion and handing it to her.

"You're already burned," he said. "Elena gave this to me; you should have put some on before we left. Your skin is like linen, and you're cooking."

"What a charming analogy," Helen replied, as he poured some into his hand and daubed it on her face. It was blessedly cool, and smelled heavenly.

"That's wonderful," she said dreamily. "What is it?"

"Coconut oil, palm oil, some other things."

"It smells like candy."

He chuckled. "That's the coconut. We have many uses for it, some of them not so savory. Have you ever had a *dulce de leche*?"

"A what?" she asked, almost purring as his strong fingers stroked the lotion along her throat.

"*Dulce de leche*. It means 'sweetness of milk,' and it's a drink made with coconut milk and rum. It doesn't taste alcoholic at all, and you can just keep belting them down until, before you know it, you're dead drunk. It's a great favorite with the locals, who like to feed them to the tourists and then take various forms of advantage."

Helen laughed, beginning to feel immeasurably better as he lifted her hair and applied the lotion to her back above the deep V of her blouse.

"I think I'd like to try one of those," she said, smiling.

"Then you will. When all this is over, I'll take you dancing, and you can sip *dulce de leches* under the stars."

When all this is over, Helen thought. Would it ever be over? For him?

"Matt?" she said as he shook more lotion into his palm and smoothed it over the exposed skin of her arms.

"Hmm?" he replied, not looking up, absorbed by his task.

"Do you think we're going to get out of this?"

He raised his head, saw the expression in her eyes. "You are, *majita*. I'm going to make sure of it."

"And what about you?" she asked, searching his face.

"I'm in it for the duration, Helen. You know that."

She dropped her eyes, following the motion of his hands. Why did she keep asking him the same question? Did she think that just once the answer would change?

"Just the front is left," he said, handing her the bottle. "You can do that."

"You do it," she replied, giving it back to him.

He stared at her, saw the seductive challenge in her eyes. Sparks kindled in his, and he spread another pool of lotion onto his fingers, slipping them across her collarbone and the tops of her shoulders. The front of the blouse had a deep round neck, and he stroked lower and lower, teasing her. When he finally reached into the cup of her bra, his big hand engulfing her breast, she moaned and her head fell forward, her hair draping over his arm.

The bottle dropped from his hand and he lifted her into his lap. Helen lay back in his arms, reaching to pull him down to her as he kissed her. The noonday sun filtered through the trees, making patterns on the two figures sprawled upon the ground. In seconds they were as lost as they had been the night before, and Matteo was reaching behind Helen to undo the buttons at the back of her blouse.

She arched her back to accommodate him, and in moving she scraped the burned skin of her arm across the rocky soil beneath her. She cried out, and Matteo sat up, looking around them.

"What is it?" he said, scanning the trees. "Did you hear something?"

"No, I just hurt my arm."

He looked down at her, lying across his thighs, and suddenly seemed to realize what they were doing. He picked her up bodily and set her against the trunk of a tree, standing himself and walking a short distance away from her.

"Now," he said in a slightly unsteady voice. "You stay there and I'll stay over here, or else we won't get to the camp today, and we might not get there at all. Understood?"

"*Sí, mi jefe,*" she replied, saluting smartly.

"That isn't funny," he said, removing two sandwiches from the backpack and tossing her one. "Now eat your lunch like a good girl and try not to taste Elena's trademark meatloaf. She thinks it's an American dish, and I've never had the heart to tell her it's like nothing I've ever tasted on this planet, much less in the States."

Helen took a bite, and had to agree that the filling in the sandwich bore little resemblance to meatloaf. It did, however, have a disturbing likeness to the Wednesday-night special at her secondary boarding school, which the students had referred to as mystery meat and which, they had it on good authority, had been responsible for the deaths of several students over the years. Helen wondered briefly how Elena had managed to get the recipe from the Parsons School for Girls in Concord, New Hampshire, and then dismissed the coincidence as one of life's little ironies.

"What are you smiling at?" Matteo asked.

"I was just thinking that this tastes like a dish I used to have at my old boarding school," she said.

He nodded. "Yeah, institutional food is pretty bad. In college we sent out for pizza every night. It's a wonder we didn't all have rickets."

"What's an engineering major like?" she asked curiously. "What kind of courses did you take?"

Matteo shrugged. "Physics, mostly."

Helen shuddered. "I had one physics course, and that was enough. All those problems with people riding bicycles up an incline, into a head wind, with this kind of pull and that kind of drag. How fast were they going? What was the thrust and the slope and the resistance? I never knew."

He grinned. "That was my favorite type of problem."

"You could actually solve those things? I would memorize the formulas for the tests, and I thought I was applying them right, but I would always wind up with an answer that had somebody riding a bicycle at the speed of light."

Matteo laughed. "And then, after having spent forty-five minutes figuring it out, you would hand it in anyway, right?"

She nodded vigorously. "You bet. I was heavily into partial credit. The professor would give you points if you picked the right law of thermodynamics, or whatever, even if you got the wrong answer. I think that's how I passed."

"Why were you taking a physics course? That seems an odd choice for an English major."

Helen made a face. "I had a counselor who told me I had to be well rounded. I was a freshman; what did I know? After that year I decided I would be narrow-minded and insular, and my grades improved dramatically."

He smiled, regarding her with amusement, and Helen thought it was an unusual conversation to be having, with this man, in this place. She could see where his rival would resent the education and the polish that made Matteo seem much more a product of the American culture than his native one. Sometimes, as now, when she talked to him she could forget what he had chosen to do with his life, but then she would be brutally reminded, by hearing the harsh tone of his voice when he issued orders or seeing the glint of the sunlight on his gun. At one moment he would seem like a young Manhattan professional at a cocktail party or a gallery opening, and at another like a guerilla, grimy and armed, looking out at her from the pages of the Sunday supplement. He sat astride his two worlds uneasily, inhabiting both, but completely at home in neither.

"What are you thinking?" he asked suddenly, his tone wary, almost unfriendly.

She blinked. "Why do you ask?"

"You were looking at me so strangely, as if you could see right through me."

"I'm sorry."

"Don't apologize. Tell me what's on your mind."

"I was thinking that your life must be difficult," she said honestly.

"And yours hasn't exactly been a party since you met me," he replied. "I carry so much trouble with me that it clings to those I touch, like pollen."

"I wouldn't have missed it, Matteo," she said softly. "This is an adventure. I've never had one before, and probably never will again."

"Did you think that yesterday, when the bullets were flying?"

"Once I realized I was still alive, I did. It's a tremendous rush, isn't it, to be in such peril, and then to escape, knowing that you got out of it through your own resources, that you won and 'they' lost. I felt exhilarated, totally alive, like I was flying."

"You felt that, too?" he said softly.

"Oh, yes. There's nothing else like it, is there?"

"Nothing," he answered, half smiling, his eyes meeting hers in perfect communication.

Helen felt the heat come up under her skin; the sensation of shared understanding was almost sexual. Then he broke the spell by striding toward her and offering his hands to pull her up. When she was on her feet he led her to the bike.

"We have to get going. The last leg of the trip will be on foot, and I don't want to be walking through the jungle after dark."

"Jungle?" Helen said apprehensively.

He leaned over her shoulder and pointed into the distance, where the slope of a mountain could be seen rising into a mist so thick that it was still untouched by the tropical sun.

"La Jungla Azul," he said softly. "The Blue Jungle."

"Why blue?"

"The vegetation is so dense that it looks blue from the air. Pilots flying over it named it."

"Is your camp on that mountain?"

"Partway up the slope. The plants produce about half the oxygen used in the whole country."

"Are you sure you can find the camp? The trees all look...the same."

He chuckled. "Spoken like a city girl. I can find it, *majita*, never fear." He handed her Elena's thermos and said, "Have another drink. And I've got candy bars. If you feel weak or faint, tell me. Eating one should take care of it."

"Okay."

Matteo replaced their supplies in the pack, and Helen climbed on the bike behind him once he was seated. His shirt was damp and clung to him, outlining his taut muscles, and when she slipped her arms around his waist she had a flash of his bare skin pressed to hers, slick and musk scented, in that oven of a bedroom at the *taberna*. She felt a falling sensation in the pit of her stomach, and she took a deep breath, steeling herself for the ordeal of the journey ahead.

"Ready?" he said, turning his head.

"Ready," she replied, and he kicked the bike into life, sending up a spray of gravel and roaring off through the trees.

They traveled at a slower pace now, picking their way through increasingly dense undergrowth, until Matteo was forced to abandon the bike and they walked. Helen followed in his wake as he cleared a path for them, breaking off low-hanging branches and occasionally pulling his knife from his belt and cutting away the leaves and vines so they could pass. Helen was finding it increasingly difficult to breathe; her lungs could not adjust to the changing oxygen content of the air, and every step was labored. As night was falling Matteo stopped and turned to look at her. Then he slipped the straps of his pack from his arms.

"That's it," he said. "You're done in. We'll have to stay the night here and reach camp in the morning."

"How far is it?" she asked, slapping away the bugs that were feasting on her hide like pork fanatics at a luau.

"A mile or so," he said, "but you can't make it."

"I can make it," she gasped.

"I'll carry you."

Helen drew herself up to her full height, not very impressive next to his six feet plus, but the best she could do. "You will not carry me. I won't make my entrance like a dead Spartan borne home on his shield."

He grinned, his teeth flashing white in the gathering darkness.

"Your entrance? Helen, we're not going to a debutante ball."

"I know that," she snapped. "Matt, I'm burned a lovely shade of coral, my bites and scrapes and cuts look like a Bactine advertisement and my hair has become the home of every insect in Central America. At least allow me the dignity of arriving on my own two feet."

"All right," he conceded. "I never argue with a woman whose skin is the color of a Hawaiian sunset."

"Do I look that bad?" she asked worriedly, feeling the vestiges of her vanity resurfacing at the prospect of being seen by other people.

"You look gorgeous," he said firmly, leaning forward to kiss the tip of her pink nose. "You look like a gorgeous blonde with a few scratches and a medium-to-well-done sunburn."

"Liar," she said. "In this light you can't even see me."

"I can see well enough. Your skin has its own glow, sort of like a radioactive isotope."

It was not the moment to tease her. Her lower lip began to tremble, and he detected the glimmer of tears in her eyes.

"Oh, no, baby, no," Matteo said, realizing that she had been pushed near her limit. He pulled her close, smoothing her tangled hair back from her forehead. "Don't cry now, it's almost over. Soon we'll arrive, and you'll have food, and a hot bath, and sleep. Doesn't that sound good?"

Helen nodded, sniffling like a five-year-old promised a lollipop after the penicillin shot.

He pressed his lips to the shell of her ear, closing his eyes. "That's my brave girl," he whispered. "Now look. Look up at that moon. Isn't it beautiful?"

"Yes," she agreed. It was enhanced by a halo, surrounded by stars just emerging from the blue void of dusk.

"By the time it's in full view we'll be there," he said. "All right?"

"Okay."

Matteo set off again, and Helen followed him, bolstered by his touch, his words. Let's face it, she thought dryly, squashing a mosquito with the flat of her hand, the man can get me to do anything.

They ascended for a length of time Helen was no longer able to measure, and then Matteo stopped, taking her hand

and pointing to a large clearing directly ahead of them. Helen could see a mass of tents and cooking fires—a sprawling encampment where people walked to and fro, appearing miniaturized by the distance.

"There it is," he said.

His step became brisker with his eagerness to get there, and Helen kept up with him, anxious for the rest he had promised. As they got closer she could pick out features she had missed before: a modern-looking motor home parked at the edge of the trees, prefab buildings that could be assembled hastily and dismantled the same way, stacked boxes of canned goods and other supplies.

She glanced at Matteo. His face was alight; he was happy to be coming home, once more joining those who shared his purpose.

They were within shouting distance now, and a guard posted nearest the path they were traveling turned at a footstep, rifle at the ready. When he saw who it was he shouldered the weapon, setting up a cry that brought the others running from tents and huts all over the camp, dropping whatever they were doing to greet their leader.

"Matteo!" he shouted, and his cry was echoed by other voices until the whole clearing seemed to ring with the sound of the name. Matteo had to halt as they crowded around him, slapping his back, embracing him joyously, some even ruffling his hair. Helen stood behind him, not wanting to intrude on his reunion, and she noticed that there were two who stayed apart from the others, lingering on the fringes of the crowd. They were a man about Matteo's age and height, but huskier, with curling sandy hair and an expressionless face, and young woman with long straight black hair and a voluptuous figure encased in a set of pea green fatigues. This couple merely watched the scene, saying nothing to their comrades or to each other, but after the excitement died down Matteo's eyes sought the man's and he said quietly, *"Vicente. ¿Qué tal?"*

That's Olmos, Helen thought with a jolt. But who was the woman?

Matteo seemed to remember Helen's presence, and he turned to take her hand, leading her forward into the light from the closest fire.

"And this," he said in Spanish, looking around at the assembled faces, "is Helen."

Chapter 6

The group, which had been setting up such a ruckus, fell silent, all staring at Helen. They couldn't imagine who she was or what she was doing with Matteo, and she felt the eyes of the dark-haired woman rake over her, taking in her dishabille.

Matteo launched into a little speech, which Helen of course did not understand. She caught one phrase, *"mi amiga especial,"* and gathered that he was telling them she was a friend and was to be treated accordingly. Helen could sense immediately that this was easier said than done; the sexy brunette looked like she wanted to roast the newcomer on a spit.

When Matteo finished talking, his followers exchanged glances, and Helen could see them all reaching the same conclusion: if that's what Matteo wants, we'll do it. They dispersed to their various activities, some of them casting parting looks, intent with curiosity, at Helen. Matteo put his arm around her shoulder and they walked the length of the camp together. Helen was fascinated by what she saw: men and women washing clothes, cleaning weapons, preparing meals, all by the light of electric bulbs strung on wires and hooked up to portable generators. Matteo paused outside the door of the motor home and said to Helen, "You go inside and rest. I'll send someone with food and clothes, and there's a working shower if you're up to taking one right now. I've been away for a while and I have to talk to some of my men, but I'll be back later, okay?"

"Okay," Helen said uncertainly, not wanting to be left alone, but aware that he had responsibilities to fulfill.

"Go on," he urged, when he saw her expression. "I'll be back before you know it, I promise." He kissed her swiftly on the forehead, and as Helen turned to go into the camper she saw the dark woman standing in the shadows, silent witness to the scene.

Helen climbed the steps and pulled open the door, wondering uncomfortably if she was to be the main attraction for the duration of her stay. The interior of the camper was furnished with ragtag items of furniture and an assortment of surprisingly modern appliances, including a coffee maker with a timer and a microwave oven. Helen didn't know if this was Matteo's place or a convenient focal point for the whole camp, but she was sure the people she'd seen living in tents would not appreciate the star treatment she was getting. She was too tired to worry about it much, however, and she was investigating the workings of the hand-held shower in the bathroom when she heard a knock.

"Come in," she said, and then changed that to "*Entrada.*"

Helen emerged into the tiny hallway running between the kitchen and the living room as the door opened and a woman in her thirties entered. She was carrying a covered tray and a neat pile of clothing. She set both on the table and gestured that they were for Helen's use, then departed without further ceremony.

Well, Helen thought. It would be tough making friends here. These people were obviously going to follow Matteo's orders to the letter, but that was the extent of it. Their natural distrust of outsiders would not allow anything more. They had to accept her presence among them, but they didn't have to like it.

Helen sighed heavily. She had never been a big winner of popularity contests, and this was just one more situation in which she would be the odd man out. Her life had prepared her perfectly to deal with any experience of emotional isolation, and she approached this one with her customary resignation.

Helen glanced at the clothes, thinking that she hadn't put on anything that actually belonged to her since she left Florida. She tried to imagine Sophia under such circumstances and had to smile. Her mother, who got a migraine if her hem was half an inch off, would never survive the rigors of life with a Puerta Lindan revolutionary.

She returned to the bathroom to shower and made the mistake of glancing in the fly-spotted mirror above the sink. She groaned aloud. Between the sunburn and the insect bites, she looked like some horrific parody of herself, a distorted figure from a beachcomber's nightmare. She looked away quickly, turned on the water and stripped off her ruined clothes.

The shower was tepid but serviceable, and after sponging off and washing her lank hair she felt much better. She dressed in the borrowed outfit, jeans and a men's army T-shirt, and sat at the table, investigating the contents of the tray.

There was a bowl of stew with beans and some kind of meat, a hunk of dark bread and a glass of milk. She polished off everything, carrying the empty dishes to the sink

and rinsing them. She left them to dry in the drainer and
then eyed the daybed with longing. Matteo had said he
would be back, but he might be gone for hours, and certainly no one could object if she took a little nap.

Helen stretched out on the sofa and was asleep within
seconds, enjoying the dreamless slumber of complete exhaustion.

Matteo dismissed his men from the tent where he had set
up temporary headquarters, but Olmos remained waiting
until the others had departed to say, *"¿Ella está americana?"*

Matteo met his challenging gaze squarely. To the question, "She is American?" he replied, *"Sí."* He didn't have
to ask who "she" was.

Olmos smiled slightly, his eyes narrowing. Matteo continued to stare at him until he raised the flap of the tent and
departed, slowly enough to suggest that he was not intimi-
dated.

Matteo sat back and rubbed the bridge of his nose with
his thumb and forefinger. Olmos would try to use that information to disturb the balance of power between them,
but Matteo wasn't going to concede his point in advance by
lying to him.

He glanced around the tent, wondering how Helen was
doing. The camper where he'd left her was ordinarily used
for meetings like the one he'd just held, but he felt that she
needed comfortable surroundings on this first night. Soon
the motor home would be left behind anyway, since they
couldn't transport it across the mountain, but he would have
to be more careful in the future. Helen's nationality would
make her enough of a target; he didn't want to add fuel to
the fire.

The flap of the tent was flung upward suddenly, and Alma Rivera stood before him, hands on hips, dark eyes flashing.

"So," she sneered, "you bring your American mistress here to flaunt her in our faces."

Matteo folded his hands behind his head and regarded her calmly. "She's not my mistress," he replied, "though it would be none of your business if she were." His tone was mild, but the tense posture of his neck and shoulders conveyed a different message.

"Hah! Matteo Montega let a pretty blonde like that escape his bed? I don't believe it."

Alma spoke the Spanish dialect of the border regions, and tonight it fell more harshly than usual on Matteo's ear. "I don't care what you believe," he answered, standing to indicate that the interview was over.

But Alma had come to have her say, and she was not going to be put off so easily.

"That skinny gringa won't last a day here," she tossed at him. "She looks like her blood is made of water."

"She's not as fragile as she appears," Matteo replied, and the note of pride in his voice stung her. "She went through a lot to get here, and more before that. Don't underestimate her."

Alma stared back at him furiously; his answer only inflamed her more. Matteo had never brought a woman to the camp. When he needed company he took one of their own, and she had been the favorite not too long ago. But now he arrived with this stranger, bringing her with him to his place, *their* place. This woman must be important to him, and that realization drove Alma to her next statement.

"She will be a problem; I can promise it!"

He fixed her with an icy stare. "Are you threatening me?"

"I don't have to threaten. I can sense the mood of the people. They aren't happy she's here. You should not keep her with you."

"Don't presume on our past relationship to instruct me," Matteo said dismissively. "I can handle my own people."

"Can you handle Olmos? Already he's stirring up the men about her."

"Olmos is always stirring up something. If I worried about him every time he got going, I wouldn't have a minute to do anything else." He paused, adopting a more placating tone. "Alma, this woman has been a great friend to me. I want you to help her, try to teach her..."

Alma spat on the dirt floor of the tent. She wasn't buying it. As far as she was concerned there was only one kind of relationship a young, pretty woman could have with a man like Matteo Montega, and she fired back nastily, "Why, certainly. Of course! Nothing's too good for my leader's yellow-haired *yanqui* whore."

Matteo crossed the room in two strides, grabbing Alma's upper arms with such strength that she would later find the imprint of his fingers stamped on her bruised flesh. But she did not flinch. Her mettle was legendary; not once had he seen her cry.

"I have never hit a woman in my life," he said in a low, dangerous voice, "but unless you want to be the first I suggest you guard your tongue. That 'gringa' saved my life. You have no idea what she's gone through for me, and if you ever speak that way about her again you will regret it."

Alma stared back at him defiantly, channeling her true feelings into a cleansing, burning rebellion. She was deeply infatuated with him, and more than that, her former claim to his bed had given her a status that had been humiliating to lose. But Matteo could see only the malice, which disgusted him, not the helpless, painful jealousy that inspired it.

"Now get out of my sight," he concluded, "and if I hear that you are giving her *any* trouble of *any* kind, you will answer to me. Do you understand?"

No response.

He shook her, not gently. "Do you understand?"

"Yes," she replied sullenly, wrenching away from him.

He let her go, turning his back on her, and didn't look around until he was sure she was gone.

Matteo exhaled sharply, combing his damp hair with his fingers. It had been a long, trying day, and the scene with Alma was just what he needed to complete it.

Why had he ever slept with that woman? he wondered irritably. He had always known better, but she'd caught him at a weak moment with her seductive body. Then he had let it continue too long, because it was easy and because he had wanted to delay dealing with the turmoil of ending it. He detested final scenes, filled with recriminations, and as anticipated, Alma had provided a beauty. She had attached an importance to the relationship that he never felt, and now she would make sure Helen found out about their past involvement.

He realized that the idea of it bothered him. Alma was clever, and once she gathered, as she eventually would, that he had told her the truth, she would find some way to make Helen feel inferior because he had slept with Alma and not with her.

Neither woman could know that the exact opposite was the truth; he had slept with Alma because he regarded her as a convenience and refused Helen because he regarded her as a treasure.

Matteo kicked a clod of dirt, fragmenting it into a dozen pieces. Why was Alma still around? He had sent her home to visit her mother and thought she would be there. Now he could add her viciousness to his list of problems. And he knew from experience that Alma was not to be discounted.

She had a crude, streetwise intelligence, and since Matteo's dissolution of their affair had been forming an uneasy alliance with the equally crafty Olmos. Through his own carelessness, Matteo had made an enemy of Alma, sending her into the waiting arms of the man who coveted his position. Like two rogue wolves on the edge of the pack, they circled the leader, waiting for the right moment to lunge at his throat for the kill, each with different reasons for wanting to bring him down.

Matteo shook his head. How would he ever be able to concentrate on liberating his country with all of this peripheral intrigue going on?

He stepped outside the tent and looked up at the night sky, seeing by the descending arc of the moon that it was very late. He hoped Helen had gone to sleep. It was odd how often he found himself thinking of her; she had become such an integral part of his life that he no longer considered himself alone, and that frightened him. He didn't want her looking to him, depending on him, but somehow it had happened. And what was worse, he dreaded cutting her loose; he understood with a sinking feeling of resignation that didn't *want* to let her go.

But he had to do it. Alma and Olmos and the others had chosen this life; Helen had been catapulted into it by a trick of fate that brought an injured fugitive to her door. And being Helen, she had not been able to turn him away. Now it was up to him to return the favor and make sure that she got home and put all of this behind her forever.

But could she do it? He didn't need her to tell him that she was in love with him; her inexperience made her as transparent as rainwater. Like Bucephalus, who, when broken to the bit by Alexander, would never after abide another rider, Helen was a thoroughbred, in mind as well as pedigree. She wouldn't turn easily from him to another man; he very much doubted she would be able to do it at all. He hadn't com-

pleted the cruel circle by sleeping with her, and for that he
gave himself some credit. But to a woman like Helen, who
lived in her head, her thoughts and feelings were just as important, perhaps more important, then her physical func-
tions. Emotionally she was no longer a virgin, and he was
totally to blame.

Matteo walked slowly through the camp, his mind working furiously. There was a raid on a government installa-
tion planned for the following night, and he would have to
leave Helen alone for several hours. He knew that his people wouldn't do anything to hurt her while he was gone, because they would fear his retribution when he returned. But
what if he didn't return? He might be killed on this foray, as
he had almost been killed on the last one. And he was well
aware that he was Helen's only protection from Olmos's
brutality and Alma's vengeance.

He shook himself slightly, dismissing such thoughts. He
would have to survive in order to take care of her, and survive he would. After all, he should have been dead several
times already; judging by appearances, he was immortal.
His lips curved in a small smile as he entered the camper,
thinking that, like his historical hero, Alexander, his real
father must have been a god.

He found Helen fast asleep, with several strands of her
damp hair, fine as angel's breath, caught between her lips.
He removed them, gently putting them behind her ear, and
she stirred. He waited until she settled down again before
getting a pillow from the closet and putting it under her
head.

Such niceties would have to be forsaken soon. They would
have to move after the raid, because the government soldiers, alerted to their presence in the area, would be combing the jungle for them. And their new quarters were sure to
be more primitive.

Matteo pulled a chair in front of the camper's door and sat in it, draping his legs over the edge of Helen's bed. No one would be able to get to her except through him, and secure in that knowledge, he slept.

When Helen awoke the next morning, she could tell by the quality of the light filtering through the camper's thin curtains that it was very early. Still, she could hear the sounds of people stirring around her: low voices, metal pots clanging, and, close by, the unmistakable click-whirr, click-whirr, of bullets being inserted into a metal chamber. She sat up and saw Matteo asleep in the chair, his arms folded, his head turned to one side and his chin resting on his shoulder.

She studied him, wondering what time he had finally returned the night before, noting the blue shadows of exhaustion staining the skin beneath his eyes. He had never had a chance to recover fully from his recent illness, and the signs were there, if you looked for them. But even they could not diminish his beauty in her eyes. When she had first seen him she'd noted objectively that he was handsome, as one might notice that a building was gracefully proportioned or a flower symmetrical. But now that she knew him, she had almost forgotten that initial impression; it was so totally supplanted by her feeling for the whole man: body, mind, and soul. So she examined him anew, seeing the broad forehead and straight, narrow nose, the firm mouth with its full lower lip and thinner upper one, the flesh redder than hers, a bequest of his heritage. The long silky lashes that lay on his cheeks like wisps of black lace were the only effeminate aspect of his features. He had shaved off his beard at Esteban's, and his olive skin, already tan, had darkened with exposure to the sun. Now, enhanced by the shadow of his beard and the dark glossy wings of his hair, it looked bronzed. Helen leaned forward, her attention caught by a ridge of scar tissue on the edge of his jaw. As if he could feel her eyes on him, his lids lifted and he looked at her.

"Hi," she said, and he smiled.

"How are you feeling?" he asked, sitting up and stretching.

"Much better. How about you? That chair doesn't look very comfortable."

Matteo stood up, rubbing the back of neck. "Oh, it'll do in a pinch." He peered at her more closely. "The burn is fading; I think you're starting a tan."

Helen smiled ruefully. "That would be a first."

"Well, Puerta Linda is your place for firsts. First motor vehicle theft, first car chase by police, first suntan. Would you like some breakfast?"

"I guess so."

"They'll have something going at the cookhouse," he said. "I'll bring it back for you."

She noticed that he didn't ask her to go with him; he was trying to minimize her exposure to the rest of the people.

"Okay."

Helen watched him go out and then looked through the window to follow his progress across the grounds. He stopped several times to speak to some of his comrades, then disappeared into a hut near the spot where they had first entered the camp. When he emerged minutes later, he was carrying a plate and was accompanied by a middle-aged woman whom Helen had seen in the crowd the night before. She sat on the couch and waited for them to arrive, wondering about Matteo's companion.

Her presence was explained soon after Matteo came through the door and handed Helen her breakfast, which consisted of an omelet, a corn cake and a cup of black coffee.

"This is Theresa Aquino," he said to Helen, indicating the woman who stood, unsmiling, at his side. "She is the only person in the camp who speaks English besides me. I'll be busy today, and she'll look after you."

So this is to be my baby-sitter, Helen thought. Well, at least she would be able to talk to Theresa, ask her questions.

"I'll leave you two to get acquainted," Matteo said. He obviously wanted to get on with his plans, and Helen nodded. Theresa, clearly a draftee, followed him out the door with her eyes and then looked back at Helen.

"I'm Helen," Helen said, extending her hand.

Theresa took it briefly, meeting Helen's eyes for a second and then looking away.

Helen cleared her throat. "I'm so glad you speak English," she began brightly. "How did you learn?"

"My father was overseer on an American coffee plantation," Theresa answered, in accented but precise English.

"Oh, I see. Well, did Matteo tell you anything about me?"

"He told me only what I was to do," Theresa replied. "Keep you with me and keep you out of trouble."

Helen sighed. That was certainly clear enough.

"Do you have some work I could help you with?" Helen asked, trying again.

Theresa's dark eyes suggested that the question was humorous.

"You want to help me?" she said, an unmistakable note of irony in her tone.

"Yes, why not? I have nothing to do, and it will pass the time."

Theresa pointed at the food Matteo had brought. "Eat. You'll need it. We cook for the whole camp, and they eat plenty before a raid."

Before a raid? Helen thought, going cold at the word despite the stifling heat. So that was why Matteo was so busy.

Say **Yes** to

romance

AND YOU'LL GET

---

4 FREE BOOKS
AN ELEGANT MANICURE SET
A SURPRISE BONUS

NO RISK • NO OBLIGATION
NO STRINGS • NO KIDDING

EXCITING DETAILS INSIDE ⟹

Say yes to free gifts worth over $20.00

Say yes to a rendezvous with romance, and you'll get 4 classic love stories—FREE! You'll get an elegant manicure set—FREE! And you'll get a delightful surprise—FREE! These gifts are worth over $20.00—but you can have them without spending even a penny!

MONEY-SAVING HOME DELIVERY!

Say yes to Silhouette romances and you'll enjoy the convenience of previewing brand-new books every month, delivered right to your home before they appear in stores. Each book is yours for only $2.25—25¢ less than the retail price.

SPECIAL EXTRAS—FREE!

You'll get your free monthly newsletter, packed with news on your favorite writers, upcoming books, even recipes from your favorite authors.

Say yes to a Silhouette love affair. Complete, detach and mail your Free Offer Card today!

She forced down the breakfast while Theresa watched, and then followed her back to the cookhouse.

She was not quite the center of attention she had been the night before but still received a number of curious glances. During the long, hot morning she helped to clean up after breakfast and get ready for lunch. The men came in groups, talking together, and the women in twos, whispering, staring at Helen and then giggling at remarks they made to each other. Helen ignored them, doing whatever Theresa told her to do, and managed pretty well until early afternoon, when Alma entered the hut alone, stopping short when she caught sight of Helen dishing out the stew.

She sauntered up to the table, accepting a plate from Helen and a glass from Theresa. She stared at Helen for a few seconds and then said something in Spanish to Theresa, who glanced quickly at Helen, then remembered that she didn't understand. Alma paused a moment longer and then added a one liner to the woman behind her, who grinned hugely and winked.

Helen continued to dish out the food, waiting until the women were seated at a table away from her to ask, "What did she say?"

Theresa didn't respond at first, devoting her attention to assembling a stack of plates on the counter before her.

Helen prodded, "You might as well tell me."

Theresa shrugged. "Alma said that Matteo must be getting tired of you already. When she was in his bed he never had her doling out rations."

Helen didn't answer, her worst suspicions confirmed.

"She was Matteo's woman before you," Theresa added unnecessarily.

"What was the rest of it?" Helen said quietly.

"What?"

"She said something else, when that other woman smiled."

Theresa hesitated again, and Helen waited patiently until she said, "Alma says she was always too busy keeping Matteo satisfied to find time for kitchen work."

Helen coughed. "Do you think I could have a glass of water?" she asked.

"In the barrel, there," Theresa said, indicating a large wooden storage tank that looked like a beer keg and was tapped the same way. Helen filled a dented metal cup and drank it dry, wondering why this information should hit her so hard.

She'd always known that Matteo must have had his share of women. Alma's reaction to Helen's arrival had certainly indicated that she'd been one of them. But it was the way these people accepted the orderly progression, Alma yesterday, Helen today, someone else tomorrow, that bothered her. Not to mention that in her case it wasn't even true. To look at Alma and know that Matteo had given to her what he had denied to Helen was almost more than she could bear.

The rest of the day passed in a blur of heat and the cloying smell of food. By the time darkness fell and they were cleaning up, Helen's feet were burning and she had a case of dishpan hands that would defy any lotion on the American market. She glanced over at Theresa, who was wiping down the counter, having put in what was for her an ordinary day.

"Theresa, how did you get involved with Matteo, with this group?"

The older woman looked at her, pushing back an errant strand of coarse, graying hair. Helen could tell that she was examining her to see if she really wanted a serious answer. Seemingly satisfied, Theresa said, "When I was a young woman my father was accused of stealing by his employer. He denied the charges but was pronounced guilty without a trial and shot."

Helen was speechless, sorry she'd asked.

"It's not the sort of thing you forget," Theresa went on. "When I saw that Matteo and the other people here were working to do something about a government that permits that kind of injustice, I joined with them. I'm getting old and can't do much, but I can cook. I've cooked all my life for my family, and I can cook now for my friends."

Helen considered that and then said, "Theresa, what is going to happen tonight?"

Theresa's face went carefully blank. "You'd better ask Matteo about that. It's not for me to say."

And he won't tell me any more than you will, Helen thought.

They walked to the door of the hut and Theresa said flatly, "You worked hard today, and you can tell Matteo I said so."

Helen had to suppress a smile. She felt like asking Theresa for a note that she could present to Matteo, like a report card from the teacher.

"Thank you, Theresa," she said warmly. "I know the others resent me, and it's nice that you were willing to give me a chance."

"It was Matteo's idea," Theresa responded, and then they both laughed.

"Good night," Helen said, walking back to the camper.

"Good night," Theresa answered, turning off for her tent.

When Helen pulled open the door of the motor home, Matteo turned at the sound, and she stopped in her tracks, frozen at the sight of him.

He was dressed, like the other men, in camouflage fatigues, combat boots and a dark knit hat to cover his hair. His face was smeared with blacking, and he had an automatic rifle slung over his shoulder. A belt loaded with ammunition was draped across his chest, and a pistol and a knife were sheathed at his waist. He was a walking arsenal.

Helen recovered her powers of locomotion and walked to the couch, sitting carefully, as if she might break. She wanted to say something, but no words made it to her lips.

"Don't look like that, Helen," Matteo said evenly. "You knew this was what I did."

"Of course," she whispered. "I just didn't know it would be so real, so much like . . ."

"Like what?" he said.

"Like war. But it is war." She closed her eyes. "Don't listen to me, I don't know what I mean."

"This is what I wanted to spare you," he said simply, and then looked up as there was a quick knock, followed by the opening of the door. Vicente Olmos entered, glancing at Helen and then saying something to Matteo. Matteo answered dismissively, and Olmos paused to smile at Helen before he left. She felt as if he had touched her.

"I have to go," Matteo said, patting his breast pocket and looking away.

Helen stood and grabbed his arm. "Where are you going? What are you going to do?"

He withdrew his arm firmly. "Stay here. I'll be back before morning."

"And what if you don't come back? What then?"

"That's a risk I always have to take. But I'm lucky. You should know that. Luck brought me to you. I'll be back."

Helen watched helplessly as he yanked open the door and ran down the steps. She followed, halting as she saw him jump into a jeep that already held several other men, all armed like him and dressed for night concealment. They took off, the driver leading the way out of the camp as several other loaded jeeps fell in behind Matteo's. Helen trailed them with her eyes until they were out of sight, and then she went back inside.

What had she expected? she thought, as she tried to accept what had just happened. That he would stay behind and hold her hand while his men went out to risk being killed? Of course not, yet she had never let herself consider in detail what his days were like, what he had been doing the night she met him, what he would continue to do in the future. She had wanted to think that the idyll at Esteban's *taberna* would last indefinitely, that her presence in his life would somehow change it, that he would make her more important than the goals that had sustained him before he arrived at her door. And now she realized what he had been trying to tell her all along, that he couldn't take responsibility for her because he had room in his life only for his country.

Helen turned abruptly and went back outside, where she walked past the groups of women who stood together, beginning the long vigil that would end only when the jeeps returned.

Alma detached herself from one of them and flung something at Helen. Helen kept walking, up to Theresa, startling the woman, who stared at her in concern.

"Would you do me a favor?" Helen asked her softly.

"What is it?"

"Would you tell Alma that I am not sleeping with Matteo, and that I'll be going back to the States as soon as he can arrange it. I'm no threat to her, and I want her to know that."

Theresa looked back at her in silence, dumbfounded.

"Please tell her for me," Helen insisted.

Theresa's brow knit, and she said, "Even if this is true, why tell her? Let her steam about it; she's been unkind enough to you."

Helen shook her head wearily. "It's not fair to let her believe a lie. Can I count on you to do it?"

Theresa shrugged. "Sure, if that's what you want."

Helen nodded and strode purposefully back to the camper. Once inside, she dropped onto the daybed and stared at the ceiling, feeling numb and drained. The physical labor of the day caught up with her, and eventually she slept.

Dawn light was filtering into the cabin when she heard the jeeps returning. She jumped up and ran to the window.

At first she didn't see Matteo, and her heart was hammering so hard she thought it would burst through her ribs. Then she saw him detach himself from the group and walk toward her. His step was tired, and she noticed that most of the ammunition was gone from his belt.

Helen went back to the couch and sat down, determined to be as self contained as the other women she had seen greeting the returning men, who acted as if they put their lives on the line every day. But of course they did, and that was one small thing, among many, that she had to learn.

Matteo entered and stopped on the threshold when he saw that she was awake.

"Are you all right?" he asked quietly, slipping his rifle off his shoulder and setting it on the floor.

"Yes. Are you?"

"Fine. No casualties this time; we all got away clean."

"Good."

Their voices were restrained, polite, covering a wellspring of feeling that neither would express.

"Your mission was a success, then," Helen added, and his face lit up.

"You bet. We not only got inside the compound, we were able to..."

Helen held up her hand. "Don't. Don't tell me about it, please. I'd really rather not hear it."

He halted in midsentence, and his expression became closed, unreadable. Helen couldn't meet his eyes, and the hot, heavy silence lengthened between them until he finally said, "I knew it. I knew that if I brought you here, and you saw what I actually do, you'd become disillusioned with me."

"What do you mean?" she replied in a low, troubled voice.

"I mean that there is nothing glamorous and wonderful about fighting. The ideals and the concepts sound good, but when you get right down to it, it's guns and knives, and dirt and sweat, and killing the people on the other side. And that's what has gotten to you, Helen. You like the thought of battling for freedom, but you can't face the reality of what's involved in the battle."

"I know you're doing what you have to do, what you think is right," she answered in a subdued tone.

"But?"

She made a helpless gesture. "Maybe everyone here is right about me."

"How are they right?"

"They all think I'm not up to it, and maybe I'm not."

He studied her without speaking for a long moment, and then said briskly, "We have to move the camp this morning. The government troops will be alerted to our presence in the area after the raid, and we have to relocate. You can help Theresa load the kitchen wagon. I'm afraid it will be tents from now on; we can't take anything but the jeeps where we'll be going. Be ready to move out in about half an hour."

"All right."

He shouldered his rifle again and said, "I'm working on a way to get you out of here, but it will take time. Just try to be patient, and you'll be home before you know it."

Helen dug her nails into her palms, but kept her voice even as she said, "Thank you. I'll do my best."

He nodded and left. She shut her eyes tightly, but a tear escaped on each side and trailed down her face.

How cold he had sounded, not like her Matteo at all. It was hard to believe that he was the same man who had caressed her so tenderly in Esteban's room and led her through the jungle with such gentle persuasion. But she had challenged the thing he lived for, and she had lost.

Helen went out to find Theresa and help her pack.

For the rest of that day they moved, carrying everything on their backs or in wagons that could negotiate the steep mountain trails. In late afternoon they reached the new site, a clearing by a stream that afforded little more than seclusion, and by nightfall the tents and prefab buildings were all up and ready to be used. The group moved so often that they had the procedure down to a science, and Helen was amazed at the efficiency they displayed in organizing their tasks and making the site their own.

Helen saw little of Matteo that day or the ones following, as he spent most of his time in conference with his men and she worked with Theresa. When they did speak their conversation was strained, and she longed for a return of the old closeness, when she could almost tell what he was thinking by the expression on his face. Once he took her aside to show her the tent she was to use, across the way from his, and she watched his clean profile as he taught her to drape the mosquito netting around her cot to keep away the bugs. She wanted to reach out and touch his mouth, the lips that had kissed hers so passionately, but somehow it seemed an intrusion now, a familiarity he would not want from a woman he longed to be rid of, so she held back. At night she would remember the feel and scent of his skin, the strength of his hard body next to hers in the *taberna* loft, and it would seem like a dream, something that had never happened but existed only in her imagination.

With the rest of the people in the camp she was circumspect, going about her business with Theresa and following the older woman's orders with meticulous precision. The only labor Helen had ever performed was mental, and it was almost a relief to engage in work that required no thought, only the physical exertion that exhausted her so that she could sleep at night. Such a routine was not intolerable, and Helen followed her natural inclination, which was to keep to herself and keep her mouth shut. She made no attempt to capitalize on her relationship with Matteo, as Alma had done, because it was not in her nature to do so. And as Matteo's comrades saw her working hard and demanding no privileges, they developed a grudging respect for her that she didn't expect and, in fact, didn't see. She still felt very much the outsider, especially since her contact with Matteo was so limited, but she lived with the feeling, going her own way, as she had always done.

But there was someone who was very concerned with her state of mind, concerned with everything about her, and that was Vicente Olmos. He watched Helen constantly—with an insinuating smile when Matteo was not around and with a carefully blank expression when he was. Helen felt his eyes on her and sensed the threat implicit in his stare the way a gazelle senses the presence of leopard: subliminally, with primordial instincts untouched by thousands of years of civilization. But she said nothing to Matteo, thinking that Olmos's deliberate intimidation of her was really aimed at his superior, and if she ignored it his ploy would fail.

Alma proved to be another matter. Helen could tell that Theresa had spoken to her, because her attitude toward Helen had changed from outright antagonism to puzzlement, as if she couldn't quite figure out what was going on between the pretty gringa and her former lover. When Helen and Matteo were together, she observed them, saw the suppressed passion that flared between them, and wondered if Matteo had lost his mind. He wanted the American and she wanted him, but it was clear that they weren't doing anything about it. This was so uncharacteristic of the Matteo she knew that her attention shifted to Helen, seeking answers there. But she found none, seeing only a quiet, reserved young woman who was trying her best to fit into an alien world until such time as she could leave it.

On a sticky, moonless night several days after the move to the new camp, Helen was trying to sleep while Matteo held a meeting with his top soldiers at the other end of the grounds. Their voices carried in the stillness after everyone else had retired, and the low murmur disturbed her, contributing to her restlessness. Finally she put aside the netting surrounding her cot and stood up, lifting her gown away from her perspiring flesh. She walked to the tent exit and lifted the flap, looking out at the few stars visible in the cloudy, overcast sky.

The humidity was thick, choking, threatening the rain that never fell but hung in the air like a pall. Heat lightning streaked the horizon and thunder rumbled distantly but ineffectively, tantalizing with the promise of the storm that might bring relief. Lifting her hair from the back of her neck, Helen remembered with amusement a teacher she'd had, a Regency buff who loved to quote Jane Austen. On the subject of a heat wave, Austen had once written that it kept her in a "continual state of inelegance." On this evening of pitiless heat, the phrase took on a new meaning for Helen. *Inelegance* was the word to describe her scattered, ragtag state. She had never felt less elegant in her life. Their precipitous departure from the San Jacinta airport had caused her to leave her luggage on the plane, and she'd been making do with whatever Matteo and Theresa could scrounge up for her. On this occasion it was a thin cotton shift that became translucent when wet and was now clinging in damp patches to her body. She was glad there was no one around to see her, because at that moment she would rather have gone naked than add another ounce of clothing to the skimpy ensemble she wore. Exhibitionism was preferable to heat prostration, she thought, giggling to herself.

Then her attention was diverted by the voices from Matteo's tent. They were getting louder and, as she turned her head to look, two men emerged. She recognized them as the bodyguards who had kidnapped her from the supermarket parking lot. They were followed by Matteo and Olmos, who were engaged in heated discussion. Matteo said something, Olmos made an obviously sarcastic reply, and they began shouting. Helen stepped back into the folds of the tent as she continued to watch. Olmos lunged for Matteo, and the other men moved in immediately to restrain him. Matteo said something derisive in a low tone, heavy with finality, and turned his back on Olmos, returning to the meeting inside the tent. Olmos stormed off, and the bodyguards took up their position near the entrance, glancing at one another uncertainly.

Helen returned to her bed, mulling over what she had seen. The situation between Matteo and Olmos was a ticking bomb on the verge of blowing sky high. It didn't matter what they were arguing about; Olmos sought every opportunity to challenge Matteo's authority, and soon Matteo would have to deal with him once and for all.

She lay down, drawing the netting around her and turning away from the glow of the oil lamp in the corner. She listened to the far off grumbling of the thunder for a while and finally drifted into a fitful, dream-troubled sleep.

When she awoke about an hour later she thought she was still dreaming, because she heard a noise in the tent but knew that she was alone. Then she realized suddenly that she was *not* alone, and she sat up, watching a moving shadow out of the corner of her eye.

"Matteo?" she said hopefully. Who else could it be, but why was he sneaking around like that? Was he trying not to wake her?

She lost sight of the shadow and was swinging her legs over the edge of the cot to get up when she was seized roughly from behind and hauled bodily into a kneeling position. A large hand was clamped over her mouth to silence her, and as she struggled she twisted around and looked into Olmos's amber eyes.

Helen couldn't scream and she couldn't move. He was terribly strong. Holding her fast with one arm, he grabbed the top of her gown with his other hand and ripped it from neck to hem, exposing her body.

Terrified and humiliated, Helen cowered as he held her immobilized, fumbling at his belt with his other hand.

So this was to be his final answer to Matteo, the ultimate blow that would end the battle and give him victory: violate the precious little gringa that Matteo kept so close and valued so highly. Helen squirmed as he shifted position to crawl onto the cot, and his hand slipped from her mouth. She saw her opportunity and bit him with all the force she could muster.

He bellowed and she dived off the cot, screaming as loud as she could. Olmos spun around, holding his injured arm, and his expression was curiously triumphant. Helen realized with horror that he had *wanted* her to scream and knew in an instant that the whole incident was a trap. Olmos was using her as bait to provoke a confrontation with Matteo, and he would be ready for it, while Matteo would not. Helen had played right into his hands.

She could hear stirring from the other tents as the people, roused from sleep, got up to see what had happened. Olmos confronted Helen, breathing heavily, his golden eyes narrowed to slits as she huddled on the ground, trying to cover herself with her arms.

Matteo burst into the tent and took in the scene at a glance. He rounded on the other man, a vein throbbing in his temple, and Helen saw the end of Olmos's life in his face.

"Matteo, no!" she shouted. "I'm all right, he didn't hurt me."

Matteo ignored her, advancing on his former comrade, who circled away from him, a half smile on his face. Come on, he seemed to say, we've known from the beginning that it would come to this.

Matteo threw the first punch, hitting Olmos so hard that Helen could hear the blow like a pistol shot. Olmos responded in kind, and they were soon locked in mortal combat, evenly matched. Matteo was faster, but Olmos was bigger, heavier, and as they rolled over and over on the dirt floor Helen prayed that they would both emerge from the contest alive.

She looked up and saw a gathering of the other men in the entrance, looking on with solemn faces.

"Stop it!" she yelled at them. "Can't you do something to stop it?"

They glanced at her, and then turned their attention back to the fight, their attitude one of resignation. They didn't have to understand English to know what she was saying, but they had seen this coming for a long time and knew that it had to run to its logical conclusion. That she had been the catalyst was unimportant.

Helen remembered that she was naked, except for the fluttering remnants of her gown, and she crawled to the cot, pulling off the khaki muslin sheet and wrapping it around her like a sari. The two men struggled upright and then tumbled headlong, almost at her feet, and she saw Olmos reach for something shiny at his belt.

"Matteo, be careful!" she shouted, gasping. "He has a knife!"

Matteo grabbed the hand that held it and shook it loose, pounding Olmos's clenched fingers on the ground until they relaxed and gave up the weapon. It skittered away as Matteo climbed on top of Olmos's prone body and punched him repeatedly about the head and face, until his nose was streaming blood and the flesh around his eyes began to swell and discolor.

Matteo didn't look much better. His lower lip was cut and puffing up like a dinner pastry, and two vivid scratches on his left cheek were oozing blood and serum. Both men were drenched with sweat, their hair soaking, their faces glistening and their clothes clinging to their bodies with dampness. As Helen watched, Olmos, who was down but far from out, reached up and throttled Matteo, who pried his hands loose with an effort that left him spent and weakened. Olmos threw him off and dived for the knife, picking it up and waving it menacingly, a glitter in his catlike eyes.

Both of Helen's hands went to her mouth as she stared at the scene in silent revulsion. She wanted to look away, but remained transfixed, like a witness to a tragic fire who can't tear his eyes from the flames.

Both men were on their feet now, and Olmos toyed with Matteo, lunging for him with the knife and forcing him to dance away. Olmos had the clear advantage and was prolonging it, enjoying the upper hand and taking the offensive with a cavalier attitude. He was going to win and could afford to make Matteo sweat before he stabbed him.

But his confidence undid him. Matteo dodged and weaved, looking for an opening, and when he saw one he leaped on Olmos and felled him, putting his knee to his chest and ripping the knife from his hand.

Matteo raised the knife above his head, and images of Olmos putting his hands on Helen filled his fevered mind. Olmos stared up at him, saw his death in Matteo's eyes, and surrendered. His whole body went limp as he waited for the blow to fall.

Helen's scream cleared the red mist obscuring Matteo's vision. His whole being cried out for him to follow through, to drive the knife into Olmos's hated flesh, but if he did so he would lose Helen forever, and he knew it. She could never watch him kill a vanquished, defenseless man and forgive him. Or forget. His fingers opened slowly and the knife fell from his hand.

He could hear Helen sobbing behind him as he grabbed Olmos's shirt and raised his bloodied face until it was inches from his.

"Get out," he said to him in Spanish. "Now, tonight. I don't want to see you ever again. I'm warning you, if I do, I *will* kill you."

He flung Olmos aside and crawled off him, hanging his head as he tried to catch his breath. Olmos, reprieved, didn't wait for Matteo to change his mind. He scrambled to his feet and plunged through the group of onlookers, who parted to let him pass.

Matteo looked up and said to the people assembled at the entrance to the tent, "Go back to your beds. It's all over."

A couple of them looked toward Helen, and Matteo added, "I will take care of the *señorita*." He turned his head and met her eyes, adding softly, "She is my affair."

They left the tent and dispersed slowly, glancing at one another but unwilling to discuss what they had just seen until they were away from their leader. Matteo waited until they were gone and then got up, stripping off his shirt and holding it out for Helen, who slipped into it, letting the sheet fall as she did so.

"Are you all right?" he asked as she turned toward him and he enfolded her in his arms. "He didn't . . ."

Helen shook her head, letting him take her weight as she relaxed against him. "No, I told you that. He just wanted to drive you to fight him, and he did. Oh, Matteo, when I thought you were going to stab him . . ."

"Shh," he said, stroking her hair with one hand as he pulled his shirt closer around her with the other. "It's finished. Don't think about it. He's gone; you won't ever see him again." He put his arm around her shoulder and guided her toward the cot, saying, "Let me help you back to bed."

"I should clean those cuts you have," she protested.

"Forget them. Come on, your legs are giving way. You need to rest."

Helen froze, clutching at his hands, burying her face on his naked chest. "Don't go," she whispered. "Stay with me."

He swung her up into his arms, sweeping her feet off the floor.

"Don't worry," he answered, pressing his lips to her ear. "I won't leave you alone tonight."

Helen closed her eyes and sighed gratefully. Her head fell back and her long hair trailed across his shoulder as he carried her, her bare legs draped over his lower arm.

Chapter 7

Matteo carried Helen to the cot and knelt to put her on it, then joined her, wedging in next to her in the narrow space. Helen curled up against his side, putting her head on his chest and slipping one hand under his broad back. The other drifted to his flat middle and stayed there, as if to reassure her of his presence.

"My fault," he murmured, his fingers combing through her hair.

"What?" Helen sighed, too happy to care much about anything. It was like a miracle to have him so close after their estrangement.

"What happened tonight was my fault," he clarified.

"Don't be ridiculous, Matt," Helen responded. "How could it be?"

"I know Olmos, how he thinks, how his mind works. I should have anticipated what he would do. He never confronts anything directly, but steps around it craftily, like a cat moving in on a mouse. It was just like him to use you the

way he did to get to me. You wound up being the victim of
my stupidity.''

"I'm all right, really," Helen said. "I *was* scared when it
happened, but I'm over it now."

"Then go to sleep," Matteo directed her. "You must be
exhausted."

"It's too hot to sleep," she answered dreamily, rubbing
her cheek on his breast. She felt his muscles tense and
planted a kiss just above his left pectoral. His skin tasted
salty from his exertions, and she licked her lips.

"Go to sleep," he said again, through clenched teeth.
"It's almost two in the morning." His words seemed to be
coming with difficulty.

"If I go to sleep, you'll leave me."

"I promise I won't," he said, thinking that if she didn't
stop moving against him he would soon be unable to conceal his aroused state.

"Do you think it will rain?" she asked drowsily, already
drifting off.

"I hope so," he said softly, "we could sure use the relief
from this heat."

He waited for her to answer, but her breathing had already deepened, become regular and peaceful. He calmed
down himself, certain that if he just held her quietly and
didn't think about what she was wearing—or not wearing—he would be able to get through the night.

Matteo stared into the half-lit gloom, watching the oil
lamp's flame cast its dancing shadows on the canvas walls
of the tent. He heard the first tentative raindrops fall, hitting the roof with individual splats, and then listened gratefully as they gathered into a torrent. The rain fell steadily,
dripping over the tent entrance, bringing with it a freshen-
ing breeze that swept through the opening, cooling his body.
It carried a fine mist that soaked into the baked earth floor
and settled on his hair and skin. The humidity broke as if a

curse had been lifted, and his thoughts ranged over the evenings events, which replayed like a tape in his mind.

The argument with Olmos had started it. Matteo was a cautious campaigner, taking out targets one at a time, following a progressive plan of gradually weakening the government's defenses until it would be easy prey for a takeover. Olmos was impatient; he wanted to launch a coup right now, before the military caught on to their methods and developed strategies to combat them. While Matteo agreed that there was such a risk, he felt that jumping the gun and attacking before significant munitions depots and fuel reserves were destroyed would be fatal. And so they went head to head about it, and this time, as never before, Olmos was ready to back him to the wall.

Matteo had wearied of arguing with him. With tolerance evaporating in the oppressive heat, excessive even for Puerta Linda, the smoldering controversy had ignited into open warfare.

Now Olmos was gone. Matteo had always hoped it wouldn't happen, hoped that he could control the other man's rivalry and keep him in the fold, because his strength and dedication to the cause made him valuable. But when he had chosen to assault Helen, he'd moved beyond the pale and become Matteo's mortal enemy.

Helen turned in her sleep, and Matteo looked at her, at the slim, perfect legs pressed along the length of his, exposed from midthigh to ankles by the brevity of his shirt. She had buttoned it hastily, awkwardly, and the swell of her breasts rose above the opening, full and inviting.

Matteo closed his eyes and turned his head, taking a deep gulp of the rain-drenched air. But when he looked back, it was worse; her movement had caused the top button to slip its confinement. One creamy breast was revealed, beyond the line of her new, red-gold tan, almost to the nipple. His fingers itched to touch it.

He lifted his hand and settled for stroking the honeyed flesh of her throat, but of course it was not enough; one sensation enticed with the prospect of more. He drew his thumb along the line of her collarbone, pressing lightly, and she sighed, her lips parting. His fingers moved lower, slipping inside the opening of the shirt, and she yearned toward him unconsciously, her breath escaping in a soundless exhalation. Overcome with desire, Matteo cupped her breast and stroked it, rising to fullness himself as her nipple blossomed into his palm.

Helen stirred and her eyes opened.

Matteo flushed scarlet and withdrew his hand quickly, muttering hoarsely, "I'm sorry."

Helen found his big hand with her smaller one and replaced it on her breast, locking her gaze with his.

With a moan of surrender, Matteo pulled her on top of him, crushing his lips to hers.

"I want you," he said thickly, against her mouth. "I can't fight myself and you, too. I just can't do it any more."

Helen lay in his arms and felt him, stallion ready, through the scant barrier of their clothes. She shifted position instinctively, her legs open, almost straddling him. He groaned—the first time she had ever heard that distinctive sound of complete, helpless male arousal—and surged upward to meet her. The cot rocked unsteadily, almost pitching them into the dirt.

"The hell with this," he mumbled, putting her aside and snatching up the sheet Helen had discarded. He shook it out and spread it on the floor. With almost the same motion he zipped the tent flap closed and kicked a storage chest in front of the entrance, blocking it. He returned to scoop Helen up and deposit her on the sheet, flinging himself down beside her and pulling her back into his arms.

"You won't stop this time?" she asked, wary of being hurt again.

"No," he answered, drawing back to look into her eyes. "I guess I made up my mind when I realized what might have happened tonight with Olmos." He traced the outline of her lips with a blunt forefinger. "I want to be the first man in your life, Helen. I want to *begin* your life."

"I want that, too," she whispered, her eyes brimming.

"Don't cry," he said, catching a tear with the back of his hand.

"You'd better get used to it," she said, smiling tremulously. "I *always* cry."

"Always?"

"When I'm happy."

"Haven't you got that backward?"

"Maybe," she answered, shrugging, as if to let it go.

"No, I guess not," he added, after thinking a moment. "If you cried every time you were unhappy, you would have washed away on a sea of tears long ago."

Helen reached up and smoothed his tumbled, sweat-dried hair. "Don't be so dramatic."

"It's true, isn't it?" Without waiting for her to reply he went on, "I hope I'm not going to add to that."

"Stop worrying about me." She examined a lock of the hair falling onto his forehead and said, "That reddish tint is all washed out of your hair, Matt."

"Thank God," he said fervently. "The hairdresser overdid it. All I wanted was to disguise the color, not to look like Maureen O'Hara."

Helen giggled. "Why did you tell her you needed it dyed?"

"I told her I was going to read for a part on television. She believed me, which goes to show how gullible some hairdressers are."

"Why gullible? I'd believe it."

"Oh, is that the acid test?" he said, laughing. "Worldly, wise, sophisticated Helen would believe it?"

"You're teasing me."

"I'm not," he replied in a warning tone. "Now, *this* is teasing." He bent to pull at the buttons on her shirt with his teeth, then snaked his tongue into the gap between two of them, swiping at her skin.

Helen sucked in her breath. His tongue was hot, scalding, and seemed to her an extension of his inner fires. Matteo put his mouth over her breast, and his lips burned her through the cloth. When he lifted his head, there was a wet circle where they had been, and she could tell from his expression that he wasn't teasing any more.

Matteo undid the buttons of the shirt he had given her with trembling fingers as she lay supine on the sheet, the dull drumming of the rain a counterpoint to their ragged breathing.

"Oh, my lady," he murmured when she was revealed. "My sad, lonely lady. Look at you. You're beautiful." He leaned forward to place a kiss in the valley between her breasts.

Helen tangled her fingers in his hair, holding his head against her. His mouth moved to one nipple, then the other, and she closed her eyes, trying to accept that this was finally happening.

Matteo raised his head and kissed her gently, moving his mouth lightly over hers, pressing, then drawing away, until she reacted as he had intended. Helen clutched him and kissed him back urgently, parting her lips to admit the invasion of his tongue. Her head fell back as he dragged his open mouth along the supple line of her throat, and the shirt trailed loosely from her arms as he molded her naked torso to his.

Matteo pulled the sleeves off and dropped the shirt to the ground. He buried his face between her breasts, enclosed by her silken flesh, and locked his hands behind her waist. Helen felt the twin sensations, exquisite in their textural contrast, of his soft mouth and his soft hair against her skin. He turned his head and laid his fevered cheek against her belly, and his lids drifted closed in luxurious abandonment to the sensuality they shared.

Helen looked down at him, at the deep flush staining his tanned skin, marred by the cuts Olmos had made, at the sweep of his black lashes against his cheeks. His lips were parted, revealing a glimpse of the white teeth that showed so starkly in the gypsy darkness of his face. His mouth was moist from contact with hers, swollen from the fight and her kisses, and reddened, as if he had sipped from her lips the wine that made them drunk on each other. His kneeling position was curiously obeisant; he seemed to be worshiping her. She put her hand on his head, felt the springy, wavy hair curl around her fingers and dug her nails gently into the flesh of his scalp. He drew a broken breath and sighed.

When Matteo moved to get up, she still watched him, fascinated by the feline grace of his body as he stood and took off his pants. The lamplight fractured his movements as he unbuckled his woven belt and stepped out of his fatigues, kicking off the canvas shoes all the men wore when not outfitted in boots. As she remembered, he was slim, but not thin, and his well-developed biceps flexed as he tossed aside his clothes and joined her on the floor.

He drew her against him, and Helen gasped. Feeling him so completely was a shock, and his strength and rigid manhood frightened her a little. Sensing this, he pulled back slightly, holding her in the curve of one arm and smoothing her hair.

"Do you want me to stop?" he asked tensely, ready to beg if she said yes, hoping she wouldn't.

"Oh, no, Matteo, no," she answered, rolling farther into his arms, hiding her face on his shoulder. She twined her legs with his, saying shyly, "I'm just, this is just . . ."

"I understand," he interrupted, running his hand along the damp curve of her spine. "It's all right."

But it wasn't. He had never been in this situation before, and he was afraid of handling it wrong. But no fear was strong enough to threaten the relentless drive that compelled him to take her.

Matteo kissed her again, falling back on the familiar to reassure her with affection. But as the embrace intensified she began to move in his arms, so sinuously that he finally lifted himself above her, letting her go. It was not wise to fondle her too much; he could feel himself surging forward, and with an experienced woman who could follow him he would have just let the tide take him. But not with Helen. She was porcelain and could be broken; she was crystal and could shatter with a careless touch.

He shifted position to lie next to her and held her loosely until she looked questioningly into his face, asking for more. He began to caress her again, stroking her breasts, rasping the nipples with his thumbs as they tightened into hard, rose-pink pebbles. She arched her back and moaned, writhing toward him as he drew the flat of his hand across her abdomen, seeking the soft mound of golden brown hair below. He hesitated slightly, to see if she would stop him. But she was too far gone; her skin was dewed with perspiration, her eyes slitted almost closed, the blue irises bright in the lamplight, like slices of sky. When his fingers trailed over her thigh she lifted herself toward him eagerly, seeking his hand. Then he cupped her, and she sighed with satisfaction. She was ready for him. As he caressed her she turned her face away to hide her pleasure, as if such delicious torment should be a hidden, secret thing. As it increased she put one hand to her mouth, and he removed it. He kissed the delicate fingers, then placed them on himself.

She did not recoil, but encircled him slowly, made bold with the joy of discovery. Her caresses were clumsy, inexpert, but Matteo found them more stimulating than anything he had ever experienced. She sought him with her other hand, touching the ribbed musculature of his stomach, and in the coiled, restrained power beneath her fingers she could feel how much he wanted her. She moved on to the marble hardness of his thighs, sculptured like a statue, roughened with wiry dark hair. When she reached between his legs to stroke his soft parts, the vulnerable underpinnings of his swollen manhood, he groaned and rolled away from her, throwing his arm across his eyes, unable to take it a moment longer.

"Matteo?" she whispered, her voice uncertain. "Did I do something wrong?"

It was several seconds before he answered. His breath was coming in short bursts, and he licked the sweat from his upper lip before he said, his voice sounding muffled, strange, "No. You couldn't do something wrong if you tried. Come here."

She obeyed, turning once more into his arms. Unable to wait any longer, he positioned her, putting her flat on her back and looming above her. He kissed her lightly, and she reached up to put her arms around the sturdy column of his neck. His skin was slick with perspiration, hot to the touch, and he fairly vibrated with sexual tension, his whole body as taut as a drawn bow.

"Helen . . ." he said, his voice hoarse with strain.

"Yes," she murmured, and he took her at her word.

He meant to go slow, he meant to be careful, but this was Helen, and he had wanted her, it seemed, for such an endless, aching time. He plunged into her, and she tensed immediately. He couldn't stop, rearing back and plunging again.

Helen cried out and pulled away frantically. Instantly contrite, Matteo withdrew, cursing his damned impatience, the bottled-up longing that had caused him to lose control.

He enfolded her tenderly, blinking back tears of frustration and regret.

"I'm sorry," he said brokenly. "Helen, I'm sorry."

"It's all right," she replied, and sounded like she meant it, but her body language told him otherwise. She was stiff, unyielding in his arms, closed against him like a clenched fist.

Matteo continued to hold her, wishing that he could relive the last minute, disgusted with himself because, even though he'd hurt her, he wanted nothing more than to bury himself in her again. She was so sweet, in those stolen seconds, fitted to him like a glove, and he couldn't forget the sensation. He knew she would feel it, too, if he could win her trust once more.

She would have to decide. He let her slip to the floor and kissed her hands, turning them over to put his mouth against her palms, ready to abandon the effort if she rebuffed him. She responded, allowing him to touch her again, and they were soon caught in the ascending spiral that had brought them to the brink before. But this time he was determined to prepare her; he kissed her body until she was weak with longing, and then pressed his lips to her navel, exploring it with his tongue. She moaned; he moved lower, putting his arms around her hips and lifting her to his mouth. She made no sound, unable even to utter one, but her legs fell apart to admit him.

The pleasure was indescribable. She was powerless before its onslaught, and he was relentless, caressing her with his lips and tongue, stroking her to a wordless, powerful climax.

She shuddered and went limp. And as she lay, relaxed and spent, he moved over her again, pulling her legs around him.

When he entered her the second time, she made an impassioned sound of pure animal gratification, and his deep groan was lost in hers. He waited for her to react and then she said, slurring her words, "You tricked me."

He smiled to himself. "Yes, I did."

"You can trick me like that anytime," she said, sighing blissfully, and he almost laughed.

"I don't think it will be necessary again," he said, beginning to move inside her.

When Matteo awoke he was alone. They had fallen asleep together, curled up like puppies. He could still hear the rain beating on the tent with a steady, incessant cadence. Where could Helen have gone?

Then he saw the drape in the back of the tent, pushed just high enough to allow a slender blonde to exit. He followed, crawling on his hands and knees and pausing before the sight that met his eyes.

The demure Ms. Demarest, who wouldn't say "hell" if condemned to it, was twirling round and round in the rain, hair flying, bare feet splashing mud, stark naked.

"*What* are *you* doing?" he called, laughing incredulously at her unself-conscious glee. She was certainly loosening up mighty fast.

"Taking a shower," she responded, flinging her arms wide. "Care to join me?"

He signaled to her to wait and ran back inside, snatching the sheet they had slept on from the floor. He dashed into the rain and wrapped her in it, practically carrying her into the tent.

"It will be light in half an hour," he said, rubbing her dry. "Did you want someone to see you?"

"Wake 'em up faster than Theresa's terrible coffee," she said, grinning, and he shook his head.

"Did you have a good time?" he asked archly.

"Not as good as the time I had with you," she whispered conspiratorially, and he smiled.

"Feeling our oats, are we?" he inquired.

"We are," she replied smugly.

He dropped the sheet and bundled her into the discarded shirt, saying absently, "We have to find you something else to wear."

"How about you?" she said, pointing to the puddle of his clothes.

He picked up his pants and put them on, saying, "I'm starving."

"Me, too," she observed. "I don't have anything here except that tin of biscuits," indicating a box sitting on top of a cardboard carton in the corner.

Matteo got it and they shared what was left, sitting cross-legged on the dirt floor.

"I wish your friends back home could have witnessed that scene," he said, gesturing to the back of the tent.

"What friends?"

He paused in the act of biting a cracker in half. "Don't you have any friends?" he asked cautiously, trying to sound as if the topic was of only mild interest.

She shrugged. "You," she said simply, looking down at the crumbs in her hand.

He was glad she couldn't see effect of her answer on his face.

"How about when you were a kid?" he asked quietly, chewing thoughtfully.

"Oh, then I had girlfriends at boarding school," she said, "but we were all at the mercy of our families, shipped around like so much luggage. We would lose touch when we were separated. And when I got older, my parents were always paranoid about people taking advantage of me, for my money, you know. So I was pretty much restricted to classmates, but even then my mother invariably hated everyone I liked. She used to say they were 'unsuitable.'"

"Why? I would think that everyone at the schools you went to would come from a background like yours."

"They did. But there's a caste system even among the rich, and Sophia was its most fervent devotee. She would say that my friends didn't have enough money or had lost too much of their money or came from the wrong kind of money—something. It never failed."

"What's the wrong kind of money?" Matteo asked, intrigued. He stretched out on the floor and supported his head with one hand, studying her.

Helen selected a morsel and popped it into her mouth. "Money that came from bootlegging, smuggling, that sort of thing. The right kind was the kind my great-great-grandfather made, through the indentured servitude of immigrants who crossed the water to escape the same slavery they found in his factories. That was legal, you see. No less immoral than the rum running or drug trafficking, but that sort of distinction doesn't cut much mustard with my mother. She would find fault with anyone I brought home and, believe me, she could make things impossible. After a lifetime of that you sort of lose the knack of making friends, you know what I mean? And the work I've been doing for the past few years is kind of solitary." She paused and sought his eyes. "Actually, I didn't mind it much until I met you. You don't miss what you've never had."

Matteo didn't know what to say. He had spent his whole life with the comradeship of others; he couldn't imagine the existence she described.

"Poor little rich girl," he murmured as she went back to her snack.

"What?" she said, looking up.

"Nothing. Your mother sounds like a monster." He was trying hard not to think about such a person raising the sensitive, impressionable child that Helen must have been.

Helen shook her head. "No, she isn't. She loves me in her way, she really does. She can't help what others made her; my grandmother, who died when I was two, was supposedly a real horror. I feel sorry for Sophia. I must have been such a letdown."

"Why?"

"She wanted a daughter just like her, who would run around the world depleting the stock of fancy boutiques and collecting rich, important husbands. And she wound up with me."

"You must be like someone along the line. I wonder who."

Helen smiled. "I think I'm a throwback. By the time I was a teenager it was abundantly clear that I had nothing in common with most of my living relatives, so I began to investigate the family tree. I discovered that my great grandfather Harold, the robber baron's son, spent ten years writing a biography of Richard Lovelace."

Matteo rolled onto his back and stared up at her. "That sounds about your speed. Who's Richard Lovelace?"

"Early seventeenth-century British poet. He wrote, 'To Althea: From Prison' and 'To Lucasta: Going to the Wars,' among other things."

Matteo shook his head, indicating ignorance.

"I guess the second poem is the better known. The narrator is a soldier explaining to his beloved why he must leave her and go away to war. He says that if he stayed, made her more important than the thing he's fighting for, then he wouldn't be the person she fell in love with, the man she wanted."

Helen was so familiar with the story that she just rattled it off without thinking and then saw that he had become very still. The falling rain suddenly sounded loud, filling the pregnant silence, and his dark eyes seared hers as she coughed nervously and added, "The most famous line goes:

'I could not love thee, dear, so much/Lov'd I not honor more.'"

He didn't reply for a long moment, then he sat up with one smooth movement and said quietly, "I think I remember it now."

Helen waited a beat before continuing. "Anyway," she said, striving to keep her voice normal, "you can imagine Sophia's chagrin at delivering into the world a dreamer like Harold Demarest rather than the minidebutante she wanted. I don't think she's gotten over it yet. No wonder she spends all her time in Europe, romancing candy barons."

"Candy barons?"

"Her latest husband is a Swiss chocolate heir."

Matteo dusted crumbs from his pants and said, "You talk like your mother raised you alone. Where was your father when you were young?"

"He was never around. He was always flying off to meetings, spending a week here, three days there. Administering a fortune like his is a full-time job. He would call home and issue orders, like a general directing troop movements from the field. When I was small, and my parents were still getting along, sometimes Sophia would join him wherever he was, but mostly it was just the two of us, with Sophia dictating who was 'suitable.' No one ever was."

Matteo smiled, and then the smile faded as a cruel thought struck him, one almost too hurtful to bear. He waited a moment before he voiced it, and then said softly, "Is that what you're doing with me?"

"What do you mean?" Helen asked, puzzled.

"Well, if you scoured the earth, I'm sure you couldn't find a man less 'suitable' for you, in your mother's opinion. Is that what drew you to me, Helen?"

She found the question so preposterous that at first she thought he was kidding. Then she saw the expression on his face and realized that he really believed it might be true.

She crawled next to him and kissed him, settling into his arms when he refused to let her go. "Matteo, listen to yourself," she finally told him. "You're saying that I fell in love with you to spite my mother. That's ridiculous."

"Is it?" he asked, searching her face.

"Of course. It may be accurate to say that you exemplify a lot of the qualities she doesn't have, but it isn't wrong to seek out a person who has the character somebody else lacks, is it?"

"Well, when you put it that way..." he said, looking sheepish.

Helen grinned. "Besides, you might be surprised. Sophia wouldn't think you're so bad. She has an eye for handsome young gentlemen, expecially dark-eyed Latino types." She ran a finger down the line of hair bisecting his middle. "She would find you very sexy, *jefe*."

He groaned. "Give me a break."

"She'd give you one. Probably put you on the payroll."

His eyes widened.

"Sure," Helen went on. "When I was growing up she had a long succession of grooms and stableboys and chauffeurs attending to her needs. Not the right class, of course, but kept around for their expertise in other areas."

He stared.

"Don't tell me, man of the world, that you're shocked," Helen said. She put her lips to his ear and whispered, "Money changes everything."

He nodded slowly. "I guess it does. My father and his wife were probably up to some games at his big house on the hill, but I wasn't around to see them."

"It must have been hard on your mother, seeing his wife with him all the time," Helen said sympathetically.

Matteo stared over her shoulder at the guttering lamp, which was almost out. "It was. I think my mother loved him. One time I sneaked up close to get a good look at his wife. I guess I wanted to compare the two women, to try to see what his wife had that my mother lacked, you know. I remember that it was weird because his wife and my mother looked so much alike. Even as a kid I could see it; the resemblance was that clear. I guess his taste didn't change.''

"Were they both dark?" Helen asked.

"Yeah. Black hair, black eyes, full figured. Faces like icons, features carved in Iberian clay."

"Like Alma," Helen said carefully.

He looked at her quickly, then away. "Like that."

"She is beautiful," Helen persisted, picking at the sore.

"No more than you," he said lightly, trying to slide out of it.

"I'll bet she really fills out a bathing suit," Helen said sadly.

"Never seen her in one."

"You've seen her in less," Helen said, unable to resist it.

He sighed heavily. "Okay, we're going to talk about this once, and never again, got that?"

She didn't answer, gazing at him stubbornly.

"I slept with Alma to scratch an itch, and that's it. I don't love her and never did. Are you satisfied?"

"Does she know you think of her as first aid?" Helen said tartly, pitying the other woman.

"She knows the score," he said shortly.

"Do I know the score?" Helen asked, her voice not quite steady.

He tumbled her to the ground, pinning her under him. "Will you stop this?" he said huskily. "That was over and done with before I met you, and it has nothing to do with us now."

"She still wants you," Helen pointed out.

"She wants the *jefe*," he replied flatly. "She would have been sleeping with Olmos tonight if he'd won the fight."

"That's terrible," Helen murmured. "You're saying that she trades her body for what she wants, like . . . barter."

"Alma's a very practical woman. She doesn't have much else to bargain with; she makes use of what God gave her."

"He gave her quite a bit. She makes me look like an undernourished Campfire Girl."

He shook silently, and she realized he was laughing. "Don't worry about it," he said at length. "In ten years she'll be going to Weight Watchers."

"In Puerta Linda?" Helen asked, smiling.

"Well, she'll be on a diet, then. And you won't."

"That's true. In my family the women don't get fat as they get older, just bony and regal, like Katharine Hepburn."

He grinned.

Helen snuggled closer, noticing with dismay that daylight was creeping under the hem of the tent. Soon she would have to help Theresa, and Matteo would be going off, as well.

"I never thought it would end up like this," she said dreamily, rubbing her nose on his shoulder. "The morning you came back after your mission, I thought you didn't want me any more."

He drew back to look at her. "I thought you didn't want me. You seemed so distant, so put off by what you'd seen."

Helen held his gaze, admitting to him what she had known since that day. "You were right. Talking about it is one thing, but actually seeing you do it is another."

"And how do you feel now?" he asked directly, never one to dodge an issue.

"I don't think anything could change my mind after last night, Matteo," she answered just as bluntly. And it was true.

She couldn't tell whether he was pleased by this or not; he was wearing his impassive, nonjudgmental face, what she thought of as his "fearless leader" expression, and it gave nothing away.

They both looked up at the sound of movement outside the tent. The rain was stopping, and people were beginning to stir.

Matteo got up and said, "You have nothing left of the clothes Theresa got you?"

Helen shook her head. "We've been wanting to wash them, but we had to wait for rain because the supply of drinking water was running low."

"I'll send something over for you," he replied.

Helen could see him changing back from her lover to the leader of the camp. His mind was switching gears, and he was already thinking about the problems of the day.

He kissed her swiftly on the forehead. "I have to go. I'll see you later, okay?"

"Okay," Helen answered. What else could she say?

She dressed after the clothes arrived and walked through the muddy center lane of the camp to the cookhouse. Water was still dripping from all of the tents, and she had to bypass huge puddles along the way. But it was about twenty degrees cooler than it had been the day before, and the dryer, rain-washed air was like a tonic.

Theresa was already at the cookhouse and surveyed her with a wry, intent expression.

"So," she greeted Helen, "things have changed between you and Matteo, eh?"

Helen didn't even try to dissemble. "How can you tell?" she countered, feeling the flush creeping up her neck.

"I figured the fight would do it," Theresa said sagely. "It took the threat of another man to bring Matteo to his senses and force him to claim you." She took a sip of her coffee and added, "Besides, Matteo didn't go back to his tent last night."

"Why are you so sure about that?"

"I saw," Theresa said airily.

"You mean everyone knows?" Helen whispered, horrified, drawing the obvious conclusion.

"Pretty much."

"Oh, no," Helen groaned, mortified.

Theresa shrugged. "You cannot keep such a thing secret; we are all in each other's pots here," she said, using a Puerta Lindan expression for closeness. "Anyway, Matteo is the *jefe*. Everyone watches him."

Great, Helen thought. And she would be on display all day dishing out the food, like people's exhibit number one.

"Tell me," Theresa said conversationally, "is Matteo a good lover?"

Helen stared at her, turning redder, if that were possible.

Theresa raised her brows, noting her reaction. "You don't discuss such things in America?" Theresa asked.

"No," Helen replied, flustered. "At least, I don't."

Theresa waved her hand. "I just wondered if he could be as good as he looks."

Helen busied herself with a stack of plates, wishing for something to deliver her from this conversation. "He is," she finally said, and Theresa burst out laughing.

"The gringa is convinced," Theresa caroled, pinching Helen's cheek, which made Helen feel even more juvenile than she already did. Theresa was a widow with four grown children and remarkably blasé about such matters.

"I think he is," Helen added defensively. "Though I have no basis of comparison."

"Eh?" Theresa said, her English not equal to the phrase.

"I've never been with anyone else," Helen clarified.

"It was your first time?" Theresa said seriously, catching on.

"Yes." Helen studied her face, past embarrassment now, wondering about Theresa's change of attitude. Her expression was no longer congratulatory, but concerned.

"Did Matteo know this when he came to you?" she asked.

Helen nodded.

Theresa considered that a long moment before she said, half to herself, "You must be more important to him than I thought."

Helen didn't know quite how to take that remark and said nothing. Theresa was sharp enough to drop the subject, realizing that this relationship was vastly different from Matteo's affair with Alma, which had been treated lightly, the subject of snickering anecdotes throughout the camp. Theresa had a pragmatic attitude about sex and felt that a man like Matteo, who had so much responsibility, was entitled to his relaxation, his little dalliances. But this thing with Helen was another matter. Matteo was highly sexed, but not without a conscience; he would never take a virgin like this little American without realizing, and accepting the consequences. For the first time Theresa saw that he might really be in love with the "*gringa blanca*," as Helen was called in the camp, and she began to worry.

Helen spent the day looking for Matteo, wondering when she would see him again. He didn't come in for his meals, but sent one of the men for food in the late afternoon. She didn't think he was actually avoiding her, just that he was preoccupied. So she went about her tasks cheerfully, remembering the previous night, certain that the coming evening would bring them together once more.

Toward dusk, as she and Theresa were packing up, Alma appeared, and Helen's stomach began to flutter. Alma was sure to have heard the gossip, and Helen didn't want an ugly scene to mar her newfound happiness. She felt no sense of triumph over the other woman, merely an empathy for her. Helen could well imagine the pain of wanting Matteo and not being able to have him.

Alma paused before her, selected a piece of fruit, newly arrived that day, and raised her brown eyes to meet Helen's. Here it comes, Helen thought, and braced herself.

Alma made a comment, looking from Helen to Theresa, waiting for the older woman to translate.

Theresa looked back at Alma, surprised, and Helen said quickly, "What is it? What did she say?"

Theresa turned to Helen, her eyes wide. "She says to tell you that she heard you didn't have anything to wear, and she has some extra clothes if you would like to borrow them."

Helen was rendered speechless. It was an overture of friendship that she would not have expected if she was running around the camp in gunny sacks.

"Please tell her that I appreciate the offer and I'll let her know if I need anything," Helen said to Theresa. After Theresa had spoken Helen added, directly to Alma, *"Muchas gracias."*

Alma nodded and went on her way. When she had left Helen said to Theresa in an undertone, "What do you think that was about?"

"¿Quién sabe?" Theresa replied, looking at the ceiling. "Who knows?"

"It was a very generous thing to do," Helen said thoughtfully.

"I'm not so sure," Theresa said, her expression calculating.

"What do you mean? She's trying to be nice, mend the fences; what else could it be?"

"More likely she senses which way the wind is blowing and wants to get on your good side to keep in with Matteo. She knows she's lost the battle and is trying to make sure she doesn't pay the consequences. You could use your influence, turn Matteo against her. That's what she would do in your place, get rid of the old flame so she's not around to provide comfort if things go wrong between you and the *jefe* in the future.''

''I wouldn't try to oust her,'' Helen said quietly.

''Oust?''

''Get rid of her.''

''Maybe not, but remember, Olmos is gone now. She must be feeling alone, and she knows how to play the game, believe me.''

''I prefer to think she wants to be friends,'' Helen said.

''You must have been raised in a church,'' Theresa observed, shaking her head. ''That one would cut your throat in a minute if she didn't know Matteo would slit hers in return, *inmediatamente*.'' She slashed her forefinger across her neck.

''Please,'' Helen said, sickened by the analogy, even though she knew Theresa was exaggerating.

Theresa threw up her hands.

''Matteo hates vindictiveness in personal relationships. He would never listen to me if I tried to do what you're suggesting,'' Helen told her.

'' 'Vindictiveness' is getting back, getting even?''

''Yes.''

''Maybe she doesn't know he feels that way. Maybe that's why she lost him,'' Theresa said. ''All I'm telling you is to be careful. You're a child in these matters, and she is an old woman.''

''I'll be careful,'' Helen assured her, trying to get off the topic. ''Should I put away this bread?'' she asked, and as Theresa answered she wondered how much of what the other woman said could be true.

It was almost dark by the time she walked back to her tent. Helen nodded to several of the people she passed, who inclined their heads in return. She sensed that she was no longer disliked, but tolerated as an eccentricity of Matteo's, like his fondness for books and *béisbol*, and Americana in general. They were disposed to forgive their leader anything, and it was obvious that they were forgiving him her presence in their midst. Helen slowed near the entrance to an alley created by the proximity of two tents, and an arm snaked out to pull her into it.

"Hey, lady, you got ten bucks?" Matteo rasped in her ear.

"What is that supposed to be," she said, laughing, "the Bronx?"

"Brooklyn," he replied, offended. "Can't you tell?"

"Matteo, all your American accents are done with a Spanish accent. It spoils the effect, if you get my meaning."

"Ah, what do you know?" he said, nuzzling her neck. "You rich girls never go to Brooklyn."

"I beg your pardon; I went to the Academy of Music all the time."

"Exactly my point. The Academy of Music isn't Brooklyn, just like Lincoln Center isn't Manhattan. Did you miss me today?"

"I did."

"Good. We'll make up for it tonight." He kissed her deeply, lifting her into the cradle of his hips so she could feel him pressed against her.

"Damn," he moaned, "I wish I could take you right here, right now."

She wished he could, too. She clung to him with her eyes closed, shutting out the world.

"Let's go to your tent," he said urgently, taking her arm.

She held back. "Matteo, everybody knows. They'll be watching us. I don't want to be on display like that."

He fell silent, thinking. Then he said, "You're right. Those bodyguards are always hanging around, and I can't wait till the middle of the night to get rid of them." He glanced over her head into the dusk and added, "There's a spot on the other side of the stream, under a big jacaranda tree. You'll find it easily. I'll meet you there in ten minutes."

"You want to have a rendezvous in the bush?"

"Sure, it'll be great. I'll bet you've never made love in a sleeping bag under the night sky."

"Until last night, I'd never made love anywhere."

He snapped his fingers. "Right. I forgot."

"Not likely," she said dryly, and he chuckled.

"Just think of the moonlight, the fragrance of the flowers," he coaxed, running his hands up and down her back, molding her to him.

"Just think of the bugs," she replied.

He grinned, his teeth flashing white in the gathering darkness. "You must be used to them by now."

"I thought I was. Until this afternoon when I found one the size of my grandfather's Bentley."

"It's the climate," he said. "Everything grows, including the insects." He planted a kiss on the point of her chin. "Last one there is a spoiled egg," he concluded, turning away.

"Rotten," she corrected, and he looked back.

"What?"

"Last one there is a rotten egg. That's the expression."

"Are you sure?"

"Absolutely," Helen said, loving him more than she'd thought possible.

"Like when you're kids, and all jumping into a pool or something," he went on, gesturing.

"I understand the concept, *jefe*. We're still talking rotten eggs here."

"I could have sworn that at Longfield we said 'spoiled' ones."

"Maybe at Longfield, but nowhere else."

"Hmm," he said, and grabbed her. "Make it five minutes," he whispered, and took off.

Helen went back to her tent, glancing around at the sparse furnishings, which consisted mainly of crates and boxes, wishing for a hairbrush and a bottle of shampoo. Though she had always found the cosmetic excesses of her mother and Adrienne ridiculous, at the moment she would have paid a king's ransom for a stick of lip gloss. She was amazed at Matteo's constant, insatiable desire for her, when she had never felt less attractive in her life. But she hadn't looked into a mirror since they left the camper behind and couldn't see the glowing finish of her deepening tan, the sun-kissed, lemony lightening of her naturally blond hair. All she knew was that her borrowed clothes fit like a cheese box, and she badly missed the absorbent effects of dusting powder. Sighing, she ran Matteo's comb—three teeth missing—through her wild locks, changed the hand-me-down shirt she was wearing—too big—for another one—too small—and, her heart racing, set off for the appointed spot.

Matteo was waiting, a dark shadow among the trees, and he moved forward to scoop her up in his arms as soon as she stepped into the clearing.

"What's a nice girl like you doing in a place like this?" he said throatily.

"I ask myself that every day," Helen replied, and he let go suddenly, easing her feet to the ground.

"I'll bet you do." He nodded, his tone subdued.

Helen threw her arms around his neck, hanging on until he responded, enfolding her against his chest.

"I was only kidding," she whispered. "I wouldn't be anywhere else, except with you."

"Do you mean that?" he asked huskily, his voice low, uncertain. "You don't know how I blame myself for bringing you here, keeping you here. And then sleeping with you just made everything worse...."

"It made everything better," Helen countered, slipping her hand inside his shirt and dragging her nails across his chest. He made a slight sound, half sigh, half moan, and turned his head, seeking her mouth with his.

He had brought along a sleeping bag, but they never actually got in it, too impatient for each other to unzip it and climb inside. Matteo undressed Helen and himself at the same time, tossing their clothes on the ground. He dropped to the surface of the bag, using it like a mat, and pulled Helen with him. She wanted no prolonged preliminaries this time; she was reaching for him eagerly when he pulled back and something rustled in the darkness.

"What are you doing?" she whispered, restless with the delay.

"Protecting you," he answered. "I wasn't prepared last night, but I'm not taking any more chances."

What thoughts she might have had on that subject fled her mind as he rolled flat on his back, lifting her above him. She settled onto him with a grateful sigh, bending forward to waft her hair across his face.

He pulled her head down to kiss her, and she rode him to completion, falling forward onto his chest as he shuddered beneath her.

"You were right," she murmured, pushing her damp bangs off her forehead and settling into his arms.

"About what?" he replied, sounding tired, but content.

"The moonlight is nice, and I do smell the flowers."

"And the bugs?"

"What bugs?" She sighed, putting her cheek against his shoulder and hooking her left leg around his right one. "I don't see any bugs, do you?"

"Just keep your eyes closed, and you won't," he answered, a smile in his voice.

"I don't think I've ever been happier than I am at this moment."

"I hope that, years from now, when you look back on this time with me, you'll still think that," he answered soberly.

Helen half sat, trying to see his expression in the enclosing darkness.

"Why wouldn't I?" she asked, a note of fear creeping into her tone.

His answer was lost in a deafening explosion that shook the earth beneath them and consumed the cookhouse in a ball of flame.

Matteo leaped to his feet, almost tumbling Helen to the ground. He caught her and steadied her, reaching for his clothes in the same motion.

"What is it?" Helen gasped, grabbing his arm, craning her neck toward the camp a few hundred feet away. Figures dashed from their tents, running, reaching for weapons and ammunition, yelling things she couldn't hear.

He shook her off, jamming himself into his clothes as another, smaller burst incinerated one of the tents, shooting sparks, like fireworks, into the air.

"They've found us," he shouted over the noise, helping Helen into her blouse and shoving it, unbuttoned, into her jeans.

"The government," he said, seizing her hand and pulling her after him. "They've found us."

Chapter 8

Helen ran at Matteo's side, her feet barely touching earth as he pulled her along with him. They had almost reached the command tent when another blast rocked the compound.

Matteo threw Helen to the ground and flung himself on top of her, shielding her with his body. She remained motionless, his weight pinning her down, until the smoke cleared slightly and he raised his head to look around.

Alma was standing not five feet away, watching them. Matteo called to her, and she answered in a flood of Spanish, gesturing wildly.

"Stay with Alma in Theresa's tent," Matteo instructed Helen, standing and helping her to her feet. "We'll set up a base for the wounded here." He glanced toward the hills, squinting, trying to see through the thinning smog surrounding them. "I can't tell where it's coming from," he said, almost to himself.

"Matteo..." Helen began.

"Go," he said, turning away from her. "You must help me now; you must do as I say."

Helen watched as he ran to one of his comrades, firing questions, and the two men sprinted off together, leaving her behind. Another barrage started, and she ducked into Theresa's tent where Alma and the older woman awaited her. There were already three injured people there who required attention, and Helen got busy, making bandages for Theresa, who was caring for the wounds.

The shelling seemed to go on forever; several times the hits were close by, and the women were forced to take cover under cots and behind boxes until it was safe to come out. Two people were brought into the tent dead, and one died before they could do anything for him. Helen prayed for dawn; Matteo had once told her that such attacks usually took place only in the dark. But the night was endless, and she kept looking for Matteo to arrive on a stretcher, maimed, or past hope. And the bombs kept falling, and the injured kept coming. Helen had never seen so much blood. She might have been sick if she'd had a chance to think about it, but she was so busy that all she could bear in mind was who was next and what needed to be done.

Finally the shelling stopped, and they had a chance to catch up. She lifted her head from the last bandage and said, "Who's next?"

"Nobody," Theresa said. "Sit down."

She shoved a folding chair under Helen, who collapsed into it thankfully.

"Do you think it will start up again?" she asked Theresa, who shook her head.

"No. Dawn comes soon. See the light?"

She pointed through the tent flap to the dark rim of the surrounding hills, just beginning to glow with the illumination of the rising sun.

"I have to find Matteo," Helen said, getting up.

Theresa placed her palm flat against Helen's shoulder and pushed her back into her seat.

"He'll find you."

"But what if he's hurt? You know he won't take care of it, he was shot just a short time ago and he..."

"*¡Cállate!*" Theresa snapped, and Helen shut up.

"Now," Theresa said, leaning in close to Helen so that only she could hear her voice. "Do you want to set an example for these people, or do you want to behave like the spoiled little gringa *princesa* they suspect you are?"

Helen looked back at Theresa, and then glanced around at the group. All eyes were on her.

"That's right," Theresa confirmed, seeing the direction of her glance. "They are all watching you. You are the *jefe*'s woman, and they know it. If you dash all over the camp to find your man and be reassured, forgetting the job he told you to do, what will they think of you? What will they think of Matteo's choice? We obey orders here, and that goes for you too. He told you to stay, didn't he?"

"Yes," Helen whispered, settling once more into her chair.

"Then you stay. He will come when he can."

They both looked up as Alma arrived with tin cups of black coffee. She handed one to each of them, smiling slightly at Helen as she did so.

Helen stared back at her, wondering if Theresa was right about her, or if she should follow her own instincts. She decided on the latter and nodded gratefully as she accepted the drink.

"Why don't you get some rest?" Theresa suggested. "We'll take turns; Alma and I will watch the patients for now."

"I *would* like to lie down," Helen replied faintly.

"There's a cot in the back, on the other side of the curtain," Theresa said. "You'll have some privacy. I'll wake you in a couple of hours, all right?"

"Okay."

Helen found the cot and stretched out on it, her whole body aching with weariness. She felt as she had when taking care of Matteo in her father's house. That reminded her of his current peril, and she tried to stay awake to worry about him but she was just too tired. She was asleep within seconds and didn't hear Matteo come in about twenty minutes later.

"Helen?" he said to Theresa, who nodded to the back of the tent.

"Sleeping," she said. "She was up all night with the wounded."

"She's not hurt?" he persisted.

"She's fine, just tired," Theresa replied, indicating that he should sit so that she could change his bandage. He had a superficial wound on his forehead, which he had bound with a handkerchief; she removed it and washed the cut, covering it with clean gauze.

Alma walked up to him as Theresa moved away to work on someone else. Alma handed him a mug of coffee laced with *baciega*, the native rum, and a hunk of dark bread smeared with honey. He took them absently, his mind elsewhere.

"Your girl did well," she said to him, using *niña*, the word for child, to refer to Helen.

"Alma, I am warning you, don't start this now," Matteo said darkly, his expression murderous.

"No, I mean it. She worked as hard as any of us; she was very helpful."

He stared at her, his eyes narrowing, wondering what was coming.

Alma sighed and pulled up a chair next to him, leaning forward earnestly.

"Look, Matteo, I hated her when she first got here. I admit it. I was jealous. I saw that you had her under your spell. I've been there myself, and I know what it looks like."

He started to protest, and she held up her hand to silence him.

"Don't argue with me. You used her to get back here, which is exactly what you should have done, but now you've put her in terrible danger."

"I'll protect her!" he said fiercely, the futile cry of a man who knew he could do no such thing.

"From this?" Alma said, making a gesture to encompass the rubble that was once the camp. "You are Matteo Montega, but as far as I know you can't work miracles. You have to get her out of here."

"There is no way," he said despairingly. "I've thought of everything."

"Maybe not everything. My brother has a helicopter."

"Since when?" Matteo said, sitting up.

"Since last week, when he deserted the army and took it with him."

Matteo eyed her thoughtfully, his mind calculating while he sat in silence. Alma came from a divided family, common to Puerta Linda, with some members loyal to the government and others agitating for change. Her brother had been a pilot, trained at the national military academy, with a future in the current regime.

"Why did he leave?" Matteo asked suspiciously.

"He got passed over for a promotion again, this time for the nephew of a cabinet minister. He finally realized that no matter how hard he worked or how well he did he wasn't going to get ahead with corrupt politicians making all the decisions." She shrugged. "He got fed up."

"Does he want to join us now?"

Alma nodded. "And he can get your girl out. All you have to do is meet him where I say."

"You're doing this because you want to get rid of Helen," he said.

She smiled roguishly. "Maybe. But are you willing to take the chance on keeping her here?" She looked down, not meeting his eyes. "I saw what happened when the shelling began and you were running back from the woods. You covered her body with yours, Matteo. Her life is more important to you than your own safety." Her voice dropped an octave, and it was husky when she added, "You love her."

Matteo didn't answer for a moment, then said, "I can't move her with this going on. It won't stop now; they'll begin again at nightfall."

"What are you going to do?" Alma asked, aware that he wouldn't wait around for that to happen.

"I think I know where the rocket launchers are. I'm going to go up there and take them out."

"And the gringa?" Alma asked, standing up as Theresa signaled her for help.

"We'll talk about her when this is over," Matteo concluded, taking a sip of his coffee and putting the cup down. He headed for the rear of the tent where Helen lay.

He pushed aside the curtain and saw her. She was sleeping on her stomach with both arms trailing to the ground, one cheek pressed against the cot. He reached out and touched her hair gently, then withdrew, not wanting to wake her.

Helen sensed his presence and opened her eyes just as he was leaving.

"Matteo!" she said, struggling into a sitting position and blinking the sleep from her eyes.

He turned and bent toward her, catching her in his arms.

"I was so worried about you," she murmured, resting her head on his shoulder as he sat on the edge of the cot.

"Nothing ever happens to me," he said quietly, sliding his fingers under her hair to cup the nape of her neck.

"You're saying that to the wrong person," Helen reminded him. "I know better."

"I made out a lot better than some of my people," he said flatly.

"Is the damage very bad?"

He nodded grimly, pulling back to look into her face. "The worst we've ever sustained, by far. They didn't stumble on us the usual way this time. This was planned."

In answer to her questioning glance, he added, "They never launched a full scale attack on us like this before. They didn't have good enough information on where we were to come so well prepared."

"But how..." Helen began, and then the answer presented itself. "Olmos," she said miserably.

"He had to have told them," Matteo agreed. "He was the only one who could have given them our location."

"Oh, Matt, if you hadn't fought with him over me none of this would have happened."

"Don't say that. It isn't true. The problem between Olmos and me wasn't about you; it had other causes, other roots. Something would have brought it to a head sooner or later; you were just handy, that's all."

"He picked me because I was unpopular," Helen said bluntly.

"Then he was mistaken," Matteo said soothingly. "Everyone has seen how you've taken hold here. Even Theresa, who would have thought Saint Joseph was lazy, has nothing but praise for you."

"He told them you were here. That's why they're pouring it on," Helen said, returning to the subject of Olmos.

Matteo didn't contradict her. "Our camps are scattered all over the country. I could have been in any one of them, and it would have been a waste of energy and ammunition they don't have for them to firebomb them all trying to hit one man." He let her go and got up, pacing in the small en-closed area. "But they're not shooting in the dark any more. This attack was intended for me."

"Cut off the head and the animal dies," Helen mur-mured.

"So they think," Matteo said softly, and the look in his eyes frightened her.

"What are your plans?" She struggled with the words, afraid to hear the answer.

"My men and I were able to pinpoint their nest on the ridge just above us. They're launching the rockets from there. If I can hit them with a couple of grenades, it'll break the back of their assault."

"You're going now?" Helen whispered, horrified. "In daylight?"

"We can't survive another night like the last one," he answered simply.

Helen jumped up, grabbing his arm. "Why do *you* have to go?"

He stared at her, puzzled. It would never occur to him not to take the risk himself.

"You're the leader, you said it yourself. You're more im-portant than the others. Let someone else go."

He took her fingers and gently disengaged them from his arm. "Helen, you've seen the people in this camp. You know how they reacted to this attack. They're scared, and with good reason. We've never been in a position like this before. They're guerillas; they're used to being the aggres-sors, hitting and running, not being picked off like sitting ducks. They need to be shown that we can endure an as-sault like this and come back from it. Will any of them fight if *I* hide? They know what has to be done, and they have to see *me* do it. Otherwise they'll run off into the jungle, scat-ter like the loners they were before I organized them. And that's exactly what the government would like to see. Do you understand, Helen?''

''I understand,'' Helen murmured, wishing she didn't. Appearances counted for everything here; she had to act courageous when she didn't feel that way, and he had to be courageous, all the time.

''Are you scared?'' she asked him, stepping closer.

He enfolded her, rocking her to and fro. ''Nah,'' he said, putting just enough emphasis into it to convince her that he was.

''Can you say Connecticut?'' she asked, and he smiled.

''Do you mind if we don't test that right now?'' he answered, looking into her eyes.

''You can fool the rest of them but you can't fool me,'' she told him.

''What? You don't believe I'm Superman?''

''No.''

''You won't tell on me, will you?'' he whispered, hugging her tighter, holding her for a moment, then letting her go.

He got up, pushed the curtain back and said to Theresa, ''Tell everyone who can walk to come to the center of the compound by the water pump. I want to talk to them.''

Theresa nodded, and Matteo took Helen's hand. ''Come with me,'' he said. ''You won't understand what I say, but I want them to see you by my side.''

Helen followed him, past the wounded reclining in Theresa's tent, out into the morning sunlight.

The debris from the fire storm was all around them. Most of the tents were down. The ground was littered with bits and pieces of everything from cookware to exploded grenades, which had gone off on the impact of the rocket bombs. Helen could see why Matteo had chosen the spot he had for the meeting; it was sheltered by a natural outcrop of rocks and thus not visible from above, where the government troops might still be watching. The members of the group assembled slowly, many wearing bandages, some with arms in slings. Matteo surveyed his ragged crew, and Helen could see him wondering how to boost their spirits, how to convince them that he had not given up and that they shouldn't, either.

When he was satisfied that all had arrived, he propped one foot, still encased in a combat boot, on an overturned crate and leaned forward intently, turning his head to look at each of them, one by one.

He began speaking in Spanish, and Helen watched the reaction of his listeners, since she couldn't follow his words. They were immobile, their eyes fixed on him, hanging on every syllable. She saw Alma in the middle of the crowd, leaning on a machine gun, looking every inch the freedom fighter she was, surrounded by faces Helen had come to identify with Matteo and his cause.

Helen yearned to know what Matteo was saying. She glanced around for Theresa and saw her not far away. Moving almost imperceptibly, she cut a slow path to Theresa's side.

"Translate for me," she said to her friend. "What is he saying?"

Theresa glanced at her, then at Matteo.

"Run," she whispered to Helen, picking up the narrative in the middle, "if you believe that what we're fighting for can't stand this test. Go back to the lives you had before, full of fear, without self-respect and without hope. But if you know, as I do, that our struggle is the only way for our country to be free, never stop working to make the dream a reality."

Helen listened as Theresa's hushed voice echoed Matteo's ringing forceful one, repeating the speech in the first person, just as he said it.

"If I don't come back today, go on without me. Find the other groups and join them. I'll die in vain if the cause dies with me. It's not one man, but all of you, together. If any of you can remember a time when I let you down, when I didn't do myself what I am asking of you now, then let my name be cast into oblivion with the weaklings and the traitors who couldn't put their lives on the line for the future."

Helen's eyes filled with tears at Theresa's emotional translation of Matteo's simple, eloquent words. She took Theresa's hand and held it, feeling closer to the other woman than she had ever felt to her own mother.

"But if you know, as I think you do, that the name of aquatar stands for a new day in Puerta Linda, then stay here and fight. Be brave, like *el jefe Montega*. Be brave, like Montega's woman," Theresa concluded, turning to look at Helen as she said the last words.

Even as the tears ran down her face, Helen could see that his tactic was brilliant. He was shaming them into a show of courage, comparing them to himself, whom they knew to be valiant, and to Helen, whom they had shunned as an outsider but were now forced to recognize for her loyalty to their leader. Walking back through the crowd, she took her place at Matteo's side and confronted them, her eyes moving from one face to the next, showing them that she was not afraid.

Gradually, as if at some unspoken signal, they dispersed, going back to the places they had come from, and everyone knew that not one of them would leave. They trusted Matteo, and on the strength of his word they would stay.

Matteo waited until they had gone and then lifted Helen into his arms, swinging her in a circle.

"What a woman I found in Florida," he exulted. "How did you know just when to appear like that?"

"I joined Theresa in the crowd, and she told me what you were saying," Helen replied, as he put her down but continued to hold her.

"I wondered why you left me," he said. "I'm glad you let them see you like that. Your presence persuaded them more than I ever could with words."

"You give me too much credit," Helen murmured. "You know how to hold your audience, Matt."

"Public Speaking 101 at Columbia," he smiled, rubbing at the wetness on her face with his thumbs.

"I doubt it," she answered, in no mood for jokes. "When are you going?"

"Now," he said flatly, releasing her. "Why don't you stay with Theresa? I'm sure she could still use your help."

"She must be sick of looking at me," Helen said. "It's hardly the glorious work of the revolution she envisioned, riding herd on a Yankee tenderfoot."

"She likes you; you know she does," Matteo replied, turning her around and facing her in the other direction. Helen could tell that he wanted her to leave so he could get moving, and she took a few tentative steps, looking back at him over her shoulder.

"Will you say goodbye before you go?" she asked.

He eyed her speculatively, and she could see him trying to decide which would upset her less, a brief farewell or no farewell at all. He opted for the former, nodding shortly.

"You have my word on it," he said, and she turned away.

Helen went directly to Theresa's tent, where she did whatever anyone asked her to do, acting as general dogsbody until, about an hour later, Theresa pulled her aside.

"Matteo is waiting for you in the back," she said, jerking her head toward the curtained-off space where Helen had slept earlier.

Feeling as if she were walking in a dream, Helen put down the basin she was holding and walked to the rear. Matteo looked up as she drew the drape back and stepped into the cubbyhole with him.

He was dressed in camouflage fatigues and loaded down with weaponry: a pistol and a knife at his waist, a sash filled with bullets across his chest and a row of hand grenades dangling from his belt. She stopped a couple of feet away from him, loath to get too close.

Matteo saw her reaction and knew its cause. One by one, he removed the offending items, setting them on a crate at his elbow. When he was clean he opened his arms and Helen walked into them.

"You're not going alone?" she said, her voice sounding strange to her own ears.

"I'm taking two of my best men. More than that might attract attention as we move through the jungle. We have to avoid being spotted until we're close enough to destroy the nest."

"You could be gone a long time."

"I don't know. We might have to wait until dusk, when visibility declines, but we can't wait until full dark. That will be too late."

"You're very good at this, aren't you?"

"What?" he said, his mouth against her ear.

"This guerilla stuff."

"I have to be. That's why I'm still alive."

"Come back," she said softly, stepping away from him.

"I will."

Helen turned her back while he reclaimed his hardware and didn't look around until she heard him leave. Then she followed, watching from the tent entrance as he joined the two men waiting for him. All three walked to the stand of shade trees at the edge of the clearing and fell to their knees. Helen stared, fascinated, as they smeared their faces and hands with mud, a product of the recent downpour, gouged from the base of the big jacaranda. Elsewhere the earth had already been dried by the hot Puerta Linda sun, but in the dim shade of the giant tree's branches the ground was still soft, ready for their use.

Matteo didn't say anything to the others, but at some hidden signal they rose together and melted into the trees, their clothes blending in with the foliage so well that after a few seconds they were invisible. She looked at the spot where they had been for a moment longer, then went inside.

"Is he gone?" Theresa asked.

Helen nodded.

"Now comes the hard part. We wait."

"For what?" Helen asked.

"The explosion. If we don't hear it by nightfall, we'll know the *cabos* got them."

The *cabos* were the government troops. The name, an abbreviation for *caballeros*, or horse soldiers, had originally referred to the mounted police and had passed into general usage as a synonym for *gentlemen*, which was ludicrous when applied to the military arm of the current regime. But the title stuck, and among the rebels it was another word for *butchers*.

The afternoon was a torment for Helen. She had thought the night before was bad, when they were under attack, but at least then she had been busy. Now there was nothing to do except change an occasional bandage, get a drink of water for a thirsty patient and listen. She listened so hard that she felt her eardrums should have burst from the strain, but she heard only the usual camp sounds, the birds in the trees and the ominous, larger silence.

She was sitting on an overturned box, staring into an empty cup, when Theresa sat on the ground next to her and handed her a banana.

Helen shook her head.

"Take it," Theresa said. "Maybe you'll want it later. If you get any skinnier even Rafaela's clothes won't fit you anymore."

Rafaela was the smallest of the women, and she'd been supplying most of Helen's things. Helen accepted the piece of fruit, peeled it and took a bite.

"The waiting is a *brujata*, no?" Theresa asked, using the peasant word for a bad dream, a nightmare cooked up by a *bruja*, or evil witch.

"Yes," Helen replied.

"Now you really know what it is like to be one of us," Theresa commented. "If you can stand this, the rest is easy."

"What can they be doing out there?" Helen asked rhetorically.

"Taking care," Theresa said. "Matteo is very careful, very..." She tapped her temple with her forefinger.

"Smart," Helen supplied. Theresa's English came and went in spurts; at times she could wax eloquent, at others the simplest words failed her.

"*Sí. Inteligente,*" she agreed. "We'd all be dead if Olmos had been in charge from the beginning. He was fearless himself, but foolish, too quick to act."

"Where do you think he is?" Helen said to her.

"Olmos?"

"Yes."

"In hell," Theresa replied. "He betrayed his friends; he is a Judas. There's no place on earth for him now."

So Matteo wasn't the only one who'd figured out the source of the previous night's attack.

"I feel responsible," Helen confessed, alluding to her role in Olmos's defection, which continued to haunt her, despite Matteo's dismissal of it.

"Nah," Theresa said, waving her hand, agreeing with Matteo. "Those two were like a couple of roosters in a henhouse; one had to give up and go away, or they would have killed each other."

"They almost did."

Helen and Theresa both froze as they heard the distant roar of a tremendous explosion. It sounded like a powder magazine had gone up—or a cache of incendiary rockets.

Helen threw her arms around Theresa's neck. "They did it!" she yelped, elated. Outside she could hear the sound of cheering as the rest of the camp shared her joy.

Theresa nodded. "So far, so good," she said. "They still have to get back, and every *cabo* left alive in the jungle will be looking for them now."

"They won't move until it's dark," Helen guessed aloud.

"You're learning," Theresa said approvingly. "Come on, help me get the food ready for tonight. It will help to pass the time."

It did. Helen worked at Theresa's side, secure in the knowledge that Matteo had accomplished his objective, hopeful that she would see him in a few hours. Her good spirits were deflated only slightly by the presence of Alma, who kept surveying "the gringa" with a curiously triumphant look that made Helen extremely nervous. Anything that made Alma happy, especially where it concerned Helen, was surely open to question, but Helen tried not to let it bother her. Matteo had survived the trickiest part of his mission, and fate would not be so cruel as to let something happen to him now. This was a routine trip for him, she told herself; he did this sort of thing all the time. So she doled out the evening meal, watching the light fade as darkness fell, hoping that the genius that always seemed to protect him would not fail him in this.

Another two hours passed, and Helen was reduced to taking inventory of the depleted stock of black market medicines, desperate for something to do. She was on her hands and knees in front of the wooden cupboard where the medicines were stored, dictating its contents to Theresa, when they both heard a shout go up outside.

Theresa's pad and pencil fell to the floor as Helen tripped over her on her way out. Theresa followed, and both women stopped when they saw Matteo and his companions making their way through the camp toward her tent.

Helen was motionless in the entrance, her eyes fixed on Matteo's face. People called to him and slapped him on the back as he passed, but he held Helen's gaze and never looked away. A silence fell as he stopped in front of her, and she reminded herself to behave with restraint, as befitted the *jefe*'s woman.

"Hi," he said, smiling into her eyes.

"Hello," she whispered, twisting her hands together to keep from touching him.

In the next moment she was whisked off her feet as he bent and swept her up in his arms, spinning her round and round. Whistles and catcalls erupted among the onlookers as he ducked his head and kissed her. Then another sound began, the insistent beating of many hands against hard objects, as if the rebels were drumming a signal. The beating fell into a pattern, rhythmic, insistent, and increased in volume, until Helen could hardly make herself heard.

"What does that mean?" she asked, pulling away from Matteo and turning her head.

"It means that they approve," he replied, grinning.

"Of me?" she said.

"Of you and me. It's what they do instead of clapping."

He strode past Theresa's tent with Helen in his arms and carried her through the entrance to her own. Behind them the sound fell away to a babble of voices as the people discussed their reprieve, thanks to Matteo's latest exploit.

"Tell everybody I don't want to be disturbed," Matteo called over his shoulder to one of the men who had gone with him. "For anything." As he set Helen on her feet he added, "They'll all be too busy celebrating tonight to care what I'm doing anyway."

As she watched he began to strip off his filthy shirt, glancing around for the tin tub she'd been using for bathing. He found it and set it on a chest, at waist level.

"The nest wasn't even guarded," he said to her, as she got water for him and he dipped into it. "They were so confident they were all off eating *dinner*, if you can believe it, when we got there. Martin and I just tossed the grenades and ran like hell; they never even got close to us. Those *cabos* will have a lot of explaining to do tomorrow."

He was exhilarated, on an adrenaline high from the experience, as he'd been when they had escaped from the airport police. After he had washed his upper body and his face, he started to rub the bar of soap over his damp hair, and then winced when he encountered the wound on his forehead, just at the hairline.

"Let me do that," Helen said. She peeled away the sodden bandage Theresa had applied and tilted his head back over the basin to wet his hair. She worked the lather into his hair, creating a wealth of creamy suds, and gently washed the cut, which was already scabbing.

"You heal fast, *jefe*," she said, smiling.

"Good thing, too," he answered dryly, and she shook her head. He would never change.

"Your hair is beautiful," she murmured as she poured clear water over it to rinse it, noticing how it gleamed wetly in the lamplight, shining with vitality.

"Your touch is beautiful," he answered, reaching back to capture her hands. He pulled her around in front of him and forgot his ablutions, taking her in his arms and kissing her. The water from his hair ran down Helen's face, but she didn't care. She kissed him back in helpless, thoughtless response, wondering if it would always be this way with him; one embrace and resistance was impossible.

He backed her against the standing chest, then took the full tub and tossed it, with its contents, out the back of the tent. He returned and unbuttoned the pair of shorts she was wearing, letting them fall to the floor. Her eyes widened as his hands went to his belt, and she realized what he was going to do.

"Matteo, wait," she said, as he freed himself from his pants and lifted her.

"I can't wait," he muttered, and entered her standing.

Helen closed her eyes, all thought fading as he moved her, adjusting her position, and she moaned, clutching him tighter. It was fast and explosive; she gasped and then went limp as he shuddered within her, then carried her to the cot, where they collapsed, replete.

There was a long silence and then she said, "Did you think about me when you left camp today?" She needed to hear that she was important to him, as he had become everything to her.

"Yes," he answered. "I was afraid to go."

She sat up to look at him. "You were?"

He nodded. "Afraid I wouldn't see you again. I have something to lose now."

"I don't like to think I'm weakening you," Helen said quietly.

He shook his head, smiling slightly. "No, you make me stronger. You make me remember what I'm fighting for, a place where people can grow up to be like you. We grow up hard in this country; the women become like Alma, and the men, well, like Olmos, and I guess me, too."

"You're nothing like him, nothing," Helen said fiercely, putting her arms around his neck and settling against his chest.

"Oh, yes, I am," he said tersely. "More than you know."

"I don't want to talk about Olmos," Helen said, not liking the trend of the conversation. "Let's talk about us."

"What about us?" he asked, absently caressing her arm with the palm of his hand. "Our sexual adventures? Now that I've taught you to overcome your maidenly reserve, that is."

It was a long moment before he realized that she wasn't going to answer him. He looked down at her to see that she was blushing, her face and neck stained pink.

"You're making fun of me," she finally said.

"What?" he responded, half laughing.

"You think I'm a prude."

He stared at her, his mouth open. He cleared his throat. "Sweetheart, you are talking to the man who just had you, still dressed, standing up, in a tent in the middle of a jungle. No, Helen, I don't think you're a prude."

It was the wrong thing to say. Her sexual confidence was still too new, too shaky; the subject could not be treated lightly. Seeing her miserable expression, he realized that what she needed more than anything was reassurance.

He turned her on her back and kissed her forehead, the tip of her nose, then her mouth. He was careful this time, gentle, as he had been with her in the beginning. By the time he got up to remove the rest of their clothes she was watching him avidly, anxious for his return.

When the cycle began again, he brought her along slowly, caressing her with lingering tenderness, finally teasing her until she was clawing at him, begging for release. When he entered her she surged up to meet him, enclosing him in the vise of her legs, taking from him as much as she gave, until they reached the peak together.

Afterwards Matteo held her as she dozed, unable to sleep himself. Finally he got up and pulled on his pants, covering Helen with his shirt and then leaving the tent.

The night was gorgeous, cooler than it had been for a long time, with a hint of the *zinflora*, the fresh wind that swept through the Puerta Lindan mountains in the spring. He could hear guitar and harmonica music coming from many of the tents as he walked through the camp. His people were having a good time, enjoying a few hours' respite, aware that they would be moving again at dawn to avoid the patrols.

The sky was spangled with stars, and he looked up at them, wishing for a cigarette. He had quit smoking over a year ago, but now he remembered how good it had been to sit under the moon and let the smoke fill his lungs, helping him to plan and to think.

One of his friends passed and he called out, *"¿Ricardo, tienes un cigarrillo?"*

Ricardo tossed him half a pack and told him to keep the rest. Matteo walked to the charred stump of a tree destroyed by the previous night's attack and sat on it. He lit a cigarette and inhaled, grimacing at the harshness of the blend. Nothing could beat American cigarettes. This was like smoking cactus leaves, but he continued, watching the tip glow as he dragged and then exhaled.

He had to get Helen out of Puerta Linda. He'd broken every promise he'd made to himself. He'd made love to her when he vowed he wouldn't, and tonight he'd forgotten to protect her again, so eager to have her that all precautions fled his mind. But he could still save her life, and that he intended to do.

It was not going to be easy to arrange her departure, or to live with her absence once she was gone. He didn't know how he was going to get along without her now. The worst had happened; she had become necessary to him. He thought about her constantly, dreamed of her when he slept, and every time he saw her he wanted to get so deep inside of her that neither could tell where one left off and the other began.

In short, he was in love.

He was too old for this, Matteo reflected, blowing a stream of smoke into the night air. This should have happened to him when he was seventeen, when boys are often hit by the "thunderbolt," as the Sicilians put it, the wild desire for a woman that would not quit until it was satisfied. But this was worse than such an infatuation, which dissipated with familiarity. No amount of contact satiated him; he needed Helen all the time.

He bent forward and looked at the ground, tapping ashes onto the grass. It was no good telling himself that he had lost perspective; he knew it and didn't care. Always before, even as a young man, he'd been able to put his goals before everything else and keep women in what he'd thought of as their proper place: at the end of the list. Maybe this relationship was different because at the beginning of it their positions had been reversed. He'd never been dependent on anyone in his adult life, and Helen had taken care of him. But he couldn't dismiss what he felt that easily; it was much more than gratitude, far more intense than the closeness one feels for a friend who has been good to him. She was a part of him, and all the old songs, which he'd once thought of as corny and exaggerated, made sense to him now.

Matteo looked up and nodded as a couple passed, intent on each other. He was thinking selfishly, he knew, worrying about how much he would miss her after she left, instead of concentrating on the need for her safety. But he had no idea how he would get along without her sweetness to neutralize the difficulty of his days, her passion to fill the emptiness of his nights. He didn't know why her generous nature hadn't been blunted by the selfishness of her family, the isolation of her upbringing, but it had endured to transform his life. While nine roses die in the cold, an old native saying went, one will survive; and Helen was the survivor, the flower in the crannied wall surmounting all odds to seek the sun.

He finished the cigarette and stood, lighting another one. He reached his decision and went to Alma's tent, ducking inside the flap as he spotted her inside, alone.

Alma saw him in the doorway and her stomach lurched. He still affected her that way, like a punch in the diaphragm, and she composed her features deliberately as he came to stand beside her.

He was wearing only his fatigue pants, and she noted, as always, the spare beauty of his torso, the patrician cast of his face. She looked away, afraid that her expression would betray her.

When she glanced back, he was still waiting, his cigarette smoldering untouched between his fingers. His hair was mussed, and he looked tired, but relaxed. Well used and well loved.

"So, your American lady is treating you well, is she?" Alma asked, to fill the silence. If he had not been so preoccupied, so intent on his reason for coming to her, he might have noticed that her smile was not quite steady.

When he made no reply she went on. "Maybe she wasn't your mistress when she arrived, but she is now. *¿No es verdad, Matteo?*"

He sighed and said, "I didn't come here to fence with you. I want you to contact your brother to get Helen across the border into Playa del Sol."

"Oh, is that the reason for the cigarettes? This was a difficult decision, to let the gringa go."

"Can you help me or not?"

"I can help you. If you can get her to Tres Luces by dawn on Wednesday, I'll tell him to meet you there and pick her up. If I leave first thing in the morning, I can get to San Jacinta in time to give him the message."

"You're sure you know where he is?"

She nodded. "He's hiding out in the Cabeza hills with some distant relatives, untraceable by the police. He has the chopper there, and they have a phone. My mother is afraid her house is being watched since he deserted, but I can go to another friend in town, a doctor who will let me call from his office."

Tres Luces was a tabletop mesa about five miles distant, with a flat, open area suitable for a landing. "Are you certain you can set this up?" he asked Alma. "I don't want to bring her all the way there for nothing. We'd have to go on foot through the jungle, and the *cabos* could be anywhere."

"I'm certain. I discussed the possibility of it with my brother before I left."

"And can he be trusted?"

"As I can be trusted," she replied, lifting her chin.

"All right," Matteo said. "You leave at dawn." He paused and looked at her closely, his gaze intent, measuring.

"Don't fail me in this, Alma. I'm counting on you."

She inclined her head. *"Sí, mi jefe,"* she answered, her tone tinged with irony. "For old times' sake."

He turned to go, tossing his cigarette on the earthen floor.

"And Matteo," she called after him.

He glanced at her over his shoulder.

"If you get lonely when she's gone, you know where to find me."

He crushed the cigarette out with his foot and left the tent without replying.

Once outside, he took a deep breath and felt better. The plan was in motion now, and he wouldn't stop it. All he had to do was tell Helen.

She was sleeping on her side when he entered, and he sat next to her, taking her hand. Her eyes opened and she smiled at him.

"Helen, wake up. I have something to say to you."

She blinked and struggled upward onto her elbows, staring at him.

"What is it?" she asked. She could tell from his voice that it wasn't the weather report.

"It's time for you to go home," he said.

Chapter 9

Home?'' Helen repeated, searching his face.

"To America," Matteo clarified.

"You're sending me away?" she said softly. She couldn't believe it.

He released her hand and stood up, pacing away from her. "Don't say it as though I'm driving you into exile. I just want to get you back where you belong."

"I belong with you."

"Didn't the last couple of days prove how dangerous it is for you to be here?" he demanded, frustrated by her look of bewildered incomprehension. Why wouldn't she understand that he was only trying to protect her?

Helen swung her legs over the edge of the cot, struggling to wake up and deal with this new development at the same time. She slipped into Matteo's shirt and buttoned it, saying, "I thought that after we, well, with everything that's happened, you would want to have me with you."

She sounded so forlorn that he almost relented, but he steeled himself to go through with it. "This is not about what I want," he said gently. "Surely you didn't think that after we became lovers I'd no longer be concerned with your safety."

"But you said yourself that I'm fitting in here, and everyone is accepting me," she protested.

"You are confusing the issue!" he replied heatedly. "I'm not talking about that and you know it. The only reason I brought you here in the first place was because you were seen with me at the airport. I had no choice. I couldn't get you back to the States on a plane; you would have been picked up before you got out of the San Jacinta terminal."

"And that's still true, isn't it? Not that much time has gone by, and they're probably still looking for me."

"There's another way," he said quietly.

"For me to get out?"

"Yes. With Alma's help."

"Alma," Helen whispered, nodding her head. So that's why the woman was looking at her with such an expression of triumph. She must have known this was coming. "What does she have to do with this?"

"Her brother has a helicopter. He'll take you to Playa del Sol, and you can fly home from there."

"He's coming here?"

"No, he can't land a chopper here, and besides, the *cabos* are all over the mountain. We have to meet him at Tres Luces, about a day's trek from this camp."

"Oh, so it's all arranged. You're bringing me to Tres . . . whatever?"

"Yes."

"And Alma's brother has agreed to this plan?"

Matteo nodded. "She was away recently to get supplies, and apparently she saw him then and discussed it."

"Anxious to send me packing, isn't she?" Helen said bitterly.

Matteo didn't answer.

"Matt, don't you see what this is? She's conveniently devised a plan for my departure because she thinks that once I'm gone you'll take up with her again."

"If she thinks that, she's mistaken."

"Is she?" Helen asked, unable to stem the tide of jealousy that washed over her as she thought of Matteo with Alma.

"Don't insult me, Helen," he said flatly, looking away from her.

"Easy for you to say," she flung at him. "I know what will happen when you're alone, and she comes sashaying around, batting those big brown eyes at you. I'll bet she's better in bed than I am, too, isn't she? I guess you didn't have to teach her anything. She knew it all already, right, Matt? How to please you, how to make you groan like you would die if you couldn't have her."

Matteo covered the distance between them in a second, grabbing Helen and forcing her to look at him. "Be quiet!" he said in a frightening, lifeless tone. Helen fell silent, closing her eyes, unwilling to meet his pitiless gaze. Tears seeped from under her lashes, and he relented, pulling her into his arms.

"Do you think I could touch her after being with you?" he whispered, holding her so tightly she almost couldn't breathe. "I can't bear the thought of your going, it tears up my guts to have to send you away like this."

"Then let me stay," she pleaded, hammering on his weakening resolve.

"No," he said hoarsely, and released her.

"What about your people, everyone here in the camp? They stay and take the risk."

"This is their country; this is the life they chose."

"What if I choose it now?" she countered, putting her hands on his shoulders and peering into his face.

"Helen, this is not a high school debate!" he replied, shrugging her off. "The decision has been made."

"Oh, the *jefe* has spoken!" she said sarcastically, saluting. "I forgot that your orders must always be obeyed. *Perdóname, lo siento mucho.*"

"Your Spanish is improving," he observed, his lips twitching.

Helen thought of something else. "Matteo, what if it's a trap?"

"What is?"

"This thing with Alma's brother. What if it's a setup?"

He shook his head firmly. "Alma wouldn't do that."

"But she was with Olmos, lining up against you."

"She was just playing the angles, keeping in with him in case he came out on top. But she would never do what you're suggesting, Helen. She knows how important you are to me."

"That's just why she might do it. She resents me—you know that—and Theresa says she's dangerous."

"She has been, to some. But not to me."

"Because she's still in love with you?"

"Because, despite what you're saying, she's loyal. She's on the level with this, believe me."

Helen considered a moment and then said, "I have no passport, no papers. I left everything in the car we abandoned."

He smiled resignedly. "You don't give up, do you?"

"Not when I want something as much as I want to be with you."

"My people will get you what you need. Playa del Sol is an open country; travel is free. You'll have no problem getting back to the States from there. I'll give you money for the plane ticket. Once Alma's brother gets you across the

border you can leave from the commercial airport in Soledad, the capital. Flights run to New York all the time."

"Haven't missed a trick, have you?" she said with a wry
glance at his impassive face.

"I try not to."

"So, when do we leave?"

"In the morning."

"I see we're not wasting any time."

"I could do without the cute remarks, if you don't mind,"
he said, passing a hand wearily over his forehead.

"It's the way I deal with terrible disappointment, Matteo, I make cute remarks. It's either that or have an hysterical fit, and of the two, I thought you would prefer the one-
liners."

He extended his hand and said, "Come here."

She hesitated, and he crooked his forefinger. Reluctantly
she moved to his side and he put his arm around her.

"Let's not waste this night," he said huskily, leading her
to the cot.

He got in with her and peeled his shirt off her shoulder,
putting his mouth against her bare skin. She closed her eyes
and forgot that it would all end soon. They had this moment, and she would have to engrave it in her mind for the
time when she would be alone again.

Helen got very little rest that night. After their conversation, their positions were reversed: Matteo could sleep
because he felt relieved, and Helen couldn't because she was
anticipating her departure. She lay awake, studying his face
as he lay in her arms, trying to memorize it. She noticed that
he had a mole at the corner of one black eyebrow and several faded scars on his jaw and chin, the results perhaps of
schoolboy brawls or adolescent accidents. She tried to picture him as a child, running through the slums of San Jacinta, skinny probably, as he was still lean, with large dark

eyes and the same wavy, unruly hair. What had happened to create this irregular lump of pinkish flesh gouged out of his jawline, or that thin slash above the slight cleft in his chin, whitened now with the passage of time? She saw these things as items of interest, not flaws; she was past the point where anything could make him look unattractive to her.

The birds began to sing, and a dawn breeze blew through the tent, presaging the rising sun. Helen slipped out from under Matteo's weight and got fresh clothes together, dressing in the thin light of early morning. By the time the familiar noises of the camp began and Matteo awoke, she was ready and waiting for him.

"I want to say goodbye to Theresa," she told him calmly, watching as he blinked and sat up, spotting her across the room.

"All right," he said quietly. "I'll go with you."

He put on his clothes and picked up her single bag, a discarded army duffel that she had appropriated. They found Theresa already at work, preparing a makeshift breakfast in her tent, since the cookhouse was a pile of rubble.

Helen looked meaningfully at Matteo, and he withdrew, standing outside and lighting a cigarette. She turned to Theresa and said without preliminaries, "I'm leaving."

Theresa glanced quickly from Helen to Matteo's still figure in the doorway, and then back to Helen.

"*¿Es verdad?*" she said, lowering her voice.

"Yes, it's true."

"*¿Por qué?* Why?"

"Matteo wants me to go. He thinks it's not safe for me to be here."

Theresa shrugged expressively. "It's not safe for any of us to be here, but here we are, just the same."

"He says it's not my fight, that I belong back home. In other words, he wants to be rid of me."

Theresa moved her head slowly from side to side. "I don't think so, *niña*. I think he wants very much for you to stay. It is his conscience that bothers him, for getting you involved."

"I wish he didn't have a conscience," Helen said, biting her lower lip, which was trembling dangerously.

Theresa put down her cooking pot and embraced her. *"Pobrecita,"* she murmured. "Poor little thing. I remember what it is to be young, when the fires burn so hot. It's like death to leave him, I know."

Helen swallowed hard, putting her head on Theresa's shoulder.

"How are you getting out?" Theresa asked, holding her off and brushing her bangs off her brow.

"Matteo is taking me to Tres…Luces, and Alma's brother is going to fly me over the border into Playa del Sol."

"Alma," Theresa said, nodding sourly.

"My sentiments exactly," Helen replied darkly.

"Eh?"

"Nothing." She threw her arms around Theresa's neck and said, "I'm going to miss you."

"I'll miss you, too. I'll forget my English again."

They laughed, as friends do to cover a painful parting, and then Theresa said soberly, "Maybe it's better this way. Matteo has only one love—his country, and what it could be. If you tried to compete, you would lose in the end."

Helen didn't answer, thinking how different Theresa's attitude was from that of Elena, Esteban's wife, who wanted Matteo to get married. But then, Theresa lived in the camp with Matteo, saw him every day, and knew him better.

"I guess I'll be going," Helen said awkwardly. "Matteo is waiting."

"Vaya con Dios," Theresa said, making the sign of the cross in the air above Helen's head. "Go with God."

"Goodbye," Helen said and hurried away out into the bright sunshine, where Matteo met her eyes as she emerged.

"All set?" he said.

"Yes."

"I asked Martin to make up a backpack for us. I'll get it, and we'll take off."

When Matteo went to pick up the provisions, Helen saw Alma standing outside her tent, watching their departure. As Matteo rejoined her, she walked over to the dark woman, who waited for her warily. Matteo observed the encounter, his posture alert, ready for anything.

"Adiós, Alma," Helen said, sticking out her hand. *"Buena suerte.* Good luck."

Alma took her hand and shook it, her heavily lashed eyes unreadable. But as Helen walked back to Matteo, Alma looked at him over her shoulder, and then turned away, unable to meet his eyes.

"You have a lot of class, do you know that?" Matteo greeted Helen quietly as she approached him.

"Don't bet on it," Helen responded. "That was very hard to do."

"But you still did it," he said. "Let's go."

Helen was surprised at the number of people who called to her as they walked out of the camp. Word had evidently gotten around that she was leaving, and they stood outside the entrances to their tents, waving and sending messages of farewell. One of the guards who first picked her up in Florida shouted something in his deep bass, and Matteo glanced at her, as if to see if she had understood.

"What did he say?" she asked.

"He said to remember him when you're back in your beautiful country," Matteo translated.

Helen halted, touched. "But they don't like Americans," she said.

"They envy Americans," Matteo replied. "And they like you."

Helen started to walk again, looking around her as they left the cleared central path and entered the woods.

"I'll never forget this place," she murmured.

"When you're an old lady you can tell your grandchildren about the time you spent in a rebel camp, and they'll look at you in your shawl and think you're making it up."

"Young people think old people were never young," she replied, and he grinned.

"Would you mind repeating that, please?" he said.

"You know what I mean."

"Yeah. When I was a kid I used to ignore my grandmother. She was just a funny woman with a black mantilla on her head and a rosary in her hand. She loved me, though, used to kiss me every time I ran past." He shook his head. "Now I wish I could talk to her."

"Your mother's mother?"

He nodded. "She died when I was eight. She lived in abject poverty all her life, but she could make the most beautiful lace. The nuns taught her when she was young, at the convent where she cleaned. She used to bring in extra money selling arm covers, things like that, to the people who could afford them. She kept it up until arthritis twisted her fingers so bad she couldn't work the needles any more." He jerked his head, as if to clear it. "I wonder what made me think of that."

"I never really knew my grandparents," Helen said thoughtfully. "They were distant, formal, unreachable. I remember them as dressed up all the time, being served dinner in a big wainscoted dining room with a crystal chandelier, giving parties where all the ladies wore gowns that rustled and smelled good. These were my father's parents; my mother's died when I was too young to recall them. Except that I have one lingering image of Sophia's mother, which everyone tells me I must have gotten from her portrait, but I swear I remember it: a black silk dress, white hair and diamonds."

"My grandmother had the black dress and the white hair," Matteo offered dryly, "but I don't recall any diamonds."

Helen glanced over her shoulder, where the view of the camp was already obscured by the enclosing foliage. "Shouldn't Alma have left the same time we did?" she asked Matteo. "If she doesn't contact her brother he won't be there to meet us."

"Alma will do what she's supposed to do," Matteo answered briefly. "Don't worry about her."

Helen let it drop, hoping that his faith in his former lover wasn't misplaced. If she were really vindictive, there were any number of ways she could screw up their plans, but Matteo didn't seem to consider that a possibility.

They walked on through the morning, and Matteo kept Helen entertained with stories of his childhood and his transition to school in America, so that she wouldn't think about their imminent parting. She couldn't imagine how he knew where they were going; the paths they followed were hardly wide enough for a person to walk single file, and every tree looked like every other tree for miles around. It was obvious they were going on foot to avoid the police on the roads, but she didn't know how he could keep his bearings without so much as a landmark or a sign. Toward noon he stopped and looked around, squinting into the sun.

"There's a clearing right around here," he said, turning his head. He pointed. "There it is."

Helen followed him into a small grassy area. There he opened their pack and handed her a sandwich made of Theresa's dark bread and thick goat cheese, which Helen had learned to tolerate.

"You're doing a lot better on the trip out than you did on the way in," he observed, taking a bite of his lunch.

"Hey, this experience has turned me into an expert hiker, climber, all-round nature girl. I'm thinking of tackling the Appalachian Trail when I get home."

He smiled, taking out a bottle of water and drinking from it. His smile faded as he said to her, "Helen, I want to tell you some things you have to know about getting home."

She separated the crust from the slice of bread she held and asked, not looking at him, "Can't it wait? There'll be plenty of time for that, won't there?"

He studied her expression and then nodded, allowing her to avoid dealing with the reason for their outing until it was necessary. They ate in companionable silence until he wrapped up the remnants of their repast and said, "Siesta. You'll be stronger this afternoon if you take a little rest."

Helen looked around. "No pillow?" she said, raising an eyebrow.

Matteo settled with his back against a tree and slapped his thigh. "Right here," he answered.

Helen stretched out in the warm grass and laid her cheek on the denim-covered surface of his leg. The large muscle tensed under her, and she looked up at him.

"Don't move," he said, "or the siesta will turn into a fiesta."

She smiled devilishly. "You were the one who suggested a nap," she reminded him.

He sighed dramatically. "Sometimes I'm just too sensible for my own good."

"Not often," she said sarcastically.

He tapped the top of her head with his index finger. "Go to sleep."

She half sat and stared at him, annoyed. "You're always telling me to go to sleep. What are you, a hypnotist?"

"That's because you talk when you should be sleeping. I've never seen anyone function on so little rest."

"Me! What about you?"

"Are we going to fight, now, or what?"

Helen shot him a look and settled down huffily, trying to find a comfortable position on his thigh, which was like a rock. But she *was* exhausted and could have slept on nails; she was asleep in no time and so was he.

Matteo shook her awake about forty minutes later, and she sat up, feeling hot and sticky. She dampened a handkerchief with water from the bottle and dabbed her face and neck, screwing her hair into a makeshift bun on top of her head.

"How much farther is it?" she asked, looking up at the sky, in which the sun shone like an open furnace.

"Ten miles. We'll make camp at dusk and walk the last little bit in the morning."

"The last little bit" was what she didn't want to consider. That would be the beginning of the end.

Matteo picked up the pack and slung the straps over his arms.

"Ready?" he said, and she nodded.

The remainder of the trek was worse; no longer as fresh as they'd been in the morning, they trudged along, battling the heat and their own fatigue. At about six Matteo held up his hand to silence Helen, and she watched as he moved forward and parted the foliage to look at something below. He glanced over his shoulder at her and gestured for her to come closer; he put his finger to his lips as he moved aside to let her see what he'd been observing.

There was a road cutting across the mountain just under the rise where they hid. It was overrun with police, armored cars and *cabos* with their distinctive tunic uniforms. Helen's heart began to beat faster as she thought about what these people would do to Matteo if they knew he was perched above them, overlooking their movements.

They crept away from the scene, and when Matteo signaled that it was all right for her to talk she whispered, "Are they looking for you?"

"They're looking for anybody. Especially me. They lost five rocket launchers when Martin and I blasted their hideout, and they don't have an unlimited supply. Your government is getting fed up with their human rights record and is holding back on the money."

"You shouldn't have come out here with me," she said miserably. "It's too dangerous."

He shook his head. "As long as we keep to the bush, we'll be okay. There's not a *cabo* in the army who can get around in here the way I can. They lug their cars and tanks with them; they have to stick to the roads."

"What about everyone back at the camp?" Helen asked worriedly. "The *cabos* know where it is."

"It's no longer there," he replied. "Everyone's gone, Helen; they moved as soon as we left. Don't think about them; I promise you they're okay."

They traveled for another two hours, and then as the light was fading from the sky Matteo pointed to a flat elevation outlined against the vanishing sunset.

"Tres Luces," he said. "In a little while you'll see where it gets its name. Three stars hang in the sky just above it like lamps."

Helen wasn't interested in tidbits of local color; she stared at the mesa, thinking that in the morning she would take her leave of Matteo there.

"There's a stream just ahead," he added. "You can take a dip if you want."

They walked until they came to the banks of the stream Matteo mentioned, and he took off his pack gratefully and dropped it to the ground. Helen sank to her knees and studied him as he took out fruit and cheese and handed them to her. She should have been hungry, but she wasn't; she settled for a long drink of water and then relaxed on the grass, easing her aching back.

"The stream has its source in the mountains to the east," Matteo said, "and it's always fresh. You can drink from it if you want."

He continued the travelogue as she listened without comment, aware that he was talking for her sake, and maybe for his own. He stretched out on the ground and put his hands behind his head, staring up at the night sky.

"Everything looks so peaceful up there," he said softly. "You'd never believe that all over the world tonight people are trying to kill each other."

"It doesn't have to be that way," she replied.

"Yes, it does," he answered flatly. "As long as some people are trying to take advantage of others, there will be those who'll fight to stop them."

And that about sums it up, Helen thought, the thing that will keep us apart. She was a "have," and he was a "have not"—had chosen to become one in fact—and all the love in the universe couldn't change that one simple fact.

Matteo didn't speak again and didn't move. After a while she concluded that he had fallen asleep. She got up quietly, taking off her borrowed clothes, and slipped into the stream. It was tepid but refreshing, and she moved around in the water almost noiselessly, rinsing the dust of the trip from her skin and hair.

"Helen."

Matteo's voice was husky with anticipation, with desire. She turned to see him standing on the bank, watching her. She went toward him, and when the water was about knee deep he could wait no longer, splashing in to meet her, seizing her about the waist and lifting her into his arms.

She was slippery, streaming, but he didn't pause to dry her off, merely set her on the pile of her discarded clothes and covered her with his body. His mouth was everywhere, hot against her flesh cooled by the recent bath. He was silent, transferring his eloquence to his hands and his lips, telling her without words how much she meant to him. Helen writhed beneath him, clutching his waist, the back of head, hanging on to the reality that would soon become a memory. When he finally rose to strip, she watched his shadowed movements in the moonlight, reaching up for him eagerly as he descended to embrace her.

Their lovemaking had the bittersweet quality of parting, and when it was over and she had settled against his shoulder, he caught the glitter of tears on her cheeks. Matteo said nothing, holding her until she drifted off and looking into the vault of stars above his head until he fell asleep as well.

He woke before it was light and saw by his watch that the sun would rise in half an hour. He dressed and waited until the last possible moment to wake Helen, who hadn't even stirred when he left her to get up.

She opened her eyes and saw the mist clinging to the water, saw the orange streaks of sunrise bisecting the sky. She dressed without saying a word, avoiding his eyes, then faced him when she had pinned up her hair and adjusted her clothes and there was nothing left to do.

"I'm ready," she said, and he picked up his pack.

The walk to the mesa took twenty minutes, and for the last eight they climbed all the way. They reached the top of the rock wall that formed its side and Matteo took Helen's arm, holding her back.

"Let me look," he said quietly, and she remained behind as he went over the top of the ridge. He was back in a minute.

"He's there," Matteo announced, and her heart sank. She had been hoping until the last second that Alma's brother wouldn't show, and she could go back with Matteo.

"I guess you were right about Alma," she said simply, and he dropped his eyes.

Helen followed Matteo over the top, taking his hand to help her negotiate some of the rocks, and then shielded her eyes from the blazing sunrise. She could see the helicopter some distance away, its rotary blade stilled, a tall man in mirrored sunglasses leaning against its side.

They approached it together, and as they got closer the man walked out to meet them, extending his hand to Matteo. Helen could see that he was dark and resembled Alma, with her thick lustrous hair and graceful movements. She wondered if there were any ugly Puerta Lindans; she hadn't seen one.

Matteo clasped the other man's hand briefly, not shaking it as he would have done with an American, and then embraced him, clapping him on the back. They talked for a few moments, and Matteo accepted a packet from him. He turned and gave it to Helen.

"These are your papers," he said. "Paolo assures me everything is in order."

Matteo drew Helen forward and introduced her. Paolo made a short courtly bow and said, *"Con much gusto, señorita."*

Matteo asked Paolo to wait and then took Helen aside as the other man glanced around nervously, obviously anxious to be on his way. They were exposed on the mesa, highly visible from the air and for miles on land because of its height.

"Listen to me," Matteo said. "I would like to go with you to Soledad but Playa del Sol has an extradition treaty with Puerta Linda, and if I'm caught there it's the same as being caught at home. Paolo is wanted, too, so all he can do is drop you off on the road to Soledad and leave."

Helen nodded, thinking that this was really happening and in a few minutes she would be gone.

"This is a compass," he said, pulling a metal object out of his pocket. "When you get to the road, face east and keep walking. You'll hit the outskirts of Soledad eventually. How long will depend on how close Paolo can get you. Make sure you get the direction right, because if you go the wrong way you'll end up in the bush."

She nodded again, taking the compass and closing her fingers around it.

"Here is some American money," he went on, handing her a stack of bills. "Soledad is a resort and all the stores accept it."

"Matteo, this is too much," she protested, looking down at the denominations.

"Take it," he said impatiently. "You have to buy a plane ticket, stay in a hotel; you don't know what might come up." He took a deep breath and put his hands on her shoulders. "When you get there, not to Soledad but all the way to the U.S., I want you to send me a cable at the Cristobal Hotel in San Jacinta. Send it to Mr. Dominguez; he's the manager there and a friend of mine. He'll hold it for me."

"What about Esteban? Wouldn't it be better if I sent it to his place?"

Matteo shook his head. "They know he's a sympathizer; Dominguez is safer. Have you got that now?"

"Dominguez at the Cristobal," she repeated.

"Good." He paused, glancing over at Paolo, who was moving around restively. "I have to know that you got home all right."

Helen stepped away from him and unzipped her duffel bag, taking out a pad and pencil.

"This is the address of my apartment in Massachusetts," she said, writing. "Just in case you might need it."

She ripped off the sheet of paper and handed it to him. He took it, folded it and placed it in the breast pocket of his shirt.

They looked at each other.

"Oh, *mi corazón*," he murmured, pulling her into his arms. "How can I live without my heart?"

"This trip was your idea, buddy," she said against his shoulder, her throat closing. "Remember that."

He held her off and searched her face. "Take care of yourself," he said huskily. "Make sure you eat and sleep, things like that."

Helen swallowed and then said rapidly, not meeting his eyes, "Look, I understand that you don't want me to stay with you, but I can still help. How about if I send you some money? You could certainly use it, for food and medicine, arms, whatever you need. I've never asked my father for a dime; he'd give it to me and he wouldn't even care what I did with it. Or I could get an advance on my trust fund. I've never done that either; the bank would go along with it...."

He put his hand to her mouth, silencing her. When she looked up at him, she saw that his eyes were wet.

"I love you," he said.

Helen felt something like despair. "Why do you tell me that now, when I'm leaving?" she asked, struggling to maintain her composure.

"Maybe because it's too late," he answered, his tone fatalistic, resigned.

As if to comment on that statement, Paolo started the helicopter's engine. Its big blade began to spin slowly, stirring up dust and creating a wind that blew loose strands of Helen's hair about her face.

"Are you sure you can get back all right?" she asked him, and he smiled.

"Don't worry about it. I'll be fine," he answered, and then there wasn't anything more to say.

"Kiss me," Matteo said and seized her, crushing her mouth with his. The blade picked up speed, and the craft hovered on its landing runners.

"Go," he said, releasing her. *"Adiós, majita. Vaya con Dios, mi princesa."*

"Stay here," she said, and turned her back on him deliberately, blinking to clear her vision. But her eyes were still misty as she ran toward the helicopter. When she got there Paolo, already in the pilot's seat, reached down to help her climb aboard.

Matteo didn't follow her, as she'd requested, but stared after her as she settled into the passenger seat and the helicopter began to rise. She glanced down and saw him standing below, his head tilted back, his arms hanging loosely at his sides. When he saw her looking he raised his hand in farewell, and she put her palm against the clear bubble by her face as if she could touch him through the glass.

Then the dirt swirling below them in the wake of their ascent obscured her vision, and when she looked again Matteo was gone.

Chapter 10

The helicopter ride was noisy, and all Helen could see below was dense vegetation that extended in all directions. Paolo looked straight ahead, monitoring his instrument panel and resting his right hand on the throttle. He was keeping to the jungle to avoid being spotted by border patrols, but Helen knew that the riskiest part of the journey would be when he set her down near Soledad and civilization was uncomfortably close. They had been flying for about ten minutes when the blue ribbon of a river appeared below them, with a road running parallel to one of its banks.

"Playa," Paolo said, nodding at it, and Helen understood that the river served as a natural boundary between the two countries. Soon after that he began to descend, and she could see a large city spreading out toward the sparkling bay that hugged the coastline.

"Soledad?" she asked, pointing into the distance.

"*Sí*, Soledad," he answered, and flew even lower, almost skirting the tops of the trees that rushed up at them.

Helen looked down and saw what he was aiming for: a flat stretch of road wide enough for a landing. He would have to drop straight down onto it, but Paolo was apparently used to operating under such conditions in this mountainous region. He approached it calmly, making adjustments in the speed of the rotor as they fell. Helen closed her eyes until she felt the jolt of the landing, and when she opened them Paolo was smiling at her.

"Está aquí, señorita," he said, gesturing to the surrounding scenery.

Helen reached over and planted a kiss on his cheek. *"Muchas gracias,"* she said, grabbing her duffel, aware that speed was of the essence.

"De nada," he replied as she pulled out the compass and stared at its face.

He took it from her and glanced at the sky, then at the instrument in his hand. "Soledad," he said firmly, stabbing his finger emphatically in the direction of the ascending sun.

Helen nodded, took the compass back and then put her hand on his arm.

"¿Por qué?" she asked. "Why? Why did you help me?"

"Por mi hermana," he answered, and she smiled to think that in Puerta Linda, as in the rest of the world, brothers loved their sisters.

They both looked up as a car approached in the distance, and Helen jumped to the ground, waving Paolo on. She dashed into the trees and the helicopter rose. The car swept past, the people inside it craning their necks up at Paolo's helicopter as he headed back home.

Helen waited a couple of minutes, making sure that the road was empty, then came out of hiding and strode off in the direction that Paolo had indicated. She made an effort to look casual until she realized that no one was paying any attention to her; the drivers of the vehicles that passed apparently dismissed her as a hiker, and she settled into a rhythm that ate up the distance she had to cover. After a while her energy flagged and she was tempted to hitch a ride but, fearful of the questions she might be asked, she continued on foot. She reached the height above the city an hour later and began the descent to Soledad.

Once inside the city limits, she saw taxis and flagged one down. She managed to make the cabbie understand that she wanted a hotel where the staff spoke English. She suspected that he took the global route to get her there, but she was satisfied when she saw it. The facade looked modern, and the people streaming in and out of it were obviously tourists. She paid the cabbie with Matteo's American money, which he was happy to get, and walked up the wide stone steps into the coolness of an air-conditioned lobby.

"I'd like a room with a bath for the night," she said to the clerk, who looked down his nose at her.

"All our rooms have baths, madam," he replied, surveying her wrinkled, dirty shorts and field blouse with disdain.

"Fine," Helen said. "And I want to book a plane ticket. Can I do that here?"

"The concierge will take care of that for you, madam," the clerk said. "Will that be cash or credit card?"

"Cash," Helen said. "Do you have a room service menu?"

The clerk extended one to her, and when she saw the prices she knew the reason for his pseudo-British accent and exalted manner. The cabbie had brought her to the most expensive hotel in the city, possibly in the country, but she was too tired to care. She stuck the menu in her bag and took her key, stopping at an overpriced boutique on the mezzanine to buy some clothes. She felt too grimy to try anything on, but guessed at the sizes. She took the package

to her room and tossed it on a chair. She debated taking a
shower, which she certainly needed, but decided it could
wait. She hardly glanced at the accommodations before she
flung herself on the bed and fell instantly asleep.

When Helen awoke it was late afternoon, and her first
thought was of Matteo. He must be well on his way back by
now. She remembered his lovemaking of the previous night,
so urgent, almost desperate, with the lingering sadness of
their coming separation, and knew that she would never
experience anything like that again. It was over, and the rest
of her life would be a pale reflection of what she had had
with him.

Helen got up and went into the bathroom, noting with
amusement the supply of soap, shampoo, toothpaste and
other toiletries, all packaged in the miniature sizes favored
by American hotels. She took a long shower, washed her
hair, and brushed her teeth with a tiny utensil that looked
like a nailbrush.

Seeing herself in the mirror was a revelation. Her skin was
a deep gold, and her hair was bleached to the shade of a ripe
lemon peel. She looked like a Malibu beach girl and smiled
when she remembered Sophia's many admonitions to stay
out of the sun because it aged the skin. Too late, she
thought. She might look eighty tomorrow, but for the moment she stared back at the thin, pale-eyed, suntanned
stranger, wondering where Helen had gone.

The clothes were all too big, including the shoes, which
seemed impossible. She had lost more weight than she'd realized. She put the belt of the slacks on its innermost notch
and tucked in the loose blouse, deciding to buy thick socks
to fill out the shoes. It wasn't worth exchanging the clothes;
she would probably put the weight back on once she got
home. She took the room service menu out of her bag and
read it, observing the comforting presence of such items as

hamburgers and grilled cheese sandwiches. The management was going all out to cater to its American guests, printing the menu in Spanish on one side and English on the other. She picked up the phone and ordered dinner. Given the hotel's desire to please the *turistas*, it was probably easier to get served promptly there than in Los Angeles. She was glad she didn't have to face the downstairs dining room, and while she waited for the food to arrive she called the concierge and arranged for her flight. It was departing the next morning for New York from the Ferdinand airport at the western end of the city, and she reflected that by tomorrow evening she would be back in Manhattan.

Helen turned on the television, which broadcast two Spanish-language stations, carrying mostly American reruns. She was treated to the spectacle of a dubbed *Bonanza*, with Little Joe referring to his brother as "José." Her dinner came and she ate most of it, forcing herself to consume more than she wanted. Then she reclined on the bed and watched *The Big Valley* and *I Dream of Jeannie*, wondering if Matteo had reached the stream where they'd made love. Finally she fell asleep again and was awakened by the morning sun shining through the hotel window.

Her trip back to New York was uneventful, even at American immigration, where she had anticipated trouble. She was prepared to call her father and have him raise hell with his politician friends to get her back into the country, but the necessity never arose. The uniformed officer merely glanced at her papers and passed her along, turning to the person behind her without change of expression. Once in the Kennedy terminal Helen felt as if she had never left home; the whole experience seemed surreal, like the memory of a fragmented dream. Impossible to believe that two days before she had been in a Puerta Lindan jungle; impossible to accept that she would never see Matteo again. She walked along, glancing at the concession stands and restaurants, telling herself that this was going to be her life from now on.

She stayed overnight in New York and sent the cable to Matteo's friend from there. She flew to Boston the next morning, rented a car at the airport, and drove to Cambridge, unhappy to see that New England was experiencing a wet spring. Her apartment was stuffy from the lack of ventilation, and she opened all the windows despite the rain, thinking how much her life had changed since she had closed them. Then she went to bed. Her exhaustion was complete and inexplicable; since she had left Matteo she'd done almost nothing but sleep. She nodded off constantly, unconsciously seeking the oblivion that allowed her to forget that she had lost him.

Gradually Helen began putting her life back together. She called the cleaning service in Florida and asked them to send along her thesis materials, so she could pick up her work again. And she resumed her research, finding that, once again, it comforted her, filling out her days and giving some meaning to her otherwise barren existence.

She had been home for over a month when she began to feel ill—dizzy and nauseous. She ignored the malaise for a while, but when it persisted she became concerned and made an appointment with her doctor. It was a fine day in late May when she went to his office to receive the report on her examination, the results of the tests he had conducted.

The nurse ushered her into his office, and she sat in the chair nearest his desk, nervously scanning the diploma-covered walls. Dr. Corrigan entered promptly, carrying her file.

"So," Helen said to him, "what's wrong with me?"

"Not a thing," he replied. "You're pregnant."

She merely looked at him.

"Haven't you missed any periods?" he asked her.

"Yes, but I've been upset and not feeling well. I've missed before for those reasons, and I've been losing weight, not gaining it."

"Weight loss is not uncommon in the beginning," the doctor said, "and the nausea will pass." He smiled. "The day will come when you'll wish you could lose some weight, believe me."

Helen sat very still, trying to absorb the fact that she was pregnant with Matteo's baby. Of course the possibility had occurred to her, but she had dismissed it as wishful thinking. Now she was being told that it was true. She began to laugh.

"Is something wrong?" the doctor said, wondering if she was about to become hysterical.

"No, no, everything is right. This is wonderful news; you've made me very happy."

"Miss Demarest, may I ask you a personal question?" Dr. Corrigan said.

"Certainly."

"You're not married, and I was wondering if you might need a referral to one of our local services. They can be very helpful to someone in your situation, to discuss alternatives, and..."

Helen stood up. "No, thank you, that won't be necessary. There are no alternatives for me." The doctor was a local man who didn't know her family and might have thought she was without resources. "I have money; I'll be fine."

"But the father..." he persisted.

"He's out of the country," Helen said, which was nothing less than the truth.

"Well, make an appointment with the nurse for your next visit, and wait for your prescriptions. You have to start taking vitamins...."

He was talking to Helen's back. She didn't mean to be rude, but she almost flew out of his office and into the street, hugging herself for sheer joy.

It had not been for nothing after all. She would have Matteo's child, and no cause or calling could deprive her of that.

She went straight home and stared at her profile in the mirror, trying to see some sign of the life growing inside her. Her stomach was still flat but soon it wouldn't be, and everyone would know her secret happiness. She remembered to call for her prescriptions and went to the pharmacy to get them filled, looking at everything she passed with new eyes. She was going to be a mother.

The next three months flew past as spring became summer and Helen finished the first draft of her thesis. She had never felt so efficient, so organized. She was checking footnotes one afternoon, humming to herself and tugging at the stretching elastic on her new maternity pants, when her doorbell rang.

She got up to answer it absently, glancing back at the pages on her desk. She pulled the door open and froze.

Sophia stood on the threshold, looking her up and down with a practiced eye. She folded her arms and sighed.

"My God, it's true," she said. "You are pregnant."

"Come in, Sophia," Helen said resignedly and stepped aside.

Her mother breezed past her on a cloud of Eau de Joy, glancing around the apartment with evident distaste. She turned and faced Helen, wearing her "an explanation is in order, please" expression.

"To what do I owe the honor of this visit?" Helen asked, shutting the door. "You haven't been to my place in what? Three years? Since Uncle Albert died in Brookline and you needed a drink after the reading of the will. He didn't leave you his antique silver collection, remember?"

"I can do without the sarcasm, Helen, thank you very much. Can you tell me why I had to find out about this from Daphne Ashmore, of all people?"

"What does Daphne have to do with anything?"

"She saw you at the Boston Public Library, my dear, looking definitely *enceinte*, as the French say."

"What was Daphne doing at the library? I didn't know she could read."

"She was looking up something for the DAR, and thank God she was. She called me in Gstaad, and I hopped the next plane right over here to see for myself. Helen, what is going on?"

"I'm going to have a baby, Sophia. Do you want me to draw you a diagram?" Helen replied impatiently, thinking about all the work she had to do. Of course Sophia hadn't called first. She knew Helen would have found a way to dodge her, so she just showed up unannounced. She favored the same guerilla tactics Matteo used: blind-siding and sneak attacks.

Sophia examined her daughter speculatively, and Helen stared back, unruffled. She had been dealing with these confrontations for years, and there was a certain familiarity about them now, a ritual pattern that had to be observed.

Sophia's hair was frosted and neatly coiffed, her makeup perfect in the eighty-six-degree heat. She was wearing a beige watered-silk summer dress of understated elegance, which must have set the bonbon king back a few francs, with matched Charles Jourdan pumps and a Hermes bag. In her ears and around her bare throat she wore the Demarest pearls, a wedding gift from Helen's father, worth ten thousand dollars at last estimate—Sophia had them appraised yearly. On her left hand the pigeon's-blood ruby that the chocolate baron had given her as an engagement ring flashed like an exit sign. She was wealth incarnate. The mugger fortunate enough to stumble across Sophia on any given day would have instantly acquired his retirement fund.

"That won't be necessary," Sophia finally said, sitting on the edge of the paper-strewn sofa and crossing her gleaming legs. "Well, Helen, I must say that pregnancy was the last condition I ever expected you to develop. Malnutrition, certainly. Cabin fever, possibly. But this..." She waved a manicured hand expressively. "It's just too depressing."

"I'm not depressed," Helen said, going to the kitchenette and taking a pitcher of iced tea from the refrigerator. "I'm very happy. Happier than I've ever been in my life."

Sophia nodded sourly. "Just like you not to say a word to a soul until it's too late to do anything about it."

"I would not have done anything about it," Helen said firmly, holding her mother's gaze. "I want this baby."

She poured tea for both of them, and when she gave one glass to Sophia she realized that the older woman was looking at her in a way she never had before. She guessed that, purely by accident, she had finally done something to impress her mother. And she knew why. Pregnancy, in most cases, required the active participation of a man, and the subject of men was one of consuming interest to Sophia.

Sophia's next question confirmed Helen's suspicions. "So who's the father?" she asked.

"No one you know," Helen answered, sipping her tea.

"That's not an answer. Is he one of those scruffy students you're always hanging around with, some graduate assistant in obscure literati?"

"No."

"Not, God forbid, a professor?"

"It's not a professor and it's none of your business."

"I beg your pardon. I'm your mother and it is my business."

"All right, fine. The father is a Central American revolutionary, and when I took that vacation last spring I really spent the time in his guerrilla camp, as his lover."

Sophia tapped her dainty foot. "Helen, you are getting on my last remaining nerve with this. Now is not the time for jokes."

Helen shrugged. "Okay."

Sophia waited a beat. "So you're not going to tell me?"

"I just did."

Sophia held her glass up to the light and examined it before she took a drink. "It's so hot for September, don't you think?" she asked conversationally.

"Boston is always like this in September," Helen answered, recognizing the old sidestep maneuver. Sophia would make chitchat for a while, then circle back to the salient topic.

"Your father and his wife just bought a chalet in Aspen," she said, fingering her necklace.

"That's nice."

"It's ludicrous. Neither one of them can ski."

"Daddy can ski," Helen pointed out. "He never has time for it."

"His wife can't. She just wants to give après-ski parties and ogle the blond European instructors."

"She can do that, if she wants. I don't think you have to pass a skiing test to buy property in Aspen."

Sophia tired of the repartee and glared at her daughter. "Helen what are you going to do?" she said in a strong voice.

"Well, I'm finishing my thesis, and then I thought I'd get my teaching certificate."

"Teaching?" Sophia said, as if Helen had suggested prostitution.

"Yes. And after that I'll look for a job."

"A job?" Sophia gasped.

"Sure, why not? I'm not going to live on the trust fund forever. I was just using it until I got out of school."

"And what about the . . . baby?"

"Sophia, people with children work all the time. I'll figure something out; don't worry about it."

Sophia took a bigger drink of her tea, then set the glass down. She folded her hands on her knees, and Helen knew that the main volley was coming.

"Look," Sophia said, "I have a solution for all of this. Claudia and Roberto will be in New York next week."

"And?" Helen said warily.

"And you know how gallant Roberto is. He would never be able to see you in such dire straits without wanting to help."

"Help," Helen said, beginning to get the picture.

"Yes. I'm sure we could work something out. You have to legitimize the child. After the baby is born, well, we could arrange . . ."

"A payoff?" Helen said thoughtfully.

Sophia glared at her.

Helen couldn't help it. She burst out laughing.

"I fail to see anything funny in your situation," Sophia observed uncomfortably.

"You can't honestly be suggesting that I *marry* Roberto Fierremonte?"

"Why not? It would only be for a few months."

"I am not going to fight Roberto for space in front of the mirror, not even for a few days," Helen said, still grinning.

"You are an ungrateful brat!" Sophia burst out, and Helen stopped cold, staring at her mother.

"Sophia, have you already contacted him about this?" Helen said, certain of the answer before she asked.

Sophia picked up her glass again, jingling the ice cubes. "Well, I just happened to be speaking to Claudia on the phone, and I mentioned your possible predicament...."

"I am not in a predicament!" Helen yelled, losing patience. "Now you get back on the phone and tell Claudia, or Roberto, or whoever you arranged this little deal with, that the bribe will not be handed over after all. What's wrong with those two anyway, don't they have enough money?"

Sophia didn't reply, and Helen sighed. "Silly of me," she said. "No such thing as enough money, is there?"

"I don't understand why you have to see it in such crass, materialistic terms. There's nothing wrong with Roberto wanting to help out a friend."

"He's your friend; let him marry you!"

"I," Sophia said imperiously, "am not about to become an unwed mother."

Helen counted to ten. She took a deep breath and said, "You know that Roberto has been trying to get his hands on some of Daddy's money for years now. He's running himself into debt with all the gambling and the high living. Do you really want to give him an excuse to stick his mitt into the till?"

Sophia's fingers knotted and unknotted in her lap. "But, Helen, what is going to happen to you?" she said miserably, and for the first time Helen saw that her mother was genuinely worried about her. Of course she wanted to avoid a scandal among her uptight, hypocritical friends, but she also thought her only child was in terrible trouble. The fact that Helen didn't see it that way only exacerbated Sophia's concern. It confirmed her lifelong suspicion that Helen was a flake who couldn't take care of herself.

Helen sat next to her mother and put her hand on Sophia's shoulder. "Mother," she said, deliberately using the title, "I have been with a man. A real man, who believes in something, who has dedicated his life to it. A man who loved me. I can't go from that to Roberto, not even for the sake of your precious reputation."

"And where is this wonderful man when you need him?" Sophia sniffed. "I don't see him, do you?"

"He doesn't know about the baby."

"When do you propose to tell him?" Sophia demanded, outraged.

"I'm not going to tell him. There are reasons why it isn't a good idea."

"Such as?"

"You'll just have to trust me on that," Helen said, smiling. "Besides, unwed motherhood, as you so quaintly put it, is *in* right now. All the movie stars are doing it."

"The Demarests aren't," Sophia responded dryly.

"They are now," Helen said, and even Sophia had to smile.

"So," she said, drawing out the vowel, "there's nothing I can say that will persuade you to change your attitude about this?"

"Nothing."

"Well, I don't know what I'm going to tell your father."

"Sophia, don't be ridiculous. He's so wrapped up in his mergers he wouldn't notice if I gave birth to the Bronx Zoo."

"He might disown the child," Sophia cautioned.

"Let him. I have enough money in my own right to support myself and the baby."

"He might disown *you*."

"He can't touch the trust fund that Grandfather left me; you know that."

"But you'll be entitled to a lot more when he dies. This sort of thing is not exactly going to encourage him to leave it to you."

"I don't care," Helen said flatly, and Sophia sighed.

"I know you don't care, and I will never understand why. Your whole life I have tried to guide you, advise you on how a person of your status should behave, and you have done nothing but disregard every word I've said. When I think . . ."

"We're not going to play that tape again, are we?" Helen asked gently.

Sophia pressed her lips together, swallowing her words. "No, I guess we're not. But I would like to know if any pressure can be brought to bear on the father. If you don't marry Roberto, I assume you'll marry him."

"Pressure? Are we talking about money again?"

"You'll find that it can be very persuasive to people who don't have it," Sophia commented dryly.

"It might interest you to know that I have already offered him money, not to marry me, but to use for something that's very important to him. He refused it."

"That sounds like someone who would fascinate you," Sophia said despairingly, and Helen chuckled.

"Cheer up, Sophia, that's good news. I wouldn't pressure him if I could. For once in my cautious, circumspect life I took a chance. Do you know what that feels like? And I'm not sorry; I'm not sorry at all. I had a wonderful experience with the man I love, and I'm going to have his baby."

"And the identity of this paragon is going to remain a mystery," Sophia stated.

Helen didn't reply, aware that reiterating the truth was futile.

Sophia nodded. "I can see that my mother will never be dead as long as you're walking around. She was as stubborn as you are."

"A bad trait that skipped a generation, as we all know."

Sophia stood, tucking her bag under her arm and patting her hair with her other hand. "We'll have to make plans," she said. "You'll have to have a shower, of course."

"No shower," Helen answered quickly. "For once, bypass an excuse to give a party." Sophia was amazing; in almost the same breath she could complain about the scandal of an illegitimate child and then plan a fete to celebrate its imminent arrival.

"You really want to do this all by yourself?" Sophia asked doubtfully.

Helen could understand her mother's incomprehension. She had never taken a step in her life without a husband, her family and an army of servants to back her up.

"I'm not by myself. The baby is with me."

Sophia shrugged. "I really don't know what I hoped to accomplish by making this trip. You'd think I would understand by now that I can never persuade you to do anything you don't want to do."

Helen smiled. "But you wouldn't by my mother if you didn't try."

"That's true," Sophia said, and they both laughed.

"Can I offer you something to eat?" Helen said politely, anxious to end the discussion of her dubious future.

"No thank you," said Sophia, who counted calories with anorexic intensity. She glanced at her Piaget watch, a gift from spouse number two. Sophia parted with the husbands, but not the perks. "I have to be running along, I'm meeting Richard Worthington for dinner."

"How is Richard?" Helen asked, of the man who had been trying to get her mother to marry him for twenty years. Poor Richard, he just never had enough assets to interest Sophia on a serious basis.

"Divorced again," Sophia replied. "I hear she ran off with a tuba player."

Helen managed not to laugh, but her grin was roguish.

"Yes, I know," Sophia said airily, "we're all very funny to you, aren't we? You think you're so superior, with your principled phantom lover and your precious little bundle on the way. I can't wait for you to become a mother. Then maybe you'll know what it's like to have your child reject you and everything you stand for. Maybe you'll understand my pain."

Helen was shocked to see that there were tears in Sophia's eyes. She went to her mother and put her arm around her shoulder, hugging her close.

"I'm not rejecting you, mother," she said quietly. "I'm just different, that's all, you know I always have been. It doesn't mean I don't love you. I do."

"And I love you, baby," Sophia said huskily, kissing her cheek. Then she collected herself and dabbed at her eyes with her forefinger, making sure that her mascara didn't smear.

"I suppose I'll be permitted to buy a layette for my grandchild. That won't be forbidden, will it?" Sophia said briskly, smoothing the unwrinkled skirt of her dress.

"Nothing is forbidden, except purchasing a husband for me."

"I've given up on that idea," Sophia said. "Never fear."

"Good."

"And you'll visit, with the baby?"

"Of course," Helen said. She knew that for all Sophia's constant traveling and partying, her mother was lonely.

"Then I suppose that's all I can do," Sophia announced. "You will call me if you need anything?"

"I'll call, but I don't think I'll be needing anything."

"As independent as ever," Sophia said, shaking her head. "If your child is anything like you, I'll wind up devoting all my time to good works."

"That might be a nice change," Helen said.

Sophia shot her a look. "Just don't disappear without letting me know, all right?"

"All right, I promise."

Sophia turned to go and then stopped, eyeing Helen with something like envy.

"You say you were in love with this man, the baby's father?"

"Very much. I still am."

"Well, that's something, anyway."

"That's everything," Helen replied, and Sophia surprised her once more by nodding slowly.

"I suppose you're right," she said softly. "I was in love with your father when I had you."

"I know," Helen whispered sympathetically.

Sophia shook her head, as if to dispense with unproductive memories. "Goodbye, darling, and keep in touch," she said, going for the door.

"Goodbye," Helen echoed, watching through the window as her mother climbed into her hired limousine and headed off to a rendezvous with her admirer.

Helen went back to her work and didn't get up from the table until dinnertime. She flicked on the television as she walked past it, intending to listen to the five-o'clock news and see if the Indian summer heat was about to break.

The announcer reviewed various domestic crises and then said, "At the top of the international news is the revolution in the tiny Central American country of Puerta Linda. Rebel orces under the leadership of Matteo Salazar de Montega ast night deposed the military government there and are now in control of the capital city of San Jacinta. The coup was bloodless, and Montega is reportedly advocating a policy of nonretaliation against the members of the previous regime. A free election is scheduled to take place in a matter of months.''

Helen sank to the sofa in silence, her hands to her mouth, her eyes filling with tears of joy.

Chapter 11

Montega," the commentator went on to say, "considered to be one of the young turks of Central American politics, was educated in the United States, where he lived and worked for thirteen years. He is a democratic thinker whose American ideas were said to offend some of his colleagues, who resented the old government's alliance with the U.S. There is little doubt, however, that these differences will fade in light of yesterday's victory, largely the result of his brilliant field tactics and charismatic leadership."

Helen sat transfixed, her gaze never wavering from the television. An old photograph of Matteo flashed onto the screen, identified as his Columbia yearbook picture. His hair was cut in the style of the mid-seventies, and he grinned confidently into the camera, totally at ease.

The hair had changed, but not the smile.

"Montega orchestrated a carefully mounted campaign of raids on government installations, gradually weakening the military's power to resist, and then struck the final blow, aking over the official buildings in San Jacinta about 1:00 .m. this morning, Eastern standard time. The leading figres of the ousted regime are in custody, and Montega insts that they will be treated fairly. He will head a rovisional government until power can be passed into the ands of ministers duly elected by the people."

"Good for you, Matteo," Helen whispered, clasping her ands at her breast. "Good for you."

"And in a related story," the newscaster said, "The FBI oday announced that it was dropping illegal purchase of irearms charges against Montega, who had been wanted for n incident involving stolen guns last March. The Bureau isists that its move has nothing to do with the coup in 'uerta Linda, but speculation is rife that this gesture of oodwill to the newly powerful Central American leader was n effort to keep an ally the United States needs in that oubled area of the globe."

The commentator moved along to another story, and lelen rose to shut off the set, still in a daze.

Matteo had realized his dream. He would now have what e'd worked so long and hard to achieve: freedom for his eople to control their own government.

At the same time Helen knew that there was no place in is life for her. Ever since she'd left him she had hoped there vould be, but as the weeks passed without word she acepted what she'd known in her heart since she climbed into 'aolo's helicopter.

There was no question in Helen's mind that Matteo had ared about her, perhaps more than he'd cared about any ther other woman in his life. But she had a rival, as Theesa said, and Helen had always come second to Puerta inda. That had never been more true than at this moment f triumph, when he could look to the future and see the ossibility of things he had once only imagined.

She wiped her eyes and got up to make her dinner, thinking that three months was too long to wait for the arrival of Matteo's child.

Matteo Montega stared out the window of the military barracks in San Jacinta, his mind in turmoil. He hardly looked up when he heard the door across the room shut, but he was forced to recognize the man who moved into his field of vision and stood there, waiting for an audience.

"Martin, what is it?" Matteo finally said.

"The temporary headquarters are ready," Martin announced. "We are still clearing out the old offices, though. Just organizing the files is going to take a long time."

"That's all right," Matteo answered distractedly. "We've had twenty-five years of those gangsters; we can wait another couple of weeks in order to set it up right." He paused and looked directly at the other man for the first time. "Any word from the United States?" he asked. "Any cables or wires, letters?"

"Plenty," Martin replied quietly. "There's a flood of mail. But not from her."

"Are you sure?"

Martin nodded. "Very sure. I checked myself."

"Massachusetts. It would be from there; that's where she lives."

"Nothing."

Matteo sighed. "Maybe she hasn't heard."

Martin shook his head. "It's been all over American newspapers and television. They love the fact that you lived there for so long, and they're playing it up big. She'd have to be hibernating in a cave to miss it."

Matteo favored him with a wry smile. "I hope that's not supposed to make me feel better."

Martin shrugged. "You asked me." He paused and shuffled his feet. "Why don't you get in touch with her?"

"I'm not sure she'll want to hear from me."

"Why not? That girl was crazy about you."

"Six months ago she was. She hasn't heard a word from me since then."

Martin simply stared at him.

"I wanted to wait until I had something to offer her," Matteo said defensively.

"Don't you think you waited a bit too long?"

"Thanks, Martin. That idea never occurred to me." Matteo stood and thrust his fingers through his hair. "I knew we were going to make the big push at the end of this summer, and it seemed like a good idea to see how things turned out before I contacted her." He shrugged slightly. "Change takes time. I couldn't ask her to come back and be camp follower again."

"What are you going to do?" Martin asked.

"Isn't it obvious? I'll have to go and get her." Matteo moved around the desk as if to leave right then.

"Shouldn't you let her know you're coming?"

Matteo shook his head. "I don't want to give her the chance to say no before she sees me in person."

"Think she won't be able to resist you, eh?" Martin said, grinning conspiratorially.

Matteo's reply indicated that he had a lot less confidence in his personal magnetism than Martin did.

"Six months is a long time," he said thoughtfully. "She could be married to someone else already. She could have moved to another country—anything."

"Do you really think she would have done something like that?" Martin asked doubtfully.

Matteo didn't answer for a moment and then said, "She had a lot invested in me. When I sent her away, well, I don't know how she reacted once she left here.'' He stopped, then whispered, ''I only hope I can find her.''

''I don't know if you should leave right now,'' Martin said carefully. ''Things are still pretty unsettled; you know that.''

''You and Ricardo can handle it,'' Matteo said firmly. ''I've given up enough. It's about time I did something for myself.''

Martin couldn't argue with him and said nothing.

''The most important thing,'' Matteo said, ''is to control the people, make sure they don't take revenge. We have to set an example, show everyone that we're better than the group we just booted out.''

''I understand,'' Martin said quietly.

''Call them all together for a meeting in an hour,'' Matteo directed him. ''I want to give some last-minute instructions before I go. I'll see if I can get a flight out this afternoon.''

Martin moved to leave, then paused and said, ''Good luck.''

''I think I'm going to need it.'' Matteo sighed and turned to pick up a sheaf of papers on his desk.

Three hours later he boarded his flight for the United States. He had covered everything he could think of in his meeting and then packed lightly for the trip, taking only one change of clothes. His stay would be brief; it wouldn't take her long to say yes, or no.

Matteo was not prepared for what happened at the airport. He was recognized and greeted as a hero; his flight was delayed for him. He finally had to detach himself from the crowds and run for the plane. He had refused to bring his bodyguards along on this trip. His mission had been accomplished, and if something happened to him now, Martin and the others would be able to go on without him. He had also declined to commandeer a military plane for himself; such abuses had been the hallmark of the previous administration, and he wanted to start off with a clean slate.

As the plane taxied down the runway and gathered speed, Matteo settled into his seat, his expression sober as he wondered what the next couple of days would bring.

Helen finished with her shower and turned off the water, bundling into an oversize terry robe and wrapping her dripping hair in a towel. As she padded barefoot into the hall the doorbell rang, and she groaned. This was becoming a regular occurrence, except that usually the bell rang while she was still in the shower, and she had to emerge to greet her visitor, while streaming suds marked up the floor. The visitor was usually a messenger from Sophia. Since she had discovered her daughter's pregnancy, Helen's mother had sent an array of wildly impractical baby gifts, such as a sterling silver bottle holder and a raw-silk baby blanket. Where Sophia found such things Helen couldn't imagine; she would have settled for a dozen cotton nightshirts, but Sophia could not be expected to descend to such a mundane level.

Helen belted the robe around her burgeoning middle, effectively concealed by its voluminous folds, and yanked open the door, ready for a solid gold pram or a jewel-encrusted high chair, almost anything.

Except what she saw. Matteo was standing on the welcome mat, holding an envelope in his hand.

Helen was speechless. A myriad of thoughts flew through her mind, but the only one she held on to was relief that her attire, albeit unglamorous, concealed her condition.

"Hello, Helen," he said, and she managed a smile that felt stiff on her mouth. She wanted to fling her arms around his neck, but too much time had passed, too many things had changed, and she wasn't sure he would welcome the attention.

"Hello, Matteo," she answered, thinking that they sounded like a couple of characters in a bad play. But she simply didn't know what to say to him, and sterile politeness was an acceptable substitute for honesty when the latter was burdened with too much risk.

"May I come in?" he asked, and she stepped aside, noticing that he signaled covertly to two men leaning against a long black sedan at the curb. They were attired in almost identical gray suits, with cropped hair and an indefinable air of competence seasoned with menace.

"Who are those people?" she asked him in a low voice, nodding over his shoulder.

"Secret-service men," he answered, flushing faintly, obviously embarrassed. "It seems I'm not a private citizen anymore. Your government insisted."

"You're sure they'll wait outside?" she asked warily.

"I'm sure," he replied firmly, and pulled the door closed after them.

They stared at one another in silence.

"I'm sorry I'm not dressed," Helen began, "I wasn't expecting you."

"I came to give you this," he replied, extending the envelope to her.

"What is it?" Helen asked, taking it and ripping open the flap.

"You'll find out."

Helen removed the slip of paper inside and saw that it was a receipt, typed in Spanish.

"There's a translation on the back," Matteo said.

Helen turned it over and realized that he had given her a voucher for the price of a motorcycle of the type and year they had stolen from the street in San Jacinta. He had done as he promised—tracked down the owner and refunded the money for the bike they'd taken.

"Thank you," she said, touched. "But you could have mailed this to me; you didn't have to come all this way. I know you must be . . . busy these days."

I want to kiss her, Matteo thought, drinking in the light blue eyes, the fine, pale brows, the edible mouth. He longed to remove the towel from her head and run his hands through her damp, golden hair.

"I am busy. There's a lot to do," he said aloud.

"Matteo, I was so happy when I heard the news about your country," Helen said quietly, feeling that the words were inadequate.

"I'm sure you were," he answered, smiling slightly.

"I felt like something had been given to me," she went on. "I know it sounds silly."

"Of course it doesn't," he murmured, taking a step closer to her.

"So how's Theresa?" Helen asked brightly. "Still running the show?"

He nodded. "There's no stopping her now. Everybody's afraid of her."

"You, too?" she asked, smiling.

"Oh, me," he said casually, "I always was."

"And . . . Alma?" Helen asked carefully.

"She's fine. She has a new boyfriend, some friend of her brother's." He reached out and touched her shoulder. "Helen . . ."

She remained still under his fingers. "Matteo, why did you really come here? I mean, this trip, those guards, you had to have a good reason."

"I do. I want you to come back to Puerta Linda with me."

"Back to Puerta Linda?" she repeated faintly, as if trying to understand.

"Yes. As my wife."

Helen backed up unsteadily and sank into a chair.

Matteo followed, looming over her, concerned. "Are you all right?" he asked.

"Yes, I'm fine," Helen managed. "I just wasn't... expecting this."

"I know it must come as a shock, my suddenly arriving and announcing this, but surely you knew how I felt about you," he said quietly.

"I thought it was over," she murmured, still trying to absorb his presence, the proposal.

"Helen," he said hesitantly, sitting next to her on the small sofa and looking into her eyes, "is there someone else?"

"Oh, Matteo, don't be ridiculous," she answered, and leaned forward to put her head on his shoulder.

His arm came around her and he said, "Does this mean you'll marry me?"

"There's something I have to tell you first," she replied, her voice muffled by the cloth of his shirt.

"What?"

She raised her head and looked at him. "It's a surprise."

"Helen, I don't care, you can tell me anything. You're a member of the secret witness program, your father is a spy, your mother is now a man, anything."

"I'm pregnant," she whispered.

His face went blank for a second, and then his eyes flashed to her middle, concealed by the oversized robe. She took his hand and guided it through the opening, allowing him to feel the full roundness of her belly.

"How long?" he said huskily, when he had recovered.

"How long do you think? Six months, I was in Puerta Linda with you six months ago."

"No, I mean when is it due?"

"In three months, Matteo. Can't you count anymore?"

He closed his eyes. "And you weren't even going to tell me?"

"I thought you had enough on your mind, what with the revolution and all."

"Oh, darling," was all he said as he pulled her into his arms. There was silence for several moments, and then he cleared his throat.

"I can't believe this," he began, "I never dreamed, I mean of course I hoped, someday, but then when you left . . ."

"You're babbling, *jefe*," she said, laughing.

"We have to get married right away," he said suddenly, letting her go and standing up, then heading for the door.

"Are you going by yourself?" Helen asked, enjoying the scene. She had never seen him like this, bewildered, at a loss. He was always in control, in command of any situation, and the thought that she, and her news, had reduced him to such a state gave her a heady feeling of power.

"Get dressed," he ordered. "We have to get papers, and I'm not a citizen; there might be a hitch with that. Maybe we should wait until we get to Puerta Linda, but no, that will take too long."

"Matteo," she said gently, and waited until he turned and looked at her.

"It's Saturday; all the registry offices are closed. And the blood tests will take several days. I've been pregnant for six months and won't give birth for another three. I think we have some time."

"But this is my child," he protested, as if that answered her objections.

"I understand that. Believe me, no one understands that fact better than I do. But I can't run off with you right now. I have things to settle, people to tell, the apartment to sublet. It will take me a few days to get my life in order."

"Of course, of course," he said, nodding vigorously. "I should have realized; I'm sorry. I'm not thinking straight."

"No!" she said in an astonished tone, and he grinned sheepishly. He joined her on the couch again, taking her hand.

"Maybe you would like a wedding here, with your relatives," he said. "Girls dream of such a ceremony, don't they?"

"Not when they have my family," Helen said dryly. "Besides, I'm a little far gone for a white dress and a march down the aisle."

"And the groom is not exactly blue chip aristocracy," Matteo added.

"I wouldn't have any other," Helen said softly, touching his face.

He seized her hand and kissed it. "Then you'll come back to San Jacinta with me. We'll have the wedding there."

"Theresa can be my matron of honor," Helen said, pleased with the idea.

"And Martin will stand up for me. We can be married in the church I attended when I was a boy; would you like that?"

"I would," Helen agreed, thinking that her whole life had changed in the space of the few minutes since his arrival.

"I love you, *majita*," Matteo murmured, bending to kiss her. She responded eagerly, and soon she was half lying in his arms and he was peeling the robe off her shoulders.

"Wait," she said abruptly, sitting up.

"What for?" he asked, nuzzling her fuller breasts. "It's a little late to worry about birth control isn't it?" he added dryly.

"As I recall, you never did worry much about it," Helen replied, a smile in her voice, and he groaned, trying to reach her nipple with his tongue as she deftly eluded him.

"I want to change," she said to him, rising as he reached after her.

"You want to change your clothes so I can take them off?" he asked incredulously.

"Will you be patient?"

"Patience was never my strong point," he called as she disappeared into the bedroom.

"Tell me about it," she answered and shut the door.

Matteo drummed his fingers on the coffee table, got up and looked out the window at his two companions and then sat down again.

"What are you doing in there?" he yelled.

The door opened and Helen emerged, carrying a two-piece negligee on a hanger. Her expression was mournful.

"What's the matter?" Matteo asked, puzzled.

"I bought this for you," she said, extending the set which was made of beige silk appliqued with Alençon lace. "In case you came back for me."

Matteo glanced down at himself. "I don't think it will fit," he said, grinning.

"It doesn't fit me anymore, either," Helen wailed. "And I wanted to look so nice for you."

"You do look nice," he said, getting up and taking the garments out of her hand. "You always look nice."

"Oh, how can you say that?" she demanded, refusing to be comforted. "I certainly didn't look nice in the camp, running around in Rafaela's clothes."

"You certainly did." Matteo held the set out at arm's length and examined it. "Do you mean to tell me you've had this hanging in the closet since you got back, in case I showed up?"

"Yes, and now I look like an elephant in it. An elephant in a silk dressing gown."

Matteo embraced her, letting the negligee fall to the floor. "Sweetheart, I don't care."

"Well, I do," she responded, stiffening in his arms. "I wanted to be so glamorous, and I feel so...maternal."

"You're beautiful. Beautifully maternal." He undid the sash of her robe, and this time she offered no resistance, closing her eyes as his lips left a heated trail on her skin.

"Look at you," he whispered. "We'll have to have more children."

"One thing at a time," Helen answered, then went limp as he lifted her in his arms.

"You're heavier than you used to be," he teased, hefting her as if weighing a bundle.

"And to think you used to worry about my weight," Helen replied.

"I'll always worry about you, *princesa*," he murmured, kissing her neck as he pushed the bedroom door open with his foot. Then he stopped short and said, "Oh, oh."

"What is it?"

"A bed, a real bed with clean sheets. I don't know if I can do this."

"Do what?"

"Make love to you in a real bed. I'm not sure I'll remember how. Cots and dirt floors are one thing, but this...I don't know."

"Very funny," Helen replied, and then they both looked up as loud knocking commenced at the outer door.

"Your friends must be wondering what happened to you," Helen said to Matteo.

He set her down on the bed and said firmly, "I'll be right back."

She lay staring at the ceiling, thinking about how perfectly happy she was, until he returned.

"What did you say to them?" Helen asked.

"I told them to take a coffee break, that I was going to make love to my fiancée and would be a while."

"You didn't!"

"Sure, why not? It's the truth." He undressed while she watched, tossing his clothes on the corner armchair and then joining her on the bed.

"I suppose we have to be careful," he said to her, taking her in his arms.

"Yes, but not too careful," she replied, and he laughed.

Matteo made love to her gently, but thoroughly, and as they lay together afterward Helen said, "Tell me what our life in Puerta Linda will be like."

"Well, I'd like to say that it will be luxurious and carefree, but that would be a lie."

"Matteo, if I wanted that I'd live with my mother."

He stirred, settling her into the crook of his arm. "It will be hard to build a country from scratch," he said honestly, "and you probably won't see that much of me in the beginning."

"That will be a lot more than I've seen of you since I left Tres Luces," Helen said tartly. "I think I'll be able to take it."

"And you'll be busy," he said, kissing her forehead, "with the *bebé*."

"*Bebé?*"

"That's 'baby,' in Spanish."

"Thank you. I never would have guessed." After a moment she added thoughtfully, "I think I'd like to teach. That's what I was planning to do, before you arrived today."

"What about your paper?"

"It's finished."

"So you haven't spent all your time pining away for me," he said, turning her onto her back and looking into her face.

"I pined," Helen said seriously. "I pined plenty."

"So did I."

"Really? I assumed you didn't give a thought to me until you had taken over the government and then you said, 'Gee, what about Helen? She was a swell girl. I wonder how she's doing?'"

He let her go, sitting up on the edge of the bed. "If you assumed that, you were wrong," he said quietly.

Helen propped herself up on her elbows, tucking the sheet about her, putting her hand on his shoulder.

"Matt, I was kidding," she told him.

"I know, I'm sorry. It's just that it was very hard for me to let you go, do what I did; and you were on my mind every day, whether you believe it or not."

"I believe it," she said softly.

He turned to look at her. "What if you had stayed and were hurt while carrying the child?" he asked.

"You did the right thing; I'm not arguing with you," Helen said, taking his hand and pulling him back down on the bed. "Though you couldn't have convinced me of that when I left." She smoothed the dark hair from his forehead. "I thought I would never see you again," she went on softly. "Do you know what that did to me?"

"I think so," he responded, and kissed her. The kiss deepened, and he lifted his mouth from hers to inquire, "Can we, again?"

"Are you asking my permission?" she said, smiling.

"What about the baby?"

"I don't think we can ask him yet."

"Helen," he said in a frustrated, anxious voice.

"Yes, we can," she said, laughing, and putting her arms around his neck.

And they did.

COMING NEXT MONTH

DESERT SONG—Barbara Faith

In order to save her brother, Christy had to depend on the help of Hassan Ben Kadiri—a man who used the mysteries of the desert to his advantage. As they struggled for survival together, she showed him the mysteries of a woman's heart.

A MATTER OF CIRCUMSTANCE— Heather Graham Pozzessere

The roles of "cop" and "threatened citizen" brought Sean and Amanda together when he protected her from being harmed by her kidnappers. But when they were held captive on an isolated island, their roles were changed by love.

NIGHT HEAT—Jan Milella

After she was relocated by the Government Witness Relocation Program, Lainie Hall's life was threatened, and the FBI put Jake Callahan on her case. Suddenly Lainie didn't know what was the greater danger: losing her life or falling in love.

HAPPILY EVER AFTER—Maura Seger

Journalist Judith Fairchild and U.S. Ambassador Gavin Penderast were charmed by the kingdom of Gregoria, but danger lurked beneath its tranquil surface. With their help the royal wedding took place, and they found their own dreams—in each other.

AVAILABLE THIS MONTH:

MONTEGA'S MISTRESS
Doreen Owens Malek

MOMENT TO MOMENT
Dallas Schulze

GOLD IN THE STONE
Diana Holdsworth

A SOLITARY MAN
Beverly Bird

ATTRACTIVE, SPACE SAVING BOOK RACK

Display your most prized novels on this handsome and sturdy book rack. The hand-rubbed walnut finish will blend into your library decor with quiet elegance, providing a practical organizer for your favorite hard-or soft-covered books.

Only $9.95

Approximately 16" x 8" when assembled

Assembles in seconds!

Silhouette Desire

**Available
January 1987**

NEVADA
SILVER

The third book in the exciting
Desire Trilogy by Joan Hohl.

The Sharp brothers are back, along with
sister Kit... and Logan McKittrick.

Kit's loved Logan all her life and, with a little
help from the silver glow of a Nevada night,
she must convince the stubborn rancher that
she's a woman who needs a man's love—not
the protection of another brother.

Don't miss *Nevada Silver*—Kit and
Logan's story and the conclusion
of Joan Hohl's acclaimed
Desire Trilogy.